HJ Bellus

BLUE

Formatting: JRA Stevens

Cover Designer: Sommer Stein Creative Pear Design

Photographer: Perrywinkle Photography

Dedication:

To all the warriors who fight to make their own dreams their reality.
Love,
HJB

“Everyone has demons…it just depends on whether you invite them in as your enemy or friend as to how your story unfolds. Make it the best one.” –HJ Bellus

Prologue

"Blue, you have mail."

My entire body freezes at the high pitched sound of my mom's voice, and I'm not sure if it's sheer panic or excitement. I've been waiting on my acceptance letter from Preston University for what seems like years, but in all actuality it's only been two weeks and three days.

"You might want to move your ass, Blue."

This time I know beyond a doubt it's the letter. Try-outs were a month ago, and I put everything I had on the line. I didn't let the other girls prevent me from focusing on the task ahead of me. Going from Boulder, Colorado to L.A. was quite the eye opener, but years of training to be the best athlete I can be came in handy and I relied on my mental strength training.

My door flies open, distracting me from staring at my MacBook and Facebook wall. My mom stands in the entrance holding one white envelope with a huge smile plastered across her face. This dream and next step in my life is as much hers as it is mine. Damn, the woman has been by my side, from baby beauty pageants to running for Miss Teen Colorado.

"I can't, Mom." Snapping the lid of my MacBook closed, I wrap my arms around my knees.

"Blue." She strums the edges of the envelope.

"No, Mom, I just can't. What if…?"

"What if you made it and you're about to start the next chapter in your life?"

"Mom, stop! Your Pollyanna Positive attitude is not working right now."

"I'm opening it."

"No." I lurch forward on my bed and snatch the

envelope from her hands. "I want Dad here."

"He's in surgery today." She glances down at the gold watch on her wrist. "He might be able to FaceTime. Let me go check."

Mom practically skips from the room, and I smile at her pep-you-up attitude. Then I begin praying my dad is elbow deep in an operation.

"Say hi to Dad." My mom bounds back in, barely making contact with the floor before landing on the bed next to me.

"Hi, Dad," I manage with a defeated voice to his face on the iPhone.

"Hey, cupcake, why the gloom face?"

"Dad, I just…"

"Stop, not another word, cupcake. You're always your own worst critic. Open the damn letter. I have lives to save here and no time to worry about some overly dramatic and very whiny cheerleader."

I crack a small grin at my dad's sarcastic words. I know he's my biggest support system, but the man is never serious about cheerleading. It's well known he wants his Blue to become a surgeon just like him. But everyone else in the Williams family gave up hope on that years ago.

"Dad," I squeal. "Not funny and not the right time."

To my surprise, I've opened the envelope while my dad has been distracting me. I don't hesitate, pulling the single piece of paper from the envelope.

"I can't do it." I toss it in my mom's direction, burying my head into her knees.

The paper rustles, and I know my mother is unfolding the letter. I hear each movement, but can't force myself to look up.

"Miss Blue Williams, it's with great pleasure we are contacting you today."

The rest of her words are blurred together in one jumbled mass of freaking words. The part of my brain that registers speech goes out of order until I hear the word "accepted."

My gaze shoots up to study my mom's face, and when I see tears rolling down her cheeks I know I've done it. I've made the cheer team at Preston. It's one of those moments in life when everything stands still while all the hard work and effort toward a certain goal replays in your mind. All those extracurricular school activities missed for another gym session, the sleepovers with friends not attended because I was away at a dance competition.

"I did it." Each word comes out individually rather than a flowing sentence. "I fucking did it."

I hear my dad in the background scold me for my language like he always does, but this time I don't pay any attention to him.

"I did it." Each time I repeat the words they get a little louder. "I did it."

I leap to my feet, jumping up and down on the bed, squealing like a stuck pig and shouting all kinds of explicit words from bitch to ho and fucking A, I did it. I catch my dad's proud smile out of the corner of my eye, and yes, he's shaking his head at me.

"Mom." I throw my arms around her and embrace her in a full throttle hug, Blue style. She drops Dad and the letter, and I squeeze harder. This moment is only truly happening because of all my mother's persistence and belief in me. Being the only child, I always felt that invisible pressure to be the best I could and to impress my parents. They always held high expectations, but never crossed the line of being lunatics.

Yes, lunatics. You know the ones. They put their baby in pageants at three months old, drive across the country for cheer camps, and buy a ten thousand dollar evening gown for Miss Teen Colorado…those kinds of parents. Yes, my parents provided me with all those opportunities, but I was the driving force behind it, pushing myself harder and faster.

"I love you, Blue Williams."

Okay, they were a bit crazy naming me Blue, but in my mother's defense, it made me stick out from the crowd.

Pulling away from my mom's hug, I deepen my smile. "Thank you for everything. You too, Dad." I wave down to him. The iPhone happened to land by our feet, so my dad is staring up at our crotches. Awkward…actually, it brings awkward to a whole new level. Using my toes, I slide him closer to my mom's side, giving him a nice view of her.

"Blue, if I have to drive out to California and pick up your knocked-up, freshman ass, I'll sell you as a slave on the black market in Mexico."

I get my looks from my mom and my humor from my dad. Never serious, that man, even in a situation like this, but from his proud smile and that twinkle in his eye I know he's proud as hell.

"Deal, Dad. I love you."

"I love you too, Blue."

Mom uses her big toe to disconnect the call, and we fall down on the mattress in a fit of laughter.

"Thank heaven you didn't make me twig."

"Mom, it's twerking, and you need to work on those skills while I'm gone."

"Blue." Her hands tighten on my thigh, and then her head drops to my shoulder. "I'm going to be so lost without you."

"We'll talk every day, and you said you'd visit once a month."

"I know, but you're my baby girl, Blue."

"Read the letter to me."

I listen to my mom finish reading the letter with a shaky voice.

Chapter 1

Thirty Days Later

I run my finger along the hem of the black and white damask bedding covering the single size mattress in my dorm room. My mom and I managed to decorate everything on my side while Dad set up my desk and chair, bitching the whole time.

"Honey, stop, I can hire someone to do that, or I can even do it. I don't want you hurting your hands."

"I'm a surgeon, not a pussy."

Yes, those are the lines I heard over and over as my parents settled me into my room. They drove me out a week before camp and stayed several days with me. It was the hardest goodbye this morning, and I nearly took off running and screaming, begging them to take me back home with them.

When my mom broke down crying during her goodbye, I had to turn away from her. Dad slapped her on the ass and then cracked some joke before he wrapped us up in one large family hug. The man pisses me off for never being serious, but in moments like those it's just what we need from him.

I have no idea when my roommate may or may not be marching through the door. We've texted a couple times. Her name is Sophia, but she gave me strict orders to call her Sophie. We were lucky enough to be roomed together since we're both freshman cheerleaders at Preston.

My dad was relentless in his efforts to have me rush and join a sorority to experience college life, but I know full well there's no way I'd have time to keep my grades up with cheer practice and then sorority life mixed into all of that, so I settled for the dorms. And to say I was nervous about my roommate would be the understatement of the century.

My stomach growls, the sound deafening in the silence of the room. I make my way over to the mini-fridge my parents bought and stocked. Nothing looks good, or even halfway satisfying. Greek yogurt…um, no. String cheese…um, double nope. Lean turkey lunch meat…um, that'd be a hell to the fucking no. I'm more in the mood for a double bacon cheeseburger spackled in grease with an extra-large order of fries.

The bonus to dorm life is all the fast food joints are conveniently placed around the outskirts of the area. Grabbing my turquoise cross-body purse from the hook, I slide it on over my head and hook it on my neck. I check the perfectly placed mirror by the door to see how out of control my hair is. *Thank you, Mom.* The bright blonde pile is still a hot mess. My hair is the one thing that sets me apart from other girls. It's long, thick, and a bright golden blonde…and all natural, at that.

I've threatened to chop it off a time or two, but every single time those words came out of my mouth my mother nearly stroked out. On my sixteenth birthday, my dad made me promise to never threaten my poor mom again, and to sweeten the pot he threw in a bright red Rover. Nothing like a brand new spanking-ass car to keep a girl's mouth shut, and yep, since that day the thought of cutting my hair has never crossed my mind.

I leave behind my car keys and choose to hoof it, knowing it will waste an ample amount of time, and I could do a little sightseeing the old fashioned way. Throwing on my aviators, I step out into the hall and notice there's bit more commotion than there has been. The football team must have arrived, hence all the hot-stacked men loitering in the hall.

For the love of all things steam and sex, these men

are tanned and gorgeous. Absentmindedly, I use my hand to keep my jaw from dropping to the floor and saliva from pooling out. Thank you, aviators, for hiding my stares. These men are nothing compared to the boys back at my high school. They're freaking giants with looks and…um…and very well-defined bodies.

I avoid the elevator because I don't trust myself and really don't want to get caught ogling on my first trip out of my dorm room. *My roommate can't get here fast enough*, I chant in my head while jogging down the stairs.

I can only hope she's the loud, obnoxious type I can hide behind. In high school, I was the leader and the forerunner, and quite frankly, I just want to fit in here. Cheer, good grades, and cheer are the only things I'm concerning myself with. The social part, well, I want to follow, be in the background, and enjoy life from the back seat. I'm sick of being the driver and navigator.

Pushing open the door to the outside, I soak up the sunrays.

"Miss Blue."

I turn to see the security guard at the u-shaped cherry wood check-in desk.

"Yes," I say, smiling brightly back at him.

"Have a nice afternoon."

"Um, thank you." I stand frozen in the middle of the lobby.

"Sorry, my name is Steve." He rounds the desk and makes his way to me. "Your father introduced himself to me earlier."

"Oh, go figure." I relax bit.

"Have a nice afternoon, and if you ever need anything, just ask." He runs his hands through this thick, greasy black hair, and I can't help but stare at the grime under his nails. Nice enough, but surely a shower wouldn't kill the guy.

"Thanks." I wave as I walk off.

I giggle and move further outside. I damn well know my dad either paid him off or scared the piss out of him with his pussy surgeon hands. Guess I can't blame the guy, since I'm the only daughter and he just dropped me off to live states away. My dad will be the first to admit he's not the biggest fan of me being a cheerleader, and trust me, he has a plethora of corny blonde cheerleading jokes to throw around, but at the end of the day he's in a tie for being my biggest supporter.

The sun in Colorado was always welcoming and highlighted my tan perfectly, but there's something about the California sun I can't seem to get enough of. It has a unique touch of warmth that I find addicting. I feel the tingle on the top of my shoulders as I stroll down the wide campus sidewalk, and just like on the inside of the dorms, there are more people loitering around outside.

I can guess most of them are student athletes since we tend to show up earlier than most to attend training camps and such. A second group of football players passes by me, and again I find myself scanning them from head to toe, mentally undressing them. Which isn't a hard task since they're only clothed in loose fitting gym shorts and shirtless, with sweat trickling down their tanned six packs.

Focus, Blue, focus, for fuck's sake. It's just a short stroll until I'm off campus and walking down a long chain of businesses ranging from strip malls with all sorts of retail stores to fast food. One small, red brick building has a line spilling out of it, so I choose that one. I mean, no one stands in line for shit, right? Well, let's hope not.

Pulling my phone from my pocket, I check it for messages, and find several texts from my parents and one from Sophie.

Sophie: I'll be there in about an hour. Be prepared to meet the most amazing person of your entire freaking life! Well, let's hope you do, because if you don't that means I've driven off a cliff, hence my annoying-ass mother and grandma Vitty driving me.

I chuckle at her text because I can hear her rambling on and on. The few times we chatted on the phone, the girl ran her mouth until my ears nearly bled, but her enthusiasm is contagious, I'll give her that.

Quickly, I slide open my mom's text and instantly bust out laughing. They sent random ridiculous pictures of them at different stops. I honestly have no idea how I turned out so normal as I study the picture of my dad riding a pink flamingo statue in front of a gas station.

"What's so funny?"

One of those hot, delicious football players is studying me, boring a hole into my chest with his dreamy blue eyes. My jaw does that drop thing, leaving my mouth hanging wide open while my hands remain planted on my cellphone. *Oh shit. Oh shit, I wonder if he'll notice if I simply turn around and sprint like a motherfucker.*

"Ethan, don't scare the piss out of the poor girl." Another dreamboat steps up, placing his hand on Ethan's shoulder.

Automatically, my gaze flashes down, triple checking my crotch for piss dribbling down my legs. *Phew, nothing…dry as dry.*

"So, what was so funny?" He cocks his eyebrow at me and sends me a panty-melting smirk.

Guarantee, my panties are wet now.

"Oh, I'm, uh…" I hold up my phone and send the two men a quick smile. "I was just reading some texts and came across a ridiculous picture of my dad on a pink flamingo."

Holy shit, Blue, that didn't sound awkward at all.

"Nice." He nods, approving of my answer.

"Ethan, you're taken, and Stephie would slit your throat if she found you flirting." The second man steps in front of Ethan, and damn if he isn't even fucking dreamier than Ethan. "Hi, my name is Lane."

He reaches out and offers a handshake.

"Oh, hi, I'm Blue." I wave like an idiot asshole from Mars, avoiding flesh contact. I have no faith in my body and know it's damn well possible I might melt in his touch.

He waves back with a goofy grin, more than likely mirroring mine. "You go to Preston?"

"Well, no, not yet. I mean yes. I'm a freshman and just settled into the dorms."

"So, are you a braniac and show up to school two months early, or…?" The man's sex appeal oozes off every single word. He's more than dreamy.

Good hell, why can't he just turn around and mind his own sexy damn business instead of assaulting me? His eyes and looks make me want to dry hump his leg.

"Um, duh, I play ball." Joke, yes, it's time to stop this guy's tactics with good ol' fashioned humor. "Recruited as a freshman and starting this year."

"Oh." He pauses a moment, scratching his head. "Sorry, I didn't pick up on that."

"Gotcha," I shout and point my finger at him. "I'm on the cheer team and here for training camp."

I decide to go with over-exaggerated humor to hide the fact I'm hot for him. A smile covers his face, and then he does the typical shit most people do when you tell them you're a cheerleader. I follow his gaze as it roams up and down my body, from the tips of my toes peeking from my sandals to the top of my messy bun. I couldn't help but notice when he let his eyes linger a little longer on my breasts.

I gesture ahead of him. "The line is moving and your friends are ditching you."

"Want to join us?"

Carefully monitoring what comes out of my mouth, I speak very slowly. "No, it's okay. I just came to grab lunch and then head back to meet my roommate."

"Well, nice to meet you, Blue."

"Same at ya, Lane."

Mr. Sex on a Stick finally turns around to catch up to his teammates. *Thank you, Jesus, my ovaries were about two seconds from imploding.*

I hang back for a little bit, allowing two new parties to cut in line as a tactic of putting space between me and the testosterone tribe. After their lingering scents have faded, I'm able to focus on the menu hanging above the counter. It's a large black chalkboard with your typical burgers, chicken strips, and salads scrawled all over it.

As I study the menu, I fan my face with my cellphone. Yeah, not the best tool for the job, but the tiny flow of air hitting my face begins to lightly cool me. The over-crowded diner is humid and hotter than Hades. And just my luck, the line stalls out a bit with the two new parties in front of me.

Booths and tables pepper the joint, along with an eclectic collection of artwork and black and white photography. There's a catchy vibe floating in the small area, and I try to take in as much artwork as possible to distract myself from the sweat beads forming on my forehead.

A lone customer catches my attention, and he only does that because he's dressed in a long sleeve black t-shirt with a backward ball cap placed on his head. Craning lower, I also notice he's wearing workout pants and not shorts. I wonder if it's the Bionic Man. How in the hell is he not having a heat stroke dressed like that in one hundred degree weather?

"The Tuck Jones," Lane calls loudly as he strides to the corner booth. I watch as he slides into the booth with the clothed man. They do the bro shake and hug and whatever else men do. It's clear Lane is deep in conversation with the man. Several moments later he nods in my direction and points. The man pulls his attention from his food up to me, and I'm busted. Yes, busted beyond a shadow of any doubt. I try to casually look away as if nothing just happened, but I'm fucked.

"Ma'am." A voice draws my attention from the embarrassing situation.

Looking forward, the two parties are gone and there's a gap the size of freakin' Texas between me and the counter. *Yep, fucking busted.*

I try to order my food, but the look on the man's face haunts me. His face is so chiseled, and even at a distance his masculine beauty is overpowering. There is something about his deep, dark brown eyes that flips my tummy. Unlike the other men who nearly caused me to piss my panties over their good looks, he is different, and different in a way my brain can't comprehend.

The lady behind the counter clears her throat, showcasing her irritation with me. I hurry up and order that burger I've been craving, along with a large order of fries, and, of course, a soda. I mean, why stop short when you're going to splurge? I'll be running later tonight when it's dark, that's for sure.

Plucking the red tray of greasy food from the counter, I find a booth, and not just any one, but the one furthest away from the group of men. As I pull out the chair, I hear someone holler my name, and I'm not shocked to see Lane standing up and holding a chair out for me.

"Join us." He puts his arm over his chest as if I were breaking his heart.

I shake my head, knowing it wouldn't be a good idea.

"Don't make me cause a scene, Blue."

I keep shaking my head, and then finally sit down in the lone seat at my table.

"Don't go breaking my heart," he belts out, and I think he's trying to sing, but I'm not quite sure. He throws my name in about every other word, and before I know it, the whole diner is staring at me.

"Asshole," I say to myself as I pick up my food and head his way. "Happy?"

I plop down in the open chair, dying from embarrassment, and completely out of lust with Lane. His 'come fuck me' eyes no longer have any power over me after his obnoxious show.

"Blue, meet my boys, and boys, meet Blue." He pauses for a moment. "I didn't catch your last name."

"Probably because I didn't offer my last name." I plop a ketchup soaked fry in mouth.

"Feisty one." He takes a bite of his burger and talks around it. "I guess you didn't like my singing."

"You call that singing?" His teammates bust out in laughter. I look up to see all of them watching us, even the man who is overdressed. "And my last name is Williams."

"Blue here is a freshman cheerleader."

"That would be me, and this would be the most awkward moment of my life." I grab my burger and go in for the kill, taking a large bite just like Lane did.

"Consider this your welcome to college life," Ethan advises. "My girl is a junior cheerleader. Her name is Stephie, and she never eats like that."

Several men choke back their laughter, but it's the one in long sleeves who holds my attention. He shakes his head and backhands Ethan.

"Well, I guess she doesn't know how to live life then."

Immediately I pray to the cheer gods that Stephie isn't that one hardcore mean girl on the squad, but with my luck, I'm probably screwed.

Ethan and Lane assault me with numerous questions, and I do my best to answer them through bites of my burger. And mother-lovin', humpin' hell, I now know why the line was so long. As I stuff my face, I watch the man in long sleeves, studying his movements and his face. I'm careful to not make eye contact with him. I can tell just from his body language that he's a closed book and doesn't want unnecessary attention drawn to him. Unlike Ethan or Lane, who'd probably strip for women ogling them.

Throwing my napkin into the now empty red basket, I glance over one more time at the mysterious man. This time I realize what it is about him that sets him apart from the other men. His face is chiseled and well defined, everything runs from his strong jawline, and his brown eyes are perfectly framed with his eyebrows. The man could walk a runaway fully clothed and still be the most gorgeous person. I can tell he's built and very athletic, just like the rest of the men at the table.

"So are you all football players?" I dig for the information on my own and almost feel guilty.

"Yes, ma'am," one of the quieter men in the booth pipes up.

"Names? I mean, I can't leave just knowing Ethan and Lane."

Ethan takes the lead and begins pointing out the men. "Gus T., redshirt freshman. Dustin, sophomore defensive end. Lane, resident pussy. Tuck, the best running back in college football, and he's a junior.

Jared, sophomore offense."

I know Ethan continues, but after learning the name of the man who's held my attention even over that glorious burger, I get distracted. His name is Tuck, and he's a running back, and obviously his teammates speak highly of him. And he's the oldest at the table, and by far the most alluring. This time I outright stare at him, not worried if he catches me or if the others notice my actions. Ethan finally shuts his trap.

"Nice to meet all of you," I say, not breaking my stare.

Tuck finally looks up at me, but only for a second as he offers me a shy little smirk. Just the brief eye contact and the slight grin has my stomach doing double time.

"Well, I'm off, boys."

I stand quickly, mentally berating myself for letting a football team turn me into a schoolgirl with a massive crush. Steadying my sea legs and getting one last look at Mr. GQ, I turn to walk toward the door. *Welcome to college life, Blue*. Good hell, I've been out of my dorm once, and heated up over several men and eaten with a group of football players. Whore, much?

My sandal catches on the leg of a booth. My upper body flies forward, while my shoulder purse nearly knocks me out as it sails over my head. The floor comes closer and closer to my face, and all I can think about is the group of men watching me. My knee grazes the tile floor—or actually thumps into the tile floor—and that's when my senses kick in. Using all my strength on my right side, I pull myself back up into a standing position before making out with the dirty tile floor.

My heart thuds so loudly, I can barely hear a thing over it, and when I turn to see if anyone happened to catch my little stumble, I see the whole table of football players staring with their mouths hung wide open. Even the booths near me are all staring.

"Don't worry, I'm a cheerleader," I say as I sprint from the restaurant, but before I make it to the door I see Tuck smiling once again.

He was stone cold and showed no emotion except for those slight and very shy smiles. *Tuck Jones, who the hell are you, and what have you done to my ovaries?*

Chapter 2

I pull up my favorite yoga videos on YouTube and do a few sessions while waiting on Sophie. Her hour turns into more like three, but then the door finally opens, and in steps my roomie.

She's my exact opposite. Similar builds, but that's it. Sophie's pale in complexion, with jet-black hair that trails down her back and bounces in curly waves.

"Hi," I squeak out, sitting up in my bed and flipping off a dumb eye mask. Being bored beyond belief, I busted into a home spa kit and ended up with a lumpy cream and an eye mask. Thankfully, I'd washed off all the green goo and just laid bored out of my mind in my bed.

"Oh my god, I'm Sophie, and you must be Blue." She bounds toward me, throwing the heap of items in her arms onto her bed. She knocks back onto my bed and lands right on me. "I've been dying to meet you. We got lost on the way here. Long story, I'll fill you in later."

I held no doubt she'd fill me in on everything.

"Can I help you?"

I tried sitting up and pushing her off to the side. I'm definitely the bubble type of person, as in stay the fuck out of my bubble until I feel comfortable enough hugging you on my own. And it's clear within thirty seconds of meeting Sophie, she has no concept of a bubble.

"Holy shit, cheer orgy."

Looking up, I see Lane standing in our doorway holding large boxes.

"Er mah god, thank you." Sophie pops up and makes her way to Lane.

Along with no bubble, the girl clearly has no shame either. Lane nods in my direction, and then a huge smile covers his face when he recognizes me.

"Blue."

"Lane."

"You've got some green shit around your eyes," he says as he walks in and gently sets down the boxes.

Springing from my bed, I go to the mirror behind the door, and holy fuck if I don't have two perfectly shaped circles framing my eyes. I'll be kicking the dog for this one when I get home. Damn spa kit. Damn Mom. And Damn Lane for pointing it out.

I snag a wet makeup remover cloth from my vanity and begin to scrub. My only saving grace is that it wipes away easily, only leaving behind a light red mark circling my eyes. Raccoon, it is.

When I turn around I'm surprised to see three more men join Lane in the room, and I find myself quickly scanning the small crowd for Tuck. I recognize one of the men from the diner, but that's it; the others are all new faces. I don't remember the name of the familiar man and feel sort of assholish for it. I'm thankful the crowd goes to setting down boxes and unpacking stuff for Sophie. I'm amazed to watch the men sort all of her shit out as she tells them where to place things and exactly how to unfold the bedding.

It only takes seconds before I know I landed the perfect roommate. She likes to talk and be loud, has men following at her heels, and will be the perfect person to hide behind and blend in.

"I'm starving." Sophie plops down on her bed and covers her stomach. Lane quickly joins her, and the other men exit the room.

"I have some food over in that little fridge. Help yourself." Feeling a bit uncomfortable, I take a seat at my hot pink office chair near my desk.

Sophie waves off my suggestion. "It's probably all healthy shit. Right?" She doesn't give me a chance to answer her question, she just continues talking.

"How do you two know each other, anyway?" she asks.

"Oh, Blue dined with me and the boys earlier."

"You little hussy." Sophie zings a pale purple zebra striped pillow toward me. I'm able to bat it away easily. "You told me you were walking downtown to get a bite."

"I did."

"Whatever," Lane pipes up. "She practically begged to sit with us and even offered us a twenty dollar bill."

Rolling my eyes, I nearly pop both eyeballs out of the socket.

"Well, let's go eat. I want to see something other than the damn dorms." Sophie stands, straightening out her tiny white shorts and shamelessly readjusting her boobies. Lane is standing right behind her like a lost little puppy.

The writing is clearly etched on the wall with these two. The only question left is whether they will be bedmates or have something a little deeper.

"I think I'll just stay behind. I'm actually going to go for a run after the late lunch I mowed down."

"Are you sure?"

"Yeah."

Lane wraps his arm around Sophie's waist, and she doesn't even flinch. "Let's go eat. I'm hungry too. Careful, Blue, it's almost dark."

"I'm going to use the running trail around the campus. My dad did some research and it seems to be pretty safe." I shrug while picking at the hem of my shorts.

"Yeah, it's well lit and the best place. The gym will be open for athletes tomorrow."

"I hate the treadmill. Actually, I despise the fucker."

Sophie giggles loudly. "I already love you, Blue Williams. I hate that fucker, too." She takes two large steps and wraps her arms around my shoulders, giving me one more hug. This one lasts a bit longer, and I realize Sophie Watson has burst my bubble and any hopes of having one.

The couple wastes no time getting out the door, and if I were a betting woman, I'd bet Sophie comes back with messy hair. Plucking the damn spa kit from the bed, I toss it in the trash and nail it from feet away. I played basketball all through high school and loved every single second of it. It's weird to think I've never cheered at a boys' basketball game because of scheduling, but thankfully my school allowed cheerleaders to participate in sports as well.

Looking out my dorm window, I notice the dusk settling in over the campus and decide to hustle my ass. We sure did luck out on the view. It's a gorgeous view of the cityscape, and with the setting sun, damn near picturesque. I wiggle into some tight spandex running pants and toss on a light hoodie.

Walking back out into the commons, it's even more crowded and rowdy. It seems all the athletes are excited to meet each other.

A different guard sits behind the desk watching a television show and doesn't even notice me as I exit the building. The running trail parallels our building and is only fifteen feet from the side of the dorm. There are several different routes you can take, lengthening or shortening your workout with different stations throughout to work your muscles.

I decide on the longest route and begin my five-mile

jog. Visualizing the map in my head, I decide about a half mile down the trail that this might not have been the best idea. Darkness envelops the night air with just enough groups of stars and a sliver of the moon lighting the way.

I find my pace, and it feels good to let my longs legs go. Signs point the directions at each crossroad, signaling which loop to take. I'm thankful and find myself melting away into my thoughts with no worries. Pushing myself to the point of breaking has become my drug of choice over the years.

I never count sets in the gym when doing weightlifting; no, I always go to failure. It's an exhilarating feeling to push my body to its limits when my brain is screaming to quit. I've never been one to listen to that tiny voice saying, "Stop." I set my mind and do it.

Mile three, and my lungs are beginning to sting a bit, but I push it away from my thoughts and dream of meeting my new teammates and coach. I met Coach Lindsey at try-outs, and she was amazing and super inspiring. It was her charisma and aura that drew me to choose Preston.

The breeze sends chills through me when it meets the sweat droplets running down my skin. I reach back and pull my hoodie up and over my Beats and focus on Lil Jon's song blaring in my eardrums. I'm able to block everything out for the next mile as I pick up my pace, forcing my body to keep up.

A dark figure comes into my peripheral, and I jump to the side. My legs tangle together as I jolt off of the trail. My upper body lands in a grassy area as my legs crash into the pebbled running track, and I feel each stone tear into my flesh.

I grab my head to protect it from anything that might

be coming next. The dark shadow hovers over me. I'm too out of breath to look up and still in a daze from whatever the fuck happened. Seconds go by before I realize I just ate shit. When I look up, I see Tuck standing above me, clothed in a black hoodie and loose gym shorts that fall right below his kneecaps, exposing very impressive calf muscles.

"Are you okay?" He squats down to face me. "Blue, are you okay?"

He finds my Beats and takes them off my ears. I'm still too startled to respond, and find my breath continuing to race out of control.

"Blue." He drags the back of his knuckles down my cheek, which only fucks up my breathing more, and the panic sets in.

"I, uh, I'm fine." I bring my legs up to my chest and see my torn running pants and the blood pooling around the ragged material.

"I was just passing you. I had no idea it was you," he offers.

"I'm an idiot and spooked." I try to bury my face in my knees and avoid the blood and cuts.

"Is this your first time on the trail?"

"Yes." My voice is muffled.

"Probably not the brightest idea to be out after dark."

"I know. I just needed to run." Tears stream down my cheeks. "I might miss home already."

I have no idea where my words came from, but they're true. My heart already misses my parents, home, and my bed.

"Freshman, right?"

I nod, suddenly feeling foolish for my psycho breakdown in front of Mr. Hunk-O-Rama.

"Yeah, sorry, I think I'm just tired." I stand and my rubbery legs wobble underneath me. "Go ahead, I don't want to mess up your workout."

He chuckles, and that slight grin dances on his serious face. "I just nearly killed a freshman cheerleader. I'm not about to run along without making sure you make it back to the dorms."

"Really, I'm fine. I may be a little, tiny," I gesture with my fingers, "itsy bitsty emotional and exhausted, but besides that, I'm good."

"When do you report to cheer camp?"

"Tomorrow morning."

We begin walking down the running trail side by side.

"Your knees may be a bit sore."

"Slightly," I respond, as my knees sting like a bitch in heat.

I break into a slow jog and look out the corner of my eye to see Tuck keeping pace with me, and just like in the diner, I find it impossible not to stare. There are so many questions I want to ask him, but know it's completely inappropriate. Like why he portrays such a dark vibe, his clothing, and if he can makes girls scream in bed.

Instead of exercising my mouth, I keep jogging, quickening my pace. My Beats bounce off the back of my neck as I find my rhythm. Tuck sticks quietly by my side.

"You can go ahead, Tuck. I'm fine, really."

"What? You don't think I can keep up with a cheerleader? Just because I'm quiet doesn't mean I'm a pussy."

I can't help but laugh at his joke.

"What's so funny, Miss Blue?"

"My dad always uses that line about not being a pussy."

I kick in the last gear at my full gait and don't say

another word. Tuck keeps up with me step for step. When we hit the next sign on the jogging trail, I decided to take the eight-mile trek back to the dorms. It feels good to be running at full speed again. With each bend of my knees, I feel the crusted blood break.

Tuck's heavy breathing makes me feel good because I know he's pushing himself just as hard as I am. The light of my dorm comes into view, and I internally groan, never wanting this run to end. It was exhilarating before Tuck joined me, but since he did, the open air with his musky scent entangled in all of it made the workout more than satisfying. I could've done without the tumble, though.

I come to a stop in front of the dorm and take a second to catch my breath, heaved over, resting my palms on my kneecaps.

"Have a good day tomorrow, Blue Williams."

I look up to see Tuck jogging in place, facing me.

"Did you Google me? How did you know my last name?"

"I have my ways," he replies with his stone-cold, serious face.

"I see. Thanks for scaring the shit out of me and nearly killing me before I start my freshman year."

My sentence rambles on, and I do that on purpose. I'm not ready for Tuck to jog away into the darkness. It's too late for dinner, and I'm betting he's not the tea or coffee type…I scramble to come up with an excuse. Tuck begins moving backward in his jogging stance.

"Where are you going?" My voice comes out more panicked than I'd like to admit.

"Home. Goodnight, Blue."

Tuck continues to jog backward until his black outline fades away into the darkness.

"Goodnight, Tuck," I holler back.

Within moments, I'm standing in front of the dorms all alone in the darkness, feeling exhausted and satisfied. Falling asleep will be easy tonight.

Tuck, who the hell are you beneath that iron-clad persona?

Chapter 3

Walking back into the dorm, it seems the crowds have gathered behind closed doors, as muted sounds escape each room I pass. Some sounds make my ears bleed. I'm surprised to see the door to our room cracked open slightly, and when I push it further open, Sophie and Lane are all sorts of tangled up…and very naked.

"Oh lord," I squeal.

"Shit, I told you to lock the door." Sophie slaps Lane's back.

I snag a medicine kit off my dresser. "I'll wait out here. No worries."

Holy shit, unbelievable. I better become a betting woman.

My mom really thought of everything when she helped me pack and buy stuff for the dorms. An emergency first aid kit was the last thing on my mind, and I do remember rolling my eyes at her when she tossed it into the shopping cart at Target. And if on cue, my phone blares out Mom's ring tone. I swear she knows everything that happens.

"Hey, Mom."

"Hi, sweetie," her voice rings out. "Hi, baby Blue."

Oish. I must be on speakerphone. My parents love this shit.

"Hi, Daddy."

"How was your first day?"

"Good, Mom. It was really good."

"Say bye to your dad. We're just checking into a hotel for the night."

"Bye, Dad. I love you."

"Love you, too, Blue. Don't go getting knocked up."

"Deal," I say.

I listen to my mom fumble with the phone while she turns off the speakerphone, and then my father slams the car door.

"Okay, I'm back. How's your roomie?"

I giggle at my mom's vocabulary and then prop the phone between my shoulder and ear. "Mom, I don't even use that term. Sophie is fine. She arrived late, and well, then…"

"Well, then what?"

"She wanted to go out to eat, and I…"

Before I have the chance to finish my thought, my mom takes control of the conversation.

"Did you offer her some of your food?"

"Of course, Mom." I roll my eyes. I really need to stop that shit. It may get me in trouble one day. "But she had already made a new friend, and they went out."

"You got ditched on your first day in the dorms?" Her tone is bathed in horror.

"No, Mom. I told them I didn't want to go, and it was a guy she'd met, and they are now currently finishing up bumping uglies in our room."

I smile to myself as I pop open the tube of antibiotic cream. I've never kept anything from my mother, but her facial expressions as I revealed stuff like this are always priceless to see. I can only imagine her now.

"Oh, dear, where are you?"

"Out in the commons room. I took a slight tumble tonight on my run, and I'm just cleaning up the scratches."

I'll leave it at scratches when it's more like craters and feels like fucking Jaws is gnawing at my kneecaps.

"How did you fall? Who were you with? Are you okay?"

And the rapid-fire questions begin.

"Just being a dumbass and running after dark. Only some scrapes."

So, I guess I don't tell my mom everything. I leave out Tuck and the larger cuts on my knees and my torn running pants. I listen politely as she gives me her motherly lecture and asks about twenty times if I need to go to the hospital. I know she's made it into the hotel room because I hear my dad chime in just like he does every single time. "Shit, just tell her to rub some dirt on it and move on."

Listening to the two of them eases my homesickness a bit, and by the time my mom's done talking, I have both knees cleaned and bandaged up.

"Okay, bye, Mom. I love you."

"Love you, too, Blue. I can't wait to hear about your first day of camp, and remember Dad and I are coming to the first home game to watch you cheer."

"Got it. Night, Mom."

I hang up the phone, knowing the goodbyes could last a century with that woman, and it's best to cut it short. I try to stand up and realize I may have gone a little heavy on the Band-Aids, as I'm unable to bend my knees. Walking like I'm on stilts, I laugh out loud at the day I've had and wonder if it's any sign of how the year will go.

"You laughing again?"

I look up to see Ethan and a beautiful woman draped off his shoulder. My butt puckers up at the realization this must be Stephie the Ball Crusher. I'm unable to form a word, not knowing which direction to take. A, admit I know Ethan and had lunch with him. Fuck, that sounds so bad and incriminating. Or B, pretend I have amnesia and peg-leg it to my door. But, there's a slight chance of naked bodies humping each other behind my door.

"Bad habit, I guess." I shrug and take a few steps away from the couple.

"This is my girlfriend, Stephie."

I cringe and turn around. I'm fully trapped and at their mercy, just like a rabbit under the teeth of a hungry coyote.

"Hi," I barely squeak out.

"And how do you know her?" Stephie places a hand on her hip and stares down her boyfriend.

His stall gives me a moment to take in Stephie. She's gorgeous from head to toe, with shoulder length blonde hair and long, lean legs.

"I had lunch with her and the boys today."

My butt fully cramps from the tight puckering, and I kiss my chance of fitting in on the squad goodbye. I'd just pissed Stephie off and painted an overly large target on my back.

"Oh, nice, and what other females were there?" she spits out.

"It was just Blue."

Might as well slit both wrists now and offer up my blood to the vampires of cheerleading hell. I'm toast.

"I went there on my own and had my own table. Lane started singing a song and being obnoxious. They really forced my hand," I ramble on and wish like hell my knees weren't locked tight with bandages. If I live past this encounter, I'm swearing off Band-Aids the rest of my life.

Stephie processes my words, but the look on her face doesn't soften. If anything, she grows more and more pissed off at the whole situation.

"Stay the fuck away from my boyfriend and know your fucking role tomorrow on the squad, freshman."

Clearly, she enjoys using the four-letter word. I only nod and carry on to my dorm in penguin fashion. This time when I open the door, Lane is standing and zipping up his fly.

"Sorry about that, Blue. We got carried away."

"You don't say." I plop down on my bed and inhale the fresh scent of fabric softener.

"Yeah, really sorry." Sophie sits up in her bed, guarding her chest with Lane's shirt.

"How about we keep the bumping and grinding to Lane's dorm?"

"Absolutely. You're not mad, are you?"

I don't have enough energy to explain how highly inappropriate her actions were, so I just shake my head.

"I told you Blue was a cool chick."

"Get the hell out of here, Lane, before I decide to kick you in the baby-maker."

And that's when their eyes land on my knees.

"Good lord, who was the lucky man?" Lane asks.

I grab the closest water bottle and sling it toward his head.

"I'm kidding, I'm kidding." He uses his arms to deflect the bottle.

Lane places one final kiss on Sophie's forehead before he exits the room, shirtless. And then, without shame, Sophie sits up in bed, exposing her tits to the world, and slides on his shirt. I'm not sure if it's an only child issue, but I'm extremely modest when it comes to lady parts. Even in locker rooms you can find me changing in a stall. I try not to stare at her perfectly shaped boobies and then wonder if they're fake.

"That will never happen again, and you have to believe me that I'm not a slut."

"Are you boobs fake?" slips from my mouth.

Sophie tilts her head in my direction. "Um, yeah, is that okay?"

"Oh, they're great," I explain.

"But really, Blue, I just got out of a bad break-up with my high school boyfriend of four years, and I guess I enjoyed the attention Lane gave me a bit too much."

"You could say that again. I mean, he had you nailed less than two hours after meeting. You slut bag."

Sophie goes pale and fumbles with the hem of Lane's shirt as she tries to stand, not knowing how to take my comment.

"Gotcha," I squeal.

She clutches her chest. "Oh my god, I thought you were mad."

"Don't mess with my cheer career or schooling and we will get along just fine."

"Really?" she asks, clearly stunned.

"Really."

"I'll be right back." Sophie cracks the door and rushes across the way to the bathroom, and I can only guess she's cleaning up or stitching up. I'm not quite sure what you do after sex.

I, on the other hand, take the moment of solitude to wiggle out of my pants, trying not to rip off my bandages, and then cozy on up in an oversized cheer camp t-shirt and boy shorts and crawl back onto my bed. Just as I snuggle in, my stomach rumbles and I decide to pop a bag of popcorn. I mean, I need to eat something on the first night since my mom supplied me with enough food for an army.

Right as I climb in bed, Sophie comes back into the room. I pat the bed beside me. Since she's already busted my bubble, I offer her some popcorn. I can tell she's uncomfortable.

"I'm really not a slut, and the more time that passes, I feel awful."

"Was his dick big?" I ask around a mouthful of popcorn.

I laugh at the shock on her face and inhale a kernel. I begin spastically choking and grabbing at my throat, indicating the internationally recognized choking signal. Sophie pounds on my back relentlessly, and then finally the kernel dislodges.

"Water," I croak out.

She bounds from the bed and grabs the bottle of water I tossed at Lane and offers it to me.

"Who needs porn with these two?"

We look up to see Lane and Ethan staring at us from the doorway. I send both of them a "what the fuck" look.

"The door was cracked open and we heard some ruckus, and since we head up neighborhood watch, we had to investigate," Lane says.

I point at Ethan. "You stay away. Stay far, far away from us. I don't want your girlfriend to eat us for breakfast."

They laugh loudly and clearly take it the wrong way, and most likely the perverts would.

"I'm serious. She already hates me."

"Calm down, Blue, she just broke up with me," Ethan says.

That's it, I'm packing my bags tonight. First flight home. I'll flip burgers before I endure the wrath of Stephie, AKA the Hulk.

"Are you freaking crazy? Now you're in here?" I whisper-scream.

"Calm down." Lane and Ethan both take a seat on Sophie's bed.

"Get out now," I demand again.

The men find it quite comical how upset I am.

"Really. It's fine, Blue. She explained it was over, and we both kind of knew that last spring. It was just convenient."

"Explain her threat then, Casanova!"

"Stephie is just a bitch," Lane pipes up, and Ethan only nods.

"How long were you two together?" I ask.

"Most of high school and on and off through college."

"And you're going to be a junior, right?"

"Yeah, we both are." Ethan signals between himself and Lane.

"She's cheated on Ethan more times than Gaga changes at an award show."

My eyebrows shoot up in surprise at how casually Lane just threw that out for us to hear.

"Whatever." I finally throw both hands up in surrender. "Both of you out. We need to bond, and clearly I need to teach numbnuts here how to shut a door and lock the sucker."

"Okay, one thing first." Lane covers his chest with his hands, and I already know he has some sort of wild proposition for us.

"Be strong," I whisper into Sophie's ear, and she nods.

"If you two survive your first week at training camp, will you do us the honor of attending a summer party with us?"

Not even a millisecond passes before Sophie bounces up off the bed and wraps her arms around Lane's neck screaming, "Yes."

I roll my eyes at her and hold back my gags. Yes, I'll admit I'm beyond excited for my first college party, especially with football players, but never would I bounce off the bed and squeal to high hell like a stuck pig.

"Out now, boys."

Chapter 4

An alarm shrills before the sun's up. Both Sophie and I do our best to ignore it. Rolling over, I see her huddled underneath her blankets with her pillow encasing her head.

"Sophie." My voice can only be heard between the bleeps and blares of the alarm. "Turn off your alarm."

"It's not mine, jackass."

She's right. My brain registers it's my phone making the god-awful noise as I sit up to grab it. When it quiets, I notice a text from my mom. Rubbing the sleep from eyes and squinting, I can barely make out her message.

Mom: Rise and Shine, love bug! I set your alarm for you today. You don't want to be late for practice. Remember Coach Lindsey said 7:00 AM sharp. Eat and show up early.

"Remind me to stab my mother." I snuggle back down into the blankets.

"Why did you set your alarm so early?" Sophie's voice is muffled through the pillow.

"I didn't. My mom did. She wants us to get up, eat, and show up to camp early."

"Well, let's go."

I peek from under the covers as Sophie springs from her bed. She's literally gone from slumber zombie mode to full-on Sophie in a few seconds. Her swift actions cause my head to spin and I groan a bit. But it's not until she pulls the covers from me that I want to outright kick her in the lady locker.

"C'mon. Your mom is right. Let's go shower—of course, not together—and then eat and head to the cheer gym. It will be good for us to show up early since there are fifteen new freshmen on the squad. You damn well know not all of them will make the second cut."

"You're killing me."

"Let's go."

In an attempt to make Sophie shut up and possibly shower, halfway asleep I get up and follow her across the hall. She makes good on her promise and does let me shower alone. Thank the good lord. Horror stories of showers and girls' dorms flood my mind.

The hot water actually does the trick of waking me up quite rapidly, and to my relief nobody joins us in the bathroom area. Sophie and I both get ready quickly and snag an apple and yogurt on the way out the door.

"Do you know the way?" I ask Sophie.

"Yes, that's why I was so damn late yesterday." She takes a large bite from the apple, letting some juices hang on her lips. "My ma and grandpa just had to make sure I knew where it was so I wouldn't fuck things up."

"Are you known as a fucker-upper?"

"That's a convo for late night with lots of chocolate."

"So, you're basically saying you're a fuck-up?"

Sophie cocks back her arm and chucks her barely eaten apple in my direction, and it gracefully nails me up the side of the head.

"What the hell?" I squeal.

"Just checking your reflexes. You suck."

We continue to poke fun at each other the rest of the fifteen-minute walk and avoid deep topics at all costs. We pass the training facility for the football team, and of course a dreamy look covers Sophie's face. I know what she's thinking about. And I'd be lying if I said I wasn't scanning the grounds for Tuck. Hopefully, practice won't kick my ass today and I'll go for an evening jog at the same time in the hopes of seeing him.

As we enter the training facility, I see the familiar

gym with mats covering the area. It's the same place they held try-outs. It's elite and has the best of the best equipment.

"Ladies."

We whirl around to see Coach Lindsey standing near a counter folding towels.

"Hi." Sophie waves eagerly.

I nod. "Good morning."

"You girls are a good thirty minutes early."

"We know. Just wanted to get here early." Sophie steps up proudly.

"Good, fold these towels while I finish today's workout schedule." Coach Lindsey sends the basket sailing across the countertop in our direction and heads down a long hall.

"That worked out well." I snag a towel and begin folding.

"Is she for real?" Sophie asks.

"I didn't pick up on any sort of joking tone in her voice."

We begin folding towels, and when the bottom of the basket comes in sight, others start entering the facility. Folding towels at the front desk isn't the way I'd imagined entering the cheer camp on the first day as a freshman. I came here to kick ass and take names, but instead I'm folding laundry and staring up into Stephie's face.

Perfect, the cherry on top of the butt-fuck cake called Blue's life.

"Well, look who we have here. Lane's new fuck buddy and the freshman who thinks she's cool enough to have dinner with our boys."

I don't miss the emphasis of the word *our*. Folding the last towel, I throw it down onto the counter and then scoop up the towering pile and set them in the basket.

"Look, Stephie, I fucking apologized for lunch and really shouldn't have, because it was harmless. I didn't come here to be best friends with you, and I sure as hell don't plan on allowing you to be a bitch to me the rest of the year. So, I have two suggestions for you. Get the fuck over it, or leave me alone." I pull the basket toward my chest and turn to leave. "Wait, better yet…both options would be best."

I don't wait for her response because I refuse to even pretend to hear the bullshit spew out of her.

"Holy shit, Blue." Sophie is on my heels, trying to keep up. "You just committed career suicide."

An evil laugh escapes me. "I used to be her and run my high school campus, and never once did I use intimidation. By hell if I'll let her treat me that way."

As my last word comes out I run straight into Coach Lindsey.

"Sorry." Mentally, I berate myself for looking over my shoulder at Sophie.

"Thanks, girls, and good for you, Blue. I don't tolerate any form of bullying or intimidation tactics from upperclassmen." Coach takes the basket from my hands. "But the first step is always a brave enough individual to stand up."

"I agree, but I shouldn't have said some of the things I did."

"It's water under the bridge, Blue, but you two better get your asses out on the mat and report for cardio."

We both nod, turn, and practically jog down the hallway, back out to the lounge, and then straight into the gym. And to my relief it's filled with several cheerleaders and a couple of other coaches. Right now the squad is at forty-five and will be narrowed down to thirty, or at least that's the email Coach Lindsey sent out last week. My mom told me it was probably just a scare tactic to push out the slackers.

"Line up," an enormous man hollers. "I want nine rows of five."

The man is wearing a black t-shirt with bold white letters printed across his chest. "Trainer." I have a feeling this man is here to kick our asses and do a damn good job at it. I try not to focus on any of the other girls as I follow Sophie to the back of a line. I keep my eyes focused on the man ahead of us. He's easily six feet tall, with broad shoulders, and no body fat at all. His dark chocolate skin is taut and defines each of his glorious muscles.

Sophie turns around to me. "Holy hell, he's hot. I'll run my ass off for him."

My stare is still locked on him and I'm unable to warn Sophie of what is about to go down. I know I should say something, but can't force my mouth to move.

"What did you say?"

I watch as the train wreck plays out in front of me. Sophie flips her head around, and her long black braid whaps him across the face, causing his eyes to bulge and his jaw to tense.

"What did you have to say?"

I pray for Sophie's wellbeing and for her tongue to produce something brilliant and talented. I know it's a far-fetched hope, though.

"I'm sorry," she squeaks.

"What was so important you had to tell your friend?"

"I told her…" Sophie pauses for a moment, and I feel my butt cheeks pucker up. "That you're extremely good looking."

Standing behind Sophie, I can't see the look on her face, but watch as she tilts her head to the side and can only imagine her puppy dog eyes going to work.

"See, we know who the resident ho-bags are this year."

I whip my head to see who said it and make direct eye contact with Satan herself, Stephie. Hot trainer man makes it over to her in three large strides and gets right up into her face.

"What did you say?"

Stephie repeats her comment, but this time not as loud or with so much conviction.

"Coach Lindsey warned me that we may have some problems with teamwork and respect, and I guess she was right."

All eyes are glued to him as he walks back up to the front of the squad and places his hands on his hips. Sophie was correct; the man is downright dreamy, and even hotter in his pissed off state.

"You'll run three miles." He points to the running track that borders the outside of the gym. "Twelve laps around that oval, and if anyone comes in over twenty minutes, we'll run it again until everyone's ass crosses that finish line before twenty minutes. Go."

I fight back the giggles threatening to escape as I watch the horror cover Stephie's face. Yes, she's gorgeous and has a drop dead body, but I can tell she's not fit nor very athletic. I take off before my damn mouth gets me in trouble, and I make sure to have a somber look on my face as I pass the trainer. Running is something I love and this task will be easy. I look over my shoulder for Sophie, who is a couple girls back, and try to nod for her to catch up with me. It takes her several seconds to do so.

"Stick with me, Sophie."

"I'm not a runner."

"I know, dumb shit, that's why I said stick with me. I'll get you to the line in time."

"We're going to die, aren't we?"

I smile. "You might."

I easily take each lap with grace, pacing my strides and making sure Sophie sticks with me. I get both of our asses over the finish line, and we were the first to finish.

"Nice work, ladies."

Sophie hunches over, fighting to catch her breath, and I watch as the rest of the girls struggle.

"They're never going to make it."

"That's real positive. Aren't you supposed to be the trainer?" My hands fly to my mouth and I shake my head. "I'm sorry. I never should've said that. No disrespect."

"I'm Jay. And you are, besides the friend of the girl who thinks I'm hot?"

"I'm Blue Williams."

"Ah, the basketball player who picked cheer."

My eyebrows shoot up in surprise.

"I know my stuff." He points to Stephie and her friends struggling on the track. "There's your weak link. They are going to come in thirty seconds too late."

Without thinking, I cut across the gym to make it to them. I know damn well Sophie can't do another mile, and judging by the look on the girls' faces, neither can they.

"You guys have to keep up with me, so we don't have to do another three miles. Can you do that?"

I turn around to see Stephie's shocked face.

"You're off pace and will force all of us to run another three miles. Look, you're the last ones. I'm not here to fight. I just want to cheer." My voice is breathy as I try to keep up my pace.

"Fine," a girl next to Stephie says.

I'd love to roundhouse kick Stephie in the crotch, but instead I turn to face the track and kick my pace up a bit.

She has to be the rudest person I've ever met and gives cheerleaders and women in general a horrible name.

We finish the half lap with only one more to go, and I'm surprised to hear the shouts of encouragement from the sideline. Even Sophie is up on her feet cheering, and Jay has a somewhat proud smirk on his face.

"Okay, girls, we have to book this last lap."

The girls keep up with me the whole way, and Stephie even finds the courage to pass me right at the finish line. I send her a slight eye roll, but then remember what my mom has always taught me. You'll meet some people in life who are simply glory hogs who demand every single ounce of attention there's to be had. And I'm a big enough person to let Hulk—I mean Stephie—have that.

The girls are all hunched over, trying to catch their breath, while the rest of our stares are fixated on Jay. He's taunting us by watching his wristwatch without saying a word or even offering any facial clues.

"All right, you made it. Now the real workout begins, and if I ever get wind of any of you treating each other that way again, it will be six miles."

Stephie gets to her feet. "Coach, I just want to say I'm sorry for my behavior, and it won't happen again."

I shut my eyes for a moment to avoid the eye roll of all motherfucking eye rolls. *Attention whores need attention to live. It is like air to them.* I repeat the saying over and over in my mind until I hear my name.

"Blue, thank you for helping us."

My eyes fly open and I realize the whole squad, along with Trainer Jay, is staring at me. My face turns beet red, and I simply shrug, repeating the attention whore mantra in my head. Oh, Stephie came to play, and I'll let her play her ruthless game while keeping my distance. I came here to work hard and push the limits on being the best. She will not distract me. I notice the nod Trainer Jay gives me before he goes on about our workout, and I know that he knows who is real and who is fake.

If any of the girls thought the three-mile run was hard, then the rest of the day is killer. Jay doesn't take it easy on us and promises we'll barely be able to walk tomorrow morning. I eat it all up, taking on each new aerobic or weight lifting task to heart. It feels good to be in the gym and being pushed like an animal. Sophie can't keep up with me, so I fly solo through most of the workout.

Coach Lindsey reminds us about the barbecue at her house tonight and that it is mandatory. Sophie assures me she has the address and can get us there on time. I love the girl already, but don't trust her, so I also punch in Coach's address on my phone.

As we exit the locker rooms, Coach Lindsey and several other coaches stand behind the counter chatting. I keep my head down as I walk by, not wanting any more conversation. My whole body aches and I need a hot shower.

"Basketball sure is missing out."

I look up to see Jay smiling at me.

"My heart is here, I can assure you of that," I say, pushing open the door.

"That was clear today."

Sophie and I make our way outside and start the path back home. We worked straight through lunch, and my stomach is just now reminding me of this.

"What's this basketball talk?"

"I played in high school." I shrug as I dig around in my bag, searching for any morsel of food, and find a half-eaten granola bar.

"You did?"

"Sure did. Was even offered a scholarship my junior year, but passed it up." Bits of granola fly out of my mouth as I talk.

"No wonder you can run like a freaking gazelle. I'm impressed."

As we pass the football training facility, a large group of men exit the building. And as if he has some sort of radar tracking system, Lane spots us and jogs over. He's freshly showered and dressed down in gym shorts, and of course Ethan follows him.

"Hey, girls."

Sophie gives Lane a hug and takes over the conversation as we all continue walking. Ethan tries to talk to me, but I don't have the energy, and quite frankly, he doesn't hold my attention. My eyes scan the sea of faces for someone else.

"Distracted." I feel an elbow contact in my left side.

"Ouch, what?"

"Distracted. Lane just said their coaches told them the showers at the dorms are down for the day."

"Are you fucking kidding me?"

"Why didn't you guys shower at the gym?" Lane asks.

"We didn't want to wait in line," Sophie answers.

"I'm jumping off a fucking bridge." I let my bag land on the ground

"Settle down on the f-bombs," a voice from behind me says.

As I turn around, I see Tuck Jones standing behind me.

"You girls can shower at my place if you want." His face is just as handsome as I remember, if not more, with his freshly wet hair and musky scent wafting off him. His face is stone cold serious.

I'm shocked at his offer, but too exhausted to reply to

him.

Sophie pipes up, "That would be amazing. Where do you live?"

"The gray house on the corner right before you get to the dorms."

God, sex even drips from the man's voice, and my legs begin to wobble. Then my body shakes a little more while my head takes another spinning dip. Before I make too big of a fool of myself, I take off toward the dorms. My legs are Jell-O as I try to walk, and I feel unstable, and then everything goes black as my body hits the pavement.

"She's starting to wake up."

When I open my eyes, I see Sophie peering down at me. I try to sit up, but she has hold of me.

"Blue, can you hear me?"

"Yes, why are you screaming?"

"I'm not. You fainted."

"Let me up."

I'm finally able to sit up and look around me. I'm sitting on a brown couch in an unfamiliar house that resembles a poster advertisement for a bachelor pad. I rub my hand over my throbbing head and then drag it down my cheek. Crusted blood and scratches line my jaw.

"Here." I look up to Tuck and his outstretched hand holding a glass of water and white pills.

I take the glass and empty the contents. Thirst is an overwhelming feeling right now.

"I'll get more water."

"I'm taking a shower. Ethan went and got us clothes at the dorms. Don't stand up."

"Okay, mother." I roll my eyes

Sophie bounces from the couch and I hear another voice join hers in the bathroom and know exactly what's about to go down.

"You should take these."

Tuck is back with another glass of water and the same two pills, with another container tucked under his arm. I don't question him and pop the pills in my mouth and easily down another glass of water. He hands me the other container he's holding—a chocolate flavored protein shake. I take it too and begin drinking it.

"I haven't watched you cheer yet, but hell, I've seen you eat shit twice."

I smile at Tuck's remark. "I try my best to entertain."

"What did you eat for breakfast?"

"Clearly not enough."

"I'd hope you'd be a smarter athlete than that."

Ouch. His words cut me and I have no response. He rises from his knees and heads back into the kitchen. I watch as his gym shorts glide with his movements, and then my gaze roams even lower to appreciate his toned, tanned calves. The man is straight muscle with an asshole attitude. Actually, I'm not sure if he's an asshole or just defensive.

I lay my head on the back of the couch and mentally spank myself for being such an idiot today. I need to be more prepared tomorrow with protein shakes and extra food.

"Here." Tuck places a large platter of food in my lap.

"Thanks. You're like a drug dealer of carbs." I look up at him with his hands placed on his hips and a pissed-off look on his face. "Sit?"

It takes Tuck several moments before he reluctantly sits on the couch, and it doesn't go unnoticed that he chooses the opposite from me.

"Am I that repulsive to you?"

Tuck makes eye contact as I stick a Twinkie in my mouth.

"Naw."

"Well, I don't want to come across ungrateful since all of this," I gesture to the pile of goodies in my lap, "but you're mean to me."

"It's just who I am."

"Wow, Sir Talks A Lot. I mean, don't go into depth or anything like that."

"I don't talk. I don't like people, and I keep my distance."

"Got it." I stuff the rest of the Twinkie in my mouth and mumble the word, "Asshole."

"I'm not deaf."

My face heats with embarrassment as I turn to look at him.

"I like you, is all," I mutter around a mouthful of food.

Tuck tries to tell me something, but we are interrupted by a group of men entering the house, and Ethan is among them. He sits on the table in front of me and tries to weasel his way in between my legs.

"Back off, alley cat." I grab the bowl of food and cradle it to my chest.

"C'mon, I'm hungry."

"No, I was talking to Tuck before you rudely interrupted us." I crane my neck to make eye contact with Tuck, but he's gone. I scan the room quickly and see no sign of him.

Ethan snorts. "That's funny."

"What's funny?" I ask, still searching for any sign of Tuck.

"You talking to Tuck. The man doesn't talk at all." Ethan successfully nabs a chocolate wrapped cupcake from the bowl. "Him scooping you up and racing back here is more action toward mankind than any of us has seen out of him."

"Whatever." I shrug and unwrap another goodie.

But on the inside my heart races with excitement hearing Ethan talk about Tuck and what he did. Dammit, if only I were conscious to feel his arms around me. If only.

"Your turn." Sophie bounds down the hall with a wet braid bouncing around.

All the noise in the small living room reminds me how delicate of a state my head is in right now. "Okay."

I set the bowl to the side and stand up, pleased to find my legs sturdy underneath me.

"Need help?" Ethan asks, with a mischievous smirk on his face.

"You haven't even been out of a relationship for twenty-four hours." Shaking my head, I step away from him, and he grabs the back of my thigh. "Don't touch me, Ethan, don't touch me ever again. I'm not an easy piece of ass and don't want anything to do with you."

His hands fly up in a surrendering motion. "No harm, no foul."

I don't respond and feel a tiny bit bad about being so harsh with him, but I want no gray areas with this guy. It's clear he's not the smartest one in the bunch. He might be the horniest, but not smartest. Lane comes jogging down the hall in a pair of loose sweats, chasing after Sophie. Scratch that, Lane is the horniest one.

I see Tuck watching me from the end of the hall, and then I look over my shoulder and realize he saw the whole scene play out with Ethan. He's standing between two doors. The one on his right is lit up, and the door to his left is open, but dark. I don't take my gaze off him as I walk straight toward him, blocking out all the noise in the background.

I stop inches from him, and Tuck doesn't move, keeping his hands firmly planted on those sexy hips and his seductive stare on me.

"I'd let you touch me, Tuck, and get to know every single part of me, but you don't do people or talking. Just know I think you're gorgeous."

His jaw clenches and he squeezes his eyes shut for a second before I turn from him and walk into the lit up bathroom. As I shut the door, I sink down the back of it until I'm on the floor, sitting Indian style and staring up at the water stained ceiling and wondering what in the hell this man has done to me. Must be the sugar high. It has to be the sugar high screwing with my thought process and the path from my brain to the words that flow out of my mouth.

One minute I'm telling Ethan off, and then seconds later I'm basically telling Tuck I'm hot for him. The most confusing part of all of this is that it's the truth. I know it, my brain knows it, and my heart keeps shouting it. *Damn, sexy fucker.*

Chapter 5

"You know Lane is a dick. Did he really think this was an outfit?"

Sophie giggles as the sunlight shines off her glossy black hair. "Hey, you'd just passed out and he was helping us."

"Whatever, he was rushing to get back to the house to bone you in the shower."

"We didn't have sex in the shower."

"Oh, really?"

"Fine, we did, and it was even better than the first time."

I try not to gag and send her a look warning her that I don't need any details, not even one. I keep my arms crossed over my abdomen, feeling naked as we walk back to the dorms.

"Slow down, Blue. I think I have shin splints from this morning."

"Too bad. I'm wearing a pink polka-dot sports bra with lime green spandex shorts. I'm really not in the mood to walk leisurely."

There's zero doubt in my mind that Lane knew what he was doing when he grabbed our clothes. Sophie wears hers proudly, strutting back to the dorms, and I just don't understand the girl sometimes.

"What do you know about Tuck?" I finally ask her.

"Who is Tuck?"

"Never mind."

"Tell me. You can't play the never mind card with me." She uses her fingers, air quoting her words.

"He's a guy."

"No shit. Spill."

"He's on the football team and intrigues me."

I pray like hell something shiny distracts Sophie from further questioning.

"And?" she pushes.

I'm tempted to scream *bear* or *fire* to see if that gets her off topic, but instead her cellphone rings and distracts her.

"My mom," she says, rolling her eyes.

I let her take the call and walk several steps ahead of her to get to my dorm room. I need a long nap before tonight's barbecue.

"Blue."

Shading my eyes from the sun, I notice Stephie walking my way. What did I do to piss off Satan now?

"I just want to say sorry for giving you the short end of the stick these past couple days."

I want to correct her and say day and a half, but decide to use my better judgment.

"Thanks."

"No, I really mean it, Blue. I know you're not a slut and didn't do anything with Ethan, and I was just being mean."

"Okay, thanks." I turn to walk off and bite my tongue to keep from congratulating her on using the word slut once again in my presence.

"I really mean it," she hollers.

What the hell does this chick want? Does she want me to hug her, hold hands, and sing? Or probably, knowing control freaks like her, she wants me to lick the bottom of her shoes and praise her for her almighty awesomeness.

I look back and send her a quick smile, not wanting her to think I'm ignoring her. Just like my dad always told me growing up, a snake is a snake no matter what skin they're wearing.

I replay today's events in my mind as I sink into my bed and burrow deep under my comforter. From the towel folding, to running, passing out, Tuck, Stephie, that Twinkie, and right back to Tuck, my mind refuses to stop analyzing every little thing, but it comes back to Tuck. My eyes close as the sweetest dreamy sensation floats through me just thinking of Tuck carrying me to his house, his posture on the couch, and then his stance at the end of the hallway. The more the man refuses to talk or let me get to know him more, the more I want him.

I guess a girl can always dream about you, Tuck.

Chapter 6

The barbeque is a hit, and I almost blush when Coach Lindsey catches me going in for thirds. Key word—almost. The food is delicious, with a gorgeous array of fish, chicken, and steak all grilled to perfection, adorned with veggies with similar grill marks. There is something about the tangy taste of the onions and green peppers that leaves my stomach wanting more. I manage to escape the looks of Trainer Jay, who is the chef for the evening, but not Coach.

"I'm real proud of you, Blue," she says as I trail down her curving, perfectly stamped, paved sidewalk. I just nod at her compliment, rub my full belly, and study each of the different colored hexagons stamped on the sidewalk. As shitty as the day turned out, tonight's dinner makes up for it.

Even Stephie is mysteriously quiet and quite polite toward me and Sophie. Snake, snake, snake…she's a snake, I repeat over and over in my mind, and then offer her a quaint little grin. I'd be a fool to make an enemy out of her and call her bluff, but I'm sure in the hell not going to go out of my way to lick her asshole.

"Ewww." I groan at my own thoughts.

"What?" Sophie stops dead in her tracks and turns to face me with a questioning face.

"Nothing." I wave her off with my right hand while I gently continue to rub circles with my other hand on my belly.

"What?" she demands once again.

I can already tell Sophie's the nosy-ass type that would take the time out of her day to figure out who farted in a room full of people, even pulling out the detective card and not giving in until the mystery was settled. She reminds me of my own mother. Not that my mother was a fart sniffer, by any means, but she sure didn't let anyone fire off a deadly one in her company. It's always best to spill it with these types of people, even if it makes no sense and contains absolutely no meaning at all, just to forgo the third degree, stare down, and guilt trips.

"I'm not going to lick Stephie's asshole." I throw up both my hands in the air, surrendering to her. "See, are you happy? My own freaking thought grossed me out, and I said eewww."

"I'm not going to even ask why you were thinking of Stephie and her butthole in the same sentence." Sophie's face dances with disgust and a tiny hint of questioning.

"Thank you." Taking two long strides, I catch up to the still half-disgusted Sophie and wrap my arm around hers. We chose to walk to the barbeque tonight, and now in the dark night without roaring traffic filling the streets, I realize it was dumb. Yes, a very dumb decision for two eighteen-year-old girls to make. We had no business being off campus at this time of night and walking alone. I know the stories of a local string of murders and rapes filling the news, which Trainer Jay shared with us over dinner, and it didn't help matters. I know three quarters of the goose bumps forming on my skin are due to my overzealous imagination.

"Quit worrying."

"What?" I freeze. "I'm not worrying."

"Oh really, you just chewing your bottom lip for an extra shot of protein?"

I shove her shoulder and then flip her the bird with my other hand. "We are two young, dumb girls walking the streets in the dark like Trainer Jay was talking about."

The roar of an engine cuts off my speech, and we turn to see an extremely jacked-up silver Dodge with all the bells and whistles.

"See, I called Prince Charming for us."

I see Lane's face as he slowly rolls down the tinted window.

"Fuck," I mumble to myself. If Lane is in there, that means Ethan is there.

As if on cue, he hollers from the back seat, "Ladies, want a ride?"

At this point, I'd rather jog home, but then I'm reminded of my full belly and screaming muscles and hesitantly follow Sophie over to the truck.

"We only have one other seat."

Lane crawls out and lets Sophie sit in the middle beside him. Ethan pats his lap from the back seat. All of the glorious food I enjoyed before now roils around and threatens to paint the sidewalk. I'm going to have to have a serious talk with Ethan about the excessive flirting and instill a strict friend code with severe consequences if the code is broken.

My glance darts to all the seats in the truck and notice every single one of them is taken by their fellow teammates, and then my vision lands on Tuck, who is huddled up in the back corner of the truck, sitting on the opposite end from Ethan.

"C'mon, it's just a seat, not a date." Ethan pats his lap again and licks his lips.

"Forget this." I continue down the sidewalk. "I'd rather walk back on my own."

The truck creeps along the road while I walk. I fight like hell to avoid making eye contact with any of them, or acknowledge the obnoxious truck inching along with me.

"Just go, you guys." I try waving them off.

I look up and see some rustling going on in the back seat, and I'm pretty sure Ethan's body was just thrown across the back of the truck. I keep walking, focusing on each time my foot hits the pavement and cuss my dumb ass out for eating so much, because I'd do anything in this moment to sprint.

Moments and several steps go by, then the silver back door opens. I don't have a chance to jump away before I'm scooped up in someone's arms and plopped down on a lap. The sound of the door shutting and the engine roaring to life fill the cab of the truck as it lunges forward, causing me to fall deeper back into my seat.

I immediately notice Tuck has me on his lap, and when I make eye contact I feel his hands move from my bare thighs. Looking down, I see he has his palms stretched out on either side of his legs, firmly planted on the seat. Glancing back to my bare thigh, I feel the sting of his hand vanishing. It was only there a second, but sent a jolting amount of pleasure strumming through my whole body.

I know we only have a few private seconds in the dark before the rest of the truck invades our tiny space. I study his gorgeous face and smile when I recognize that strong jawline in the moonlight shining through the window. A slight stubble peppers his face, and it's something I've never picked up before, but then again I've never been this close to the man. However, his black hoodie is familiar, with the hood hooked up over his head and beanie safely tucked underneath it.

Without breaking eye contact, I grab his left hand that rests next to the door, and his muscles go taut as I do. I'd give anything to feel his skin instead of the hoodie between us, but my thigh will have to do. And I thank the creator of very short shorts. I guide his hand back on to the top of my thigh and am slightly shocked when he follows my lead.

I lean back on his chest and realize how expansive the man is. I fit perfectly on one side of him and know I could easily snuggle in, throwing my arms around his neck and flexing my hips back into him, but I don't. My back simply relaxes on his left shoulder. Turning my head, I let my lips lightly brush against his stubble and feel the tickle of each tiny hair, and a large smile spreads across my face. I take the path back to his ear very slowly.

And when I finally get there and that stubble is gone, my smile slowly fades. "You are the only one allowed to touch me."

His hand tightens on the flesh of my leg, and I gasp.

"Blue."

His whisper is more of a growl, and I know exactly what's coming next. And I have no idea why I'm so magnetized to him.

"I know, Tuck, you don't do people or talk or anything human. I know."

The cab of the truck fills with Outkast singing *Roses,* and I'm a little stunned when both of Tuck's hands connect with my hips as he centers me in his lap. My back immediately mourns the loss of his solid chest. He pushes up as we settle in our new position and his message takes no words to convey. It's clearly pressed against my ass, and it makes me smile. Peeking over my shoulder, I let Tuck see my smile, but he only shoots back his dark gaze.

Our ride comes to bitter end, and I notice we are outside Tuck's house.

"Stop one, boys."

Without a word or as much as a glance back in my direction, Tuck hops out, leaving me on the cold seat of the truck. The remainder of the guys also get out, with the exception of douche bag Ethan, Lane, and Sophie. Of course Sophie and Lane are practically humping while he starts driving in the direction of the dorms.

My heart breaks. Wait, it can't break because I don't technically love Tuck, so maybe my ego fucking shatters with his reaction to me. I want to get to know the man, flirt with him, spend time with him…all the shit Ethan wants to do with me, I want with Tuck, and yet it seems he finds me as annoying as I find Ethan.

When the truck comes to a stop, I let all my manners fly straight out the window as I bolt for the dorms. I even forget to greet the security guard. I'm beyond being nice and just want my bed. It's a welcome sight being greeted by a dark dorm room. I strip down and find an over-sized cheer shirt I got at camp years ago and go snuggle deep down in my bed. My sheets smell like home, and it might be the only thing that can hold me together. I grab my phone and FaceTime my mother.

Of course she answers immediately. Her screen is as black as mine, and I know she and my father are in bed as well. Even in my high school years, I'd cuddle between the two of them when I'd endured a difficult day, and that's what I want now.

"Blue, you look so black." I hear my dad laugh at his corny-ass joke.

"I miss you guys."

I roll my eyes at the sound of my mom sighing and my dad saying, "I told you so, I won the bet."

I get lost talking to the black screen as all three of us share our days, and I know my mother cringes just like I do when my father shares some of his experience in the ER. The man is the best surgeon around. My mom warns me about the crime that Trainer Jay talked about at the barbecue, and I tell her to keep her ass off of Fox News. We all get our fill of giggles and chuckles before we hang up, and even as silly as it seems, I kiss the screen two times before hanging up.

I lazily begin to drift off as I keep my cellphone clutched to my chest, and I wish I had Tuck's number. I have to get him off my mind. When sleep is about to finally win out, the door flies open and reveals one silhouette. Sophie hurries to shut the door and uses enough courtesy to not flip on the lights. I hear her rustle around in her drawers looking for clothes to wear, and then she climbs in my bed.

"That was the best sex ever, Blue."

"Eww! Get your sex-soaked body out of my bed." I push her away as her giggles fill the room.

"We did it in the showers." She flicks a lock of her long hair on my shoulder.

"How?" I don't believe a word she says.

"Ethan was lookout, and we took our time. He even went down…"

"Whoa, whoa. Shut up."

Sophie laughs hard, shaking the bed. The little fucker loves taunting me with their sexcapades.

"But, Blue, for reals, Lane and Ethan both told me to warn you about Tuck."

Now the little ass has my full attention. "Why?"

"Because they say they've never met an angrier person than him."

I roll my eyes. "He's not angry, just reserved."

"They've known him a bit longer than you and are on the team with him. They're genuinely concerned for you."

"Tell them not to be."

Sophie slaps me hard across the face with another lock of wet hair, leaving behind a stinging trail on my cheek.

"He sounds dangerous, Blue."

"Well, I'm saying don't worry because he has no interest in me at all. Period. End of story. Don't want to talk about it again."

Chapter 7

Routine. It's the vitamin that keeps my blood pumping through my veins. It's taken two weeks to get a routine down pat, and I can say I'm finally over the homesick stage. Cheer practice, lunch, more workout, a yoga class, and then more cheer practice. Learning all new dances and cheers has been difficult, and not because of my skill level, but learning to work with new teammates. Stephie has been true to her word and kept her distance. She and Ethan made up days after their dramatic break-up, and I couldn't be more thankful because he treats me like a flesh-eating disease. I love it.

Sophie still enters the dorm room late at night sated and with rubbery legs from Lane's rabid love-making skills, and she sure as shit still tries to give me blow-by-blow action. I always act disgusted, but deep down I'm jealous, and pretend it's Tuck doing those things to me.

Ah…Tuck. Unfortunately for my heart, but fortunately for my lady parts, he also became part of my routine, and I tingle every night when his scent joins me. Damn, I really make that sound hot and sexy, when in reality it's only hot. He finds me each night on the jogging trail when I'm sweating and hot as hell as I push my body harder and faster. I've never spooked and performed gymnastics for him since the first night. When he catches up to me or I catch up to him, we find a steady pace and finish our workouts together.

Some nights he picks the paths, and some nights I do, and it all happens with no words. It's just the sound of his pounding feet and the scent I have, and trust me, I soak it all in each night and then memorize it as I fall asleep.

I refuse to be the first to talk to him. He knows I want to be friends, and I clearly know he has the ability to pop a boner for me, so yeah, I'm pretty sure the ball is in his court. It may be a deflated ball with no hope, but it's still in his court. And I hate to admit it's my favorite part of the day. Even when my muscles are pushed to the edge of ripping, I go running just to see and smell Tuck. And when I say see, all I see is a dark hoodie or long sleeve shirt with a beanie on his head and long gym shorts.

I want more of him. I yearn to see more of his gorgeous skin, and every single time we run underneath a light I take the chance to study his beautiful face. Most of the time he's doing the same to me, and I know I get to him whenever I see his strong jaw flex.

Tonight is one of the biggest mixers before school starts. All the athletes will be in attendance along with their coaches, so it's not going to be a rager or anything. But leave it up to Sophie and Lane to have the hook-up on the after party. My body lies limp on the bed, exhausted and with no motivation to go to this mixer.

Sophie tosses dress after dress out of her closet. Some she holds up to her body and checks the view in the full size mirror, and others are an automatic no. She stands in a matching bra and undies, and I know it's only a matter of hours before those babies get shredded.

She's left with an empty closet and a mound of clothes behind her, and some that landed around me on my bed.

"Well, shit. I have nothing. Absolutely nothing. Why didn't I schedule in a shopping trip this week?"

"Probably because you were too busy fucking Lane from one end of the campus to the other." I don't look up as I mindlessly scroll through my Facebook wall on my iPhone. It's filled with old high school classmates and their selfies and bragging posts. It's like my crack; it makes me sick, but I can't seem to look away.

I spot a hot pink sun dress at the bottom of my bed and hook it with my big toe. I try to fling it over to Sophie, but it lands right on my face, and I giggle. Sophie is so distracted now, digging through her mole pile of clothes, that I re-adjust the dress on my toe and send it flying. This time it lands right on the top of her head.

"This one was my favorite. Pair it with your silver flats and pull up your hair." I lie about the dress since I wasn't paying attention. The simple fact is that Sophie would look drop dead gorgeous in a gunnysack, and Lane would fuck her right out of it.

"Thanks, Blue." She bounds from the floor and begins getting ready.

Every once in a while I look up from my phone and admire the transformation Sophie is going through. I adjust the pillows under my head into a more comfortable position, cross my legs, and go back to Internet stalking. I've typed in Tuck's name over and over and even stalked friends we might have in common…and nothing. Which is really not that surprising since he's so damn private.

Our door bursts open and Lane grins over at his princess, who is now fully dressed and just finishing her make-up. I've come to terms with the fact we have an open door policy and don't lounge in my panties and camisoles like I would at home. Nope, it's always fully clothed here.

"Hi, Prince Charming." I throw my phone to my side and smile at Lane. All in all, he's turned out to be a great guy for my homefry.

He plops down on Sophie's bed and tosses me a bag of candy. And he's also discovered my vice…candy, anything sweet and sour. He also knows Sophie is never ready to bounce out the door unless it's a late night booty call.

"Damn, Sophie, you look so fucking hot." He sends her a wink, and she giggles. Their actions are actually genuine and super cute, but I'll never let up on my front of gagging or rolling my eyes.

"Sit up." Sophie stands at the bottom of my bed armed with a brush and some other hair items.

I raise an eyebrow at her.

"Sit up, I'm going to do your hair." She throws the hair products on the bed. "You have the prettiest hair here and only keep it pulled up in a messy bun."

"You do have gorgeous hair," Lane adds around a mouthful of taffy, and then quickly remedies his comment to make mine second best to Sophie's. I just giggle and sit up and let her have her way with me. I can smell styling products, heat from the curling iron, and Sophie's perfume.

"What are you reading now?" Lane asks.

"Facebook. I haven't started a new book."

"You mean a new porno?"

I toss a wrapper in his direction.

"You know, Blue, YouTube has all sorts of good free porn," Lane says through his laughter. Well, his laughter cuts off when he gets a sharp look from Sophie. "Baby, it's research. I learn new moves."

She shrugs and then blows him a kiss, and I promptly make a gagging noise.

"I read romance stories. They are not porn. It's more like fairytales."

"Okay, done. Look in the mirror."

I stand from the bed and have to give it to Sophie. She has my hair spot-on perfect. Loose curls lay all over with my long bangs pinned off to the side and some slight volume on the top. My curls are even soft enough to run my fingers through.

A tiny grin covers my face and I shrug. "It's okay."

"Shut up. Pick a dress." She points to the mounds and mounds of clothes on the ground.

"I'm wearing this." I point to my shorty shorts and lacy tank top.

"No, you're not."

"Yes, I am."

"No, you're not. I'm done hanging out with a perma-athlete who never dresses up. Pick a dress, bitch."

Lane always gets uncomfortable when we throw naughty words at each other.

"Okay, I'll wait out there with Noah." He points toward the lounge.

"We've brought a date along for you. Now wear something nice."

"You what?" I yelp.

There's nothing quiet or nice about what just came out of my mouth.

"A date."

"No."

"He's not Ethan. Trust me. He's one of Lane's teammates. He is very polite, quiet, and a good catch."

"You're a bitch and totally just broke the fucking friend code. I'm wearing this, end of fucking story."

I toss on my plainest pair of flip-flops and follow her out the door. The two men stand up, and I can't deny the man-candy they dragged along for me is fucking hot. His tan biceps bulge from his team t-shirt, and his sandy brown hair is long and shaggy, hanging in his eyes, but there's just enough of the blue shining through to make my heart pitter a bit.

Sophie makes introductions, and he's kind enough to extend a hand, so I react and shake it. Sophie makes an *awing* noise, and then I remember how many forks I want to stab in her eyeballs right now.

"I'll be right back. I forgot my purse."

Sophie gives me a sideways stare, fully knowing I'm a pocket girl. I'm going to show that twat-waffle just how much I appreciate being surprise-attacked via a gorgeous muscle man. Racing back into the room, I throw my hair up into a ponytail, erasing all of Sophie's styling, and then notice my Aztec print balloon style pants crumpled in a corner and decide to throw those bad boys on as well. Now looking back into the mirror, my normal high pony stares back at me with my short tank top and crazy ass pants. A hint of my skin shines through above the hem of my hammer-time pants, and I feel the desire to hike the bad boys up Urkel style, but giggle and decide against it.

Sophie hates these pants, and they just happen to be one of my favorite pairs. I've always been known to have a different sense when it comes to style. Yep, I'm usually a month or two ahead of the current trends, so I'm used to others harassing me about my hideous choices.

"Blue, let's go," Sophie hollers from the lobby in a spine-chilling cheer voice that I'm pretty sure floors four through seven heard as well.

I don't waste another moment and bustle out of the room. I stare right at her and silently give her the "paybacks suck, you bitch" stare.

"All right, let's go."

We all make our way to the elevator, and it's not until we are out in the sunshine of the parking lot that Noah speaks up.

"Your purse. You went back for you purse and you don't have it."

His concern is quite swoony, and, well, downright panty melting. I'll give it to Sophie; he is nothing like

Ethan at all.

I wave him off with a sly little grin. "Oh, it's fine."

As we all climb in Lane's friggin' monster truck, Sophie just has to pipe up.

"Quite the magician, purse to hobo outfit change."

I didn't miss the snark lacing Sophie's voice. I just shrug back at her. Lane picks up on the uncomfortable mood and takes over the conversation. I'm thankful he doesn't require me to be an active participant as he goes on about football practice and how hot the defense is this year.

Noah, like the perfect gentleman, takes a seat behind Lane on the driver's side, as I'm on the other side, behind the empty passenger seat. Sophie is nearly dry humping Lane as he drives. I glance over at Noah and am relieved that he's immersed in Lane's conversation. I take him in from head to toe and realize he's a freakin' god with a perfect face and the most beautiful body. Only his strong biceps are visible, but I can imagine what's under the rest of his clothes. Maybe, just maybe, he might be my perfect escape from my lust for Tuck, or at least curb my desires for the mystery man.

"So, Noah, you play football?" My fingernails dig into the skin of my palms, regretting such a lame conversation starter.

"Yeah, junior year, quarterback." He shifts politely in his seat to make eye contact.

And if I were any normal girl, with his baby blue eyes, sandy curls, and deep voice, my panties should've spontaneously combusted. Hell, adding quarterback to the mix, I should've been on fire with hot lust and using some of Sophie's quick-to-fuck moves. But nope, I just smile, admire his looks, and appreciate all the hard work he's no doubt put in to be the quarterback for the University in which football is everything.

"Wow, quarterback. That's huge. Congrats." My butt slides a bit over on the navy blue leather seat, closing our distance.

"Yeah, Momma swears I came out holding a football." He flashes his pearly whites at me.

I just picked up on his thick Southern accent. How in the hell I missed that before is beyond me. I think it was because I was trying to convince my panties to light on fire for this Adonis. Sophie sends me a quick little wink over her shoulder, not interrupting our conversation.

"That's funny. My dad swears my mom went to a hypnotist and ate pom-poms while she was carrying me." My hand lands on his thick thigh as we enjoy a moment of laughter, and I expect to feel a zing or at least a tingle. I'm no prude and know the excitement that courses through your body when new love or even lust is in the air, but nothing, zero, zilch.

Sophie takes a moment to interrupt our conversation and fills Noah in on my basketball scholarship and those talents, and how she swears I can run like a gazelle.

"Well, with legs like those, I'd pegged you for a b-ball kind of girl."

I feel a blush cover my cheeks, and it's not from his compliment, but from my asshole move and covering them up. This time his hand lands on my leg, and I don't flinch. We carry on in conversation about our upbringings and high school days filled with nothing but one athletic venture after another. We even compare notes on high school practices compared to the University level. And I'm not quite sure when it happened, but I slide all the way over to him, now sitting in the middle of the back row. Shoulder to shoulder, we both have our iPhones out, sharing pictures of our homes, parents, siblings…well, siblings in his case.

"Why the name Blue?" Noah asks randomly.

I shrug; I'm used to being assaulted with this question all the time. "Well, you've probably picked up that my mom is a freak. Actually, beyond freak, probably more along the lines of an OCD gorilla. She knew I'd be an only child because of complications." I twist my lips awkwardly, not really wanting to go into the history of my mother's ovaries with Noah. "Anyway, I'd be an only child, and she's always been determined to have me shine and stick out from the crowd."

"That's cool," he replies.

I usually get the look of shallow disgust from people when I tell that story. In all honesty, I generally avoid the question, but Noah is easy to talk to and I can tell he's really down to earth.

The truck comes to a halt and I realize we talked non-stop to our destination. An apology or four may be called for. It was fun having someone to talk to in a civilized fashion. Tuck treats me like a vile weed, Sophie and Lane are always humping like rabbits, and Ethan…well, Ethan is just rabid.

Noah slides out of the truck, and I glide back over the smooth leather to my side.

"Here."

I look down to Noah standing on the black asphalt in his loose jeans and tight team t-shirt, smiling with his hand held out and gesturing to me. A smile instantly shines from me just like a giddy little eighth grader. Damn, these pants sure do make it easy to slide back and forth on this leather…always looking for the silver lining. I place my hand in his and let him guide me from the truck.

And yes, I glide out just like a princess in a modern day fairytale down into the arms of a knight in shining armor who melts panties in his kingdom. Or at least that's how I picture it.

My damn pants catch on a piece of the door, sending me sailing down toward the not-so-cottony-soft asphalt. It's kind of like when you see a snake or bear in the wild and you piss yourself and run. Yeah, I literally tinkle a bit before crashing into the surface and clenching my eyes shut. I let all common sense float up to the clouds.

As I wait to land face down, two arms wrap around me, and I squeal and pee a little more from being startled.

"Easy there, tiger."

I look up to Noah's dazzling smile and know this is the moment any other girl would wrap her arms around his neck and pull him down into her, thanking him with a kiss and savoring his taste on her tongue. Me, nope, just damp panties from a slight tinkle or two.

Fuck you, fuck you, no, I really mean fuck you, Tuck. Fuck you for ruining me and whatever curse you've bestowed upon me.

"Thank you," I ramble out with a clear shake in my voice.

Noah places me on my feet, and like a true gentleman, holds me to his side for a couple seconds until I get my legs underneath me. I'm nestled into his side when I finally pick up on his scent, and let me tell you, it's grade-A delicious. All sorts of masculine musky aroma wafts from him, and I should be wanting to lick the man from head to toe, but I don't.

"All right, I think I'm good to go now," I say, sending him a quick smile. "Thanks for saving my face from becoming hamburger."

"Yeah, we wouldn't want that to happen, now, would we?" He gives me one final squeeze before he lets go. "And thank god you changed into those pants to protect to those pretty legs."

Ah, shucks, and he is sweet to boot. My feet are under me, senses clear, and when I glance up to see where everyone is walking, I stare into Tuck's eyes. And from the look of his locked jaw and very pissed off expression, I think he saw the whole scene play out. But then again, he looks pissed most of the time, so maybe he couldn't care less.

The little devil perched on my right shoulder screams for me cuddle right back into Noah's side and even place a thank you peck on his clean-shaven cheek. But in the end it's just not me to play a guy, especially not one as nice as Noah.

I break eye contact with the incredibly sexy asshole and begin mentally comparing the two men. Noah, a god, deep southern accent, quarterback, clean-shaven, all-American, Abercrombie and Finch type shit. Then Tuck, dark, mysterious, bold, built like a brick shithouse, there's no finesse or grace to the man, brown hair, stubble, and melts my panties and pisses me off more than anyone I've ever met in my life.

It's as if Tuck put me in a coma as we enter the large hall adorned in crimson, silver, and white. School colors paint everything in the room, and school spirit rings loudly, and all I can do is scan the crowd for Tuck. I'm sure he's slunk off to some dark corner and the rest of his team will soon crowd around him. I just don't get it.

I'm jerked by the elbow, not giving me much time to analyze the problem or scan any further.

"Blue, stop."

"Stop what?" I ask in disgust.

"Stop looking for him. I told you to stay away. Lane's a good judge of character and told me Tuck has his fair share of problems."

The automatic eye roll, bite of the tongue, and I want

to puke on Sophie and tell her how ridiculous she is, first off for saying Lane is a good judge of character when she's been humping him since the day they met, and then secondly I want to scream in her face that I don't give a flying fuck what she thinks.

"You really need to stop, Sophie. I don't care. And the man can barely look at me, let alone talk to me, so there's no worry there."

"I'm just worried that you have so little social life."

And this is when I can't manage to tamp back the wealth of anger pooling inside of me. I could throw some really mean words in Sophie's direction, and I fight to keep them back.

"I do have a social life, Sophie. It may not be what you equate to one, but I came here to cheer—nothing else."

I don't leave room for another comment, and she takes the hint. We settle into a table with a good mix of athletes. I'd guess there were a few soccer players, cross country runners, and of course football players and cheerleaders seated with us.

It only takes me minutes to notice an extremely large group of football players at one table, and I'd bet my left tit Tuck is hidden away in them. I'm not sure if the group looks large because of the number of people huddled around the table, or if it's because of the sheer size of the men. Some of them are practically giants.

Our table falls into an easy conversation between athletes. Noah took the seat by me, but has been a perfect gentleman, keeping his hands to himself. He cracks me up with all his southern phrases and sayings. Every time I raise an eyebrow at him, he stops and explains the phrase.

Coach Lindsey's voice rings out through the dining hall, demanding everyone's attention on her small frame up on stage.

"At this time, I need all cheerleaders to meet me in the back. Again, all cheerleaders in the back."

The woman is all business as she sets the mic back on the stand, hops from the stage, and jogs to the back. I waste no time in hustling my ass. Sophie lip locks Lane, which reminds me I should do something to Noah. I pat him on the back and give him a wink. As I walk away, I shake my head at my swoony move. It was more like a coach sending a player into the game. I'll be lucky if I don't send the poor guy running toward the hills.

My long legs close the distance, and I'm one of the first cheerleaders to make it to the back of the room.

"Good hell, did you steal those from Coach's closet?"

Trainer Jay is glaring at my pants, and I let out a giggle and then give him my best running man with a sassy little head swivel to finish it off.

"You win." He throws his hands up in surrender. "You have the moves, so you're allowed to strut them."

We form a quick circle with Coach in the middle of it.

"Surprise, girls." She pauses and we stare around at each other with raised eyebrows and some head scratches. "Tonight is your first performance. Get your asses to the locker room and change. There's a pinned up list of who is performing what, and which outfits you are wearing." Forcefully, she places her hands on her hips and puts on her no bullshit face. "Don't mess up. I'll be announcing squads and leaders as you go on. No pressure, girls."

We break fast, almost racing to find something that resembles a locker room. Once we find a tiny bathroom, we push and shove around the one list posted on the wall. My eyes scan over three or four times before I locate my name. My heart is pounding so loudly I can't concentrate on reading.

I'm in a group with sophomores and juniors, and we are doing a dance to *Without Me* by Eminem. I recognize the song immediately, since the other day at practice we were assigned songs and the chore of choreographing moves to them. I don't spend a ton of time analyzing my group, but I do see Stephie's name and some other really talented teammates.

Tears instantly prick and threaten to overflow. My one single goal was to make squad leader, and that just flew out the friggin' door. I knew it was unrealistic, but I worked my ass off and stepped up as a leader time and time again at practices. My brain knew it was unattainable, but I never convinced my heart of that simple fact.

When I find the box with our outfits in it, I shrug and lose all sorts of enthusiasm, but dig deep and muster up school spirit, still willing to give it my all. The sequined outfits are sexy and will showcase my legs. Silver and black. I hold my tears back and focus on what my dad would be telling me in this moment, and of course it would be something ridiculous to get me to giggle.

Looking around the tiny space and at the different outfits, I can tell this is a type of celebration, rite of passage, initiation, something of that sort, and it's clear that upperclassmen knew it was coming. I'm impressed not one of them leaked this fact, but then again I've kept my head down and worked my ass off. When my sight lands on Sophie, her giggling and positive attitude finally makes me crack a grin. The girl is simply content with life, and I know it's because she doesn't hold herself to super high expectations. But I'm starting to wonder if she has the right idea. I should be humping Noah and taking cheer as it comes…but the sad fact is I'm not wired that way.

"Let's go, girls," Sophie squeals and leads her group out as if she's already been titled.

I tug down on the shiny bikini top and adjust the girls. I guess the one good thing is that this is my song. It's the one I connected with and made most of the moves to during practice. Coach Lindsey picked an array of songs, and we were expected to know and learn each of the routines and work together as a team. At the time, I thought the objective of the lesson was teamwork, so I guess this is the final test.

Stephie leads us to the back of the stage, and it's only a few short steps until the red velvet curtain hides us. Coach Lindsey calls out all the group names, and I'm relieved to know we don't perform first. We are the third squad out of five.

"It'll be okay, Blue."

I feel a hand pat my shoulder. I turn my head to see Trainer Jay standing next to me, and it's as if he can read the disappointment on my face. I know I really need to suck it up and put on my game face. Sophie's group goes first and is dressed in a similar outfit as my group's, except the colors are gold and white. She dances her ass off with her squad to a Sean Paul song. Even though she wasn't titled leader, her genuine enthusiasm does warm my competitive soul a bit.

The next group performs to another upbeat song by Outkast. The sound blares from the speakers with the deep bass heightening the school spirit in the hall, but even through all the joyous celebration I don't miss the fact that another upperclassman was given the title of leader. The song trails off and the girls make their way from the stage, some carried off by other athletes and others simply taking a leap into the crowd.

My skin pricks and my mind has never been so rattled. All mental toughness just flew right out the fucking window. I want to turn and run back home to Colorado and go to a community college, forget Tuck and his smells, and my goals and dreams. I don't have long to plan my escape route as I'm pushed from behind. I'm second to last in line and realize Coach has already started announcing our group.

"Here we have our third group of Preston cheerleaders." She pauses a moment until we are all lined up on stage in our ready position. "This squad group will be cheering on the east side of the field at football games, entertaining our rowdy student section."

Well, that makes my smile glow a little brighter with thoughts of cheering at Tuck's games…and Noah's, that is.

Coach demands attention again as she begins speaking in the microphone. I wait for any second to have my heart shattered. "Trainer Jay and some of our guest judges had a hard time with this group, as the talent is deep and beyond anything I've ever seen in my years of coaching. I have no doubt the leader will take the entire team to new levels, including all the squads."

Stephie literally has the motherfucking audacity to inch forward a bit as if to presume the title is all hers. My eyes quickly scan our line-up and I pick out several other talented upperclassmen who could beat her out and pray like I've never prayed before to any god who exists that Stephie wouldn't be the leader. Anyone but that snake.

Coach goes on and on about the strength and amazing qualities of her whole team, and I just want her to cut my pain short and name the leader, let us dance, and then I'll make my escape back to the dorms to wallow. Not even the threat of the recent crimes on women all over the campus could hold me back from running to my room.

"It's with great honor that I announce Blue Williams as the squad leader for the school year, and all I have to say is what a feat, young lady." Coach's eyes stare me down and send chills up my spine.

I hear each word and I think processed them correctly. I catch sight of Sophie standing on a table and screaming, and even catch a quick glance of Tuck with something that resembles a smile on his face. Yet, I don't move.

"Blue." Coach nods at me, and that's when it hits me.

My body jumps into action, and I don't let the fact that I just overcame the impossible skew my judgment right now. I send a quick nod to the girls, and we line up for the dance and wait for the music to start. Once it does, I've never danced with so much pride, honor, and conviction in my life.

Once the song started, the lights were dimmed, so it is difficult to make out faces in the crowd. Especially ones who like to wear a dark hoodie or beanie at all times. But when I spot Tuck, I never break eye contact with him.

Our few minutes finish on stage, and I stride off with most of the girls, while others bounce off the front or are grabbed by other athletes.

Someone calls my name, and I see Noah standing with his hand once again stretched up to me with that smile covering his face. Several other football players also surround him.

"What?"

"Jump. We got you."

I shoot him a raised eyebrow, but don't have time to ask too many questions before Coach announces the next group, so I jump down into their arms and they carry me above their heads, chanting *Blue* all the way back to our table. I'd be lying if I said it wasn't the most awesome thing that has ever happened to me. As they gently set me down, my eyes do the scan thing they are so used to doing, but don't find the person they want to see.

"Thanks, guys," I squeak out and then take my seat, my heart still thundering.

Sophie bolts into the middle of my lap within seconds, squealing, hugging, and kissing all over my face.

"I'm so proud of you, Blue. I knew you'd get it."

I squeeze her back just as tightly, and still can't believe what just happened. It takes everything inside of me to watch and cheer on the next two groups. All I want to do is bolt from this chair and sprint straight outside to call my mom. No, a call won't do for this, but a quick FaceTime will.

Once the final group is finished and my cheeks are beginning to prickle from my perma-grin, I excuse myself from the table.

"You okay?" Noah asks with concern lacing his voice.

"Never been greater. Just going to use the restroom real quick." I place a peck on his forehead, and my actions shock me. I know it's from the pure and undeniable adrenaline coursing through my blood, but in no way do I have any intentions of leading him on.

"Okay." He sends me a little wink.

It makes me cringe, and I mentally note to never send any mixed signals again. Noah's too sweet to use or break.

My ass finally finds a perfect curb to plop down on out in the night air. California's evenings are amazingly warm and welcoming. I know my whole table would kick my ass if they knew I was out in the dark all alone with the monster the news and our coaches keep warning us about, so they'd triple shit their pants if they knew I ran in the dark every single night.

My fingers strum the edge of the cement as I wait for my parents to answer the FaceTime. I know they're spending a relaxing evening at home tonight.

Mom's face is the first to beam back at me, but it's Dad's voice I hear first.

"Baby Blue."

I shake my head and giggle a little bit at one of his many nicknames for me. But it's that one I always scold him for using. All I can manage to do is give a squeal scream combo back into the phone. My mom immediately picks up on it and smiles back at me and begins screaming nonsense right back in my direction. Dad finally appears in the background and can't help but smile.

He's been around the two of us and knows our idiotic squeals of delight only mean one thing.

"I got it."

Something catches my attention, and I turn to see Tuck leaning against the brick wall with his arms crossed over his chest. He only nods at me, and not taking time to analyze it any further, I turn back to my parents.

"Holy hell, is Preston having serious cutbacks?" my dad asks.

Titling my head, I ask, "What?"

"I mean, my hell, I'd hope they could afford a bit more fabric for you."

I peer down at my outfit and know exactly what he's talking about.

"I'll be on the phone with the athletic department first thing Monday making a donation to the cheer squad for clothes."

The low rumble of a chuckle fills the night air, and I

know it's Tuck admiring my dad's antics. It doesn't even bother me that he's listening to the conversation. I give my mom a blow-by-blow replay of the whole thing, and tell her even Stephie was in my group, and this was all sprung upon the freshman. I don't miss the worry that flashes across her face, and I know she's nervous about me being able to handle the job.

"I got this, Mom."

"I know you do, Blue. I've never doubted you for a second."

My dad's attention has been lost, and I see him reading a golfing magazine.

"Well, I better go. I just had to see your faces." My dad pulls down the magazine and grins back at me.

"I love you, baby girl. Be good, and if the b-ball team comes after you, take it, please."

I roll my eyes at him. "I love you too, Dad. Thanks for everything, Mom, and I love you. Bye."

I literally have to force my finger to push the red circle to end the session, and when I finally do, I feel that homesickness that long ago left wander right back in.

I push it all down and try to focus on the positive of the whole situation. Standing up, I brush off my sequined ass and shake some loose twigs from my legs and begin to walk up the stairs.

"Don't ever go out in the dark without me."

I freeze at his words and pierce him with a glare. "Excuse me?"

"You heard me, Blue."

"Tuck, you won't even talk to me, or fucking look at me most of the time. How the hell do you know when I go out in the dark?"

"I run with you every night. It's no coincidence I pass you."

I roll my eyes and don't let him creep into my happiness right now. Walking the rest of the way up the stairs, I just hear a growl from the man.

Chapter 8

"I'm not sure we should be doing this, Sophie." I nervously fiddle with the hem of my tank top.

"Everyone," she drags the word out, "is going. The whole team. It's tradition."

I climb into the back of Lane's truck, filled with reservations about going to a party. Noah was nabbed by some of his teammates and I nodded to him to go ahead. I clutch my sleek iPhone and debate updating my Facebook status, but in the end decide against it. Everyone in my hometown would just chalk it up to my parents buying me the spot once again, because seriously, I could never work hard at anything. Insert sarcasm. I guess it was the thing to do when jealousy took over…make up lies.

"You could've ridden with Noah." Sophie turns back to me.

I look to the empty spot in the back seat and wonder why in the hell I'm back here. Surprising Sophie and causing Lane to swerve across the road, I catapult myself into the front seat.

"Nah, he's nice and all. Will be a great friend, but no spark."

"He's a good guy, Blue." Lane's deep voice fills the cab of the truck.

"He is."

We pull up to an extremely large house—or castle—that's already bumping and grinding with activity.

"What is this?" I ask.

"Brett, he's a senior and a local. This is his house, the party pad."

"Holy shit," Sophie mutters as her eyes take in the

scene before us.

The full moon and streetlights illuminate the perfectly manicured lawn adorned with a pearly white picket fence. The house is framed with a gigantic front porch where several bodies are congregated. The music from the house is easy to hear. Lane jumps from the truck while Sophie and I follow him with deer in the headlights looks.

Finding some comfort, I stuff my hands in my pockets of my ever so comfortable pants. Sophie is still dressed in her cheer outfit. I neatly folded mine and stowed it on the back seat of the truck with plans of having it framed in a shadow box. *Thanks, Mother, for making me neurotic like you.* I shake my head at my thoughts, but still plan on shadow boxing that bitch.

We wind through an endless sea of bodies, some with drinks in hand, while others just chat away the night. We finally make it to the center of a large area where people are dancing. I'm startled by a booming voice.

"She's here."

The music instantly cuts off and a voice fills the air, and I notice a makeshift DJ standing in the corner of the room.

"It's that time, cheerleaders. Get on with your bad selves."

Instantly, music is blaring once again. Laney, another team leader, snags me by the elbow and propels me up onto a table with the other leaders. I stand like a fucking idiot as the others start freestyling to *Hot in Herre* by Nelly. The rest of the cheerleaders surround the table and start dancing as well. It only takes me minutes to find my rhythm and groove with the girls and finally fully accept the position as a leader. I let my hair down and even swing it around as I carelessly twerk a bit too aggressively. I make sure to pooch my tush when the infamous part of the song comes on and then break out into the running man, letting my pants have some of the limelight.

The DJ picks up on my moves and switches to the classic *Can't Touch This*, and the other leaders just shake their heads. It's evident there's no old blood lingering in them. My dad insisted if I was going to dance and cheer that I know some oldies, and granted, MC Hammer wasn't at the top of his list, but I learned it.

The crowd's response is ridiculous, in turn causing me to dance harder and with sharper moves. When the song ends, I give the signal across my throat that I'm done and take a bow. My heart couldn't handle another song as my lungs struggle to inhale and exhale the stifled air filling the room. Hopping from the table, I look for an exit, or at the very least a window to get some fresh oxygen.

It doesn't take long to find one off to the side of the dance floor, and it is already opened. My hip rests against the frame, and I try to calm the adrenaline and my rapid breathing. Pulling out my phone, I text the new developments to my mom. *Damn, I do really need to get a life.*

I know she won't see it until morning, but I still give her play-by-play action.

"Damn, can't stand to be away from him that long?"

At the sound of a familiar, dark voice, I glance up into Tuck's eyes. I shoot him a questioning look, and he only nods over his shoulder. Noah has his phone out texting as well. Just as I have calmed myself down, my fucking blood boils at his words. Part of me wants punch him in the baby-maker, and the other part is thankful the asshole is talking to me.

Without much thought I whip the phone in his face. "I'm texting my mommy, asshole." He just shrugs and isn't fazed much by my words, but I do sense some tension leave his shoulders. "And why would you care, Tuck? You can't stand me."

"It's not that, Blue."

"Then?"

He just simply shakes his head once again, not even attempting to offer an explanation. The lights in the whole house go out, leaving us wrapped in a pitch-black cocoon. A strobe light above the dance floor flicks out some lights, but not near enough to be able to see anything. Cellphones start waving back and forth with their flashlight apps on to the slow and steady beat of a song. And when I hear what song it is, I realize it may be one of the saddest love songs ever. *Let Her Go* floats in the air as the tone of the party slows way down, and I'm guessing this is when several bodies will clear out and boy parts meet girl parts behind closed doors in any slice of privacy they can find.

I turn to walk away from the window and am halted when Tuck wraps his hand around my wrist. His fingers easily overlap my tiny wrist, way overpowering me. I am about to finally lay into him and just let him know much he has ruined me, my ovaries, and hot man radar.

Before I have the chance to rip him a new asshole, he lowers his face to mine.

"I didn't get a chance to say congratulations, Blue."

He sweeps his sweet lips over mine with a little taunt of a kiss, and my knees buckle, and I literally sway. His hand goes to the small of my back, dragging me into him while his lips fully land on mine. I'm so stunned I don't even attempt to be a partner in the kiss.

Tuck lets out a low growl that vibrates off my lips, awakening something within me, and my lips come alive. I kiss him back hard, trying to soak up his taste in one long, hard swallow. I'm the first to open my mouth to him, and he doesn't hesitate as his tongue darts into my mouth. The room is still black and the song plays. I know once the lights go on that I'll lose this Tuck, so I take full advantage of this opportunity.

The sweet taste of the man in my mouth drives away all common sense, and boy, does he know how to kiss as he runs his tongue all over the inside of my mouth. He shoves the small of my back into him, and I can tell just how excited he is. I want him like I've never wanted anything in my life.

I finally snap out of the luscious trance his mouth spun me into and kiss back and begin to explore the inside of his mouth with my tongue. I raise my hands to run them through his hair. Two fingers reach below his beanie, and he shakes his head, not breaking the kiss. I rest my shaking palms on the top of his shoulders and let him spin me around and push me up against a wall. He hikes one of my legs up and around his hip, and grinds up into me. My head drops back and I moan.

His lips trace down my neck, licking and sucking on anything he can find. I know the song is almost over and go in for the kill.

Firmly I place both of my palms on his cheeks and make him look at me.

"I want you, Tuck. I want you as a friend, and I want to touch you. Let me in."

Just another growl and he's devouring my lips like a hungry, wild beast. This time my hands trail from his cheeks back behind his ears with the intention of wrapping my arms around his neck. I feel Tuck tense up and don't give two fucks. My right hand stalls a bit when it hits the bumpy and marred flesh behind his ear. I don't leave it there long in fear of Tuck pulling away. My fingers interlock around the back of his neck and I kiss the fuck out of him, putting everything I have out on the line. I bite down on his bottom lip, and it's not a subtle move as my hand reaches down between us and I grope his hard erection.

Still sealed to his lips, I tell him again, "I want you, Tuck." My words are lost in our heated passion. The song ends and he pulls away, leaving no body contact at all.

"Congrats, Blue." He steps back and slides his hands in the pockets of his jeans. "Noah is a good guy. We've played together for years. He'll take care of you."

"I want *you*, Tuck."

He slowly but steadily begins to walk away while staring at me, and with each step I slide down the wall until I'm on my butt with my head buried in my knees and tears are streaming down my cheeks. I don't look up to see if he's still watching me, and I sure as hell know I won't feel his touch again. That greedy bastard, taking me like that and then leaving me and trying to deflect my feeling to his teammate. My blood boils with the sheer selfishness, but then again, I was the greedy one soaking it up.

God did give Tuck lips to kill a girl.

Chapter 9

The radiant California sunlight beams through the window and perches right upon my eyelids as if targets are covering them. I growl knowing Sophie left the blind open once again.

"Sophie."

No response, and I don't need to turn to see that she's not in her bed. It's something that's becoming more and more common. I swear Lane pays off our dorm supervisor to allow so many sleepovers.

Bitching and moaning the whole way, I force myself out of my warm blankets, scamper across the cold tile, snap the blinds shut, and then jet back into my warm blankets. I close my eyes and wait for sleep to come to me again. The damage is done with the bright sun and the chilly, tingling pads of my feet.

"I swear, one day I'll twat tap your ass, Sophie," I bark out into the empty room.

My fists ball into the soft comforter, trying not to replay last night over and over in my mind. It's not like I dreamt about the sound of my name being called, dancing at the house, and then those lips. Yes, each one of those haunted my dreams, and now I'm up to face it in full-force reality.

I do what every college student does and grab my phone from my nightstand to mindlessly troll shit on Facebook and Instagram. I make the huge mistake of stalking Stephie's profile and can practically feel her venom pricking me from her nasty statuses. She's clearly not thrilled and looks to be my biggest obstacle. I would've paid to see the look on her face. I bet it was the equivalent of having her lady nuts chopped off when my name was announced.

I grin and know Karma is a bitch, so quickly stop relishing Stephie's pathetic life. This may be the longest and most miserable day of my life. No cheer practice. A whole day of nothingness, and it practically makes my skin crawl at the very thought. I lose myself in my phone, call my mom and listen to her ramble, shower, chow some yogurt, watch inappropriately funny-ass videos of people doing dumb things on the Internet, until Sophie waltzes into our dorm.

I'm happy for her and her relationship with Lane, but it would be nice to have a close friend to hang with. It just means I need to make friends with some of the other girls on the team, but I've been way too focused on practices.

"Hey, queenie leader," Sophie sings as she bounds on me.

"Please do tell me that you showered off all your hot animalistic sex."

"I did, but then we did it in the shower. Does that count?'

I flip her off me as we both erupt in a fit of laughter. She knows nothing of last night's encounter with Tuck, and I'm bound and determined to keep it that way. Seeing her sends thrills of excitement coursing through my body, and I'm not sure if it's because of human contact or the fact she reminds me of everything cheer team.

"Hey, Lane and I are heading out to the beach for the rest of the day. Want to go?"

My ass is up and off my bed bounding around the room, and while I'm ripping through my drawer to find my bikini, she keeps talking.

"Noah's going too." She sounds nervous, so I turn to look at her and smile.

"Cool. He's really nice."

Her shocked expression is hilarious, but I don't pay attention to it, as I need to get out of the room five minutes ago. Boredom nearly killed me off. I find my favorite black bikini and hurry to put it on and then begin packing a beach bag. Since I'm from Colorado, I'm probably going to look like quite the tourist with my matching beach tote and towel, but I grab them anyway and throw in a couple bottles of water, jerky, and some serious junk food. The last thing to land in the bag is an apple, and I only toss it in there to alleviate the guilt.

"I'm ready."

I turn to Sophie, who is moving slower than slow, fiddling with her hair and then readjusting her bikini while studying all of it in the mirror. I'll never understand girls like her who take more time than needed. I mean, hell, she already has Lane wrapped around her little finger.

"I'll wait in the lounge," I say, hoping she'll hurry up.

When I walk out to the area with couches and a big screen TV, it's deserted except for two people. Lane and Noah. I actually spark up at the idea of another individual accompanying us, so it's not just a suck-face-fest with an awkward third wheel attached.

"Boys." I flop down on the oversized yellow chair and prop my tan legs up on the ottoman.

They both nod at me, but I don't miss the huge smile on Noah's face when he sees me, and it makes my gut hurt because I don't want to send him the wrong signs. I need to keep it in the friend mode with this guy and make sure it's clear to both of us.

Lane is the first to break the silence. "Congrats on last night."

"Thank you. I'm still in shock." I rub my knobby

kneecaps and try to play it cool.

"Yeah, I bet." Noah winks at me.

"Lane, get in there and drag your girl out. I'm going stir crazy in this place." I stand and start pacing.

"You got it."

"And no funny business in there," I holler.

Lane is in full stride, but takes a moment to look over his shoulder with a devilish grin.

"Oh my god, those two hump like bunnies. I'm not sure how Sophie can manage to walk sometimes."

"Young love. I'll take you in my car and send Lane a text to meet us." Noah grabs my bag and heads toward the elevator before I have the chance to say yes or no, so I just follow him.

Friend mode, friend status, I repeat over and over in my mind, because after last night's kiss, it's clear my body is hardwired for only one man. And clearly that man has some attachment issues.

"We could wait." I stall at the entrance of the elevator.

"I won't hurt you, Blue, I know where your heart is." Noah reaches out his hand to me once again, and still no combustion happening down in the lady parts. I grab it and hop on the elevator. I guarantee his reference was to cheering, and he was right, and that will be the perfect excuse to keep it in friend mode only.

Just like last night, he keeps everything relaxed and light-hearted. He opens the door to his sleek black sports car for me, and I raise an eyebrow at him.

"Damn, this is fancy for a college athlete. Someone paying you?"

He chuckles at my reference to the biggest no-no in college sports.

"Nah, it's from back home."

"Southern boys drive things like this?" I point to the

dash.

"Some of us." He dusts his shoulder with his hand as he settles in the driver's seat. "The good ones, that is."

I laugh at his joke as the engine roars to life. Everything about this man should turn me on. The more I analyze it, the more pissed I become at Tuck. I'll give it one more day. One more day of hanging with Noah and see what happens.

Noah turns on the music to some extremely loud and very thumping tunes. It's upbeat, and before I realize it my thoughts and the music have consumed the whole trip. When I look up, the beach is amazing, and it's the first time I've been since arriving here in California. I squeal as I get out of the car and wrap Noah up in a great big hug from the sheer excitement. It's just something about the sounds of the waves crashing in and the peaceful lull encompassing the atmosphere.

I didn't even realize my legs had taken off around the front of the car. Thank god Noah is a star quarterback and wasn't thrown off by my leap into his body. Brushing my hair back over my shoulder, I step back and try to play it real cool. The slight ocean breeze has the top of my hair swirling in circles. I try to calm it down when I notice Noah is staring at me.

"What was that for?" he asks with that sly grin.

"I needed this, Noah, I needed out of the dorms, and I mean…this is gorgeous."

"It's my favorite place here. Spent a lot of time here my freshman year coping with homesickness and going from top dog to low man on the totem pole." Noah tosses my beach bag over his shoulder and I giggle.

"What?" he asks with a raised eyebrow.

"You look so cute packing that bag." I point at the neon colored tote, scrunching my nose up. "You know I can carry it."

"I'm a gentleman. I'd carry a pink purse for a lady."

I just shake my head at him and wonder why in the hell god gave someone all the swoon factor. He bottled it all up in Noah and didn't leave an ounce of it for Tuck.

"Why don't you have a girlfriend?" My hand flies to my mouth when the question comes out. "I'm sorry. You don't have to answer that, it's just…"

Noah picks up on my embarrassment and rambling words. "It's okay, Blue. It's pretty simple. Football is number one in my life and always has been, and the right girl hasn't come into my life. Still waiting on my princess who doesn't mind if I live in a gym and can share me with football."

"Guessing there's not too many of them out there," I reply.

"Right. I could ask you the same question."

And with a silent stare he waits for my answer.

"Same as you." I grab my towel and lay my claim on a piece of the sandy goodness, kicking off my flip-flops and letting my toes sink into the warm sand.

"Sometimes I want a girl, but other times I know it will never work out."

I shrug, full well understanding the words that just came out of his mouth. I didn't date much in high school, and now it seems the only man I want has no desire to be with me.

"Noah."

"Blue."

"How well do you know Tuck?"

He grins as he pulls his tank off over his head, sending his sandy brown locks flowing in that light breeze. God, I should be dry humping my towel for this hunk of a man in front of me, but I'm not. I hear some giggles and look over my shoulder and notice a small crowd of college girls whose ovaries just melted from the blonde Adonis.

"Why?" he finally asks.

I just shrug and really don't know how to answer him, so I don't.

"Tuck's a good guy."

And he simply leaves it at that. No more information is given, and I sure as hell don't want to act overly interested. Lord knows Sophie is already on a rampage about me even looking at Tuck. She'd flip if she knew I was digging for information from one of his teammates.

"Quarterbacks and running backs have to be close, right?" I strain my neck to look up at him.

"We do, Blue, and we are. Tuck isn't the number one running back in the country for no reason."

I just nod at the information and realize it may be the most positive thing I've ever heard about Tuck, and in an odd sense it pulls me even further into his orbit. It's clear Noah is a great guy, and he just totally gave the green light on Tuck.

"Ever been in?" He nods in the direction of the raging blue waters.

It takes me a minute to process his words, as I was in a knee-deep mental affair with Tuck.

"No. I'm just here to tan, not get eaten by a shark."

"C'mon, you have to put your toes in, Blue."

Noah nabs me by the elbow and guides me to the water, and I pull back every single step of the way.

"You better take that little dress off or you're going to be soaked," he warns as we near the ocean.

"Noah," I try to yell through my laughter. "Stop, I don't want to be shark poop in the morning."

He doesn't quit tugging, so I pull my sundress off over my head and toss it back behind me. Noah's grip slips on my wrist, and I try to bolt back to my safe place on my towel, but before I know it, his large hands are grabbing me around my waist and throwing me over his shoulder.

"Noah," I squeal.

He doesn't answer me, but simply begins jogging toward the aqua blue water. I don't know how close we are or when I'll be going in. I just see my towel and happy place moving further and further from my vision.

"I can't die." I whap his ass with my palm.

He laughs, and when he does, I catch movement out of the corner of my eye. It's hard to focus on it since I'm bouncing up and down on Noah's shoulder, but when I steady myself just enough I can make out a black hoodie and long pants running down the beach. Then I make direct eye contact with Tuck and my world stops when he pierces me with dark brown eyes. They seem nearly black as coal right now, and it pains me to the core.

He doesn't break our stare and has a stone cold mask covering his face. I reach my hand out to him as if a final silent gesture asking for him to accept me in his life, and that's when my back hits the ice-cold water and I freefall down into the depths of the ocean with it hugging every single part of my body. With clenched eyes, I relive the moment Tuck kissed me and the way it made me feel. I let it all take over as I float below the surface for a few seconds. And when my breath nears the end and panic mode is about to hit because of lack of oxygen, I finally get it. Tuck makes me feel this with his simple presence. He sends my whole body into a panic mode just wanting and needing more, even during our dark, silent runs. He's as powerful to me as an ocean is to Mother Nature.

Popping up from the water, my hair mats to my face, and quickly I wipe it from my eyes while gasping for air and searching for Tuck, but he's gone.

"Blue, you okay?"

I hear Noah, but can't reply to him. My eyes continue to scan the beach for Tuck.

"Blue."

I'm swooped from my treading water into Noah's arms.

"Hey, are you okay?" he asks again.

I manage to nod and let him swim back to the beach with me.

"I'm sorry, Blue."

"No, no. It's not you at all. Trust me." I sit in the sand, letting the waves run up and down my legs.

"What was that?" He sits next to me, drawing lines into the soaked sand.

"What?" I turn to face him.

"You were on another planet, Blue. I thought you were seizing or going to drown. I feel like an ass."

"No, it wasn't you." I slap his thigh. "The water was just cold, and then I stayed under too long. I had to catch my breath."

I'm pretty sure Noah takes the bait and relaxes a bit. I take a handful of wet sand and throw it on his legs.

"Payback."

He just chuckles at me and I keep a close eye on his hands in the sand, knowing he too has a competitive heart.

"But did you die?" he asks with a crooked eyebrow.

Another handful of sand hits his chest, and I nearly die from laughter at the shocked look on his face.

"You little shit," are the only three words that come from his mouth before he's on his feet and dragging me back out in the water and trying to dunk me. I squeal and fight against it, but then again I'm under the water. We goof around for several minutes, then I let my body float peacefully among the mild waves before we hear

Sophie's voice and see her waving from my towel.

"We better go." Noah grabs me again, dragging me back to the beach to join our friends.

With one foot out of the water and on the soaked sand, I feel myself wrapped up in Noah's arms once again.

"You're such a sucker. I always win." He flashes his pearly whites at me before tossing me back into the water, and right before I go under I see him run up to the towels. And the most ironic part of the whole situation is Noah just gave me the sweetest gift he could—another glimpse of that kiss.

Chapter 10

The first week of college kicked my trash. Learning the ropes of courses and where everything was on campus about put me under, but then add in cheer practice, and my own workouts, plus my nightly runs, equals my ass thoroughly kicked. On the fourth day of college, I called my mom sobbing about the walk around campus and the lack of parking, and I'm pretty sure I ugly cried for about an hour to her, and I know most of the meltdown stemmed from sheer exhaustion. The next day a baby blue cruiser bike with a wire basket on the handlebars showed up for me, and I never wanted to lick a piece of metal so badly in my life. The bike is my lifesaver on campus, running from class to class.

During my senior year of high school I completed my freshman year of prerequisites, so academically I'm in second year courses, but still considered a freshman. Now three weeks in, I'm adjusted with my bike and schedule, and the schoolwork is easy enough for me.

I've seen Tuck every night while running, and lately he's been staying closer to me while we complete our route. However, not a word is ever exchanged between us. Cheer practice has been great, and Stephie has actually stepped back and followed suit, which nearly made me choke from shock. Keep your friends close and your enemies closer, the silence before the storm, and all sorts of warnings always flash through my mind when I'm around her. But I'm seriously starting to think she's just miserable with herself.

"Sophie, I'm going to the gym."

It's a rare afternoon that she's actually in the dorm room. Unlike me, when she's not doing homework or working out, she's sleeping. I swear she and Lane must fuck all night, every night. I take every moment I can to try and encourage her to get more involved in cheer and less in Lane, or at least her academics, but she never takes the bait.

"Naw, I'm going to take a nap, then I have class."

"You should really get your lazy ass up."

"Worry about yourself."

It's the same response I get every time.

"Okay, bye."

I don't feel so badass driving my bike to the sports gym and then back to the dorm, so I always walk, even though it's a good mile or two with rolling hills to straight up mountains. The walk is one hell of a workout itself. I've found the best time to access this gym is in my spare time in the afternoon. It's after my last class of the day and before cheer practice. I love and hate the gym. I love running so much I tend to get very lean and always need to tone my muscles.

When I finally arrive, a sheen of sweat covers my forehead and my water bottle is already empty while my bladder is full. As soon as I open the gym door the noise level is extremely loud when it's usually a dull roar.

I bolt for the bathroom to drain and refill. Sprinting around the corner, I run into someone. I was so preoccupied doing the pee-pee dance I wasn't paying a lick of attention. I bounce back hard from the collision, dropping my gym bag and water bottle to the ground. A hand catches my wrist, helping me steady myself, and when the blur of the clash comes to a halt, Tuck is holding me to his sweaty chest.

"Fuck, Blue," he says breathlessly, "I just about steamrolled your ass."

"I have to pee." It comes out as a squeak as my cheek is pressed against his dampened white t-shirt.

It's evident he's in the middle of a grueling workout as his heart throttles against his chest and I can feel the blood pumping through his veins at a rapid rate, but I still don't move. Moments go by as he holds me to his chest, but then icy reality sets in and he lets go, stepping back with caution and making sure I'm okay. He bends over and picks up my water bottle, and when he does, I see Noah watching the whole exchange.

"Here." He hands me the green Gatorade bottle. I make sure my fingers brush against Tuck's as I grab it. He then hands me my bag and I do the same thing, grasping for as much contact as possible.

"Watch where you're going next time, Blue," he growls and walks around me.

I'm shameless and watch him go, enjoying the view of his long gym shorts riding on his hips and the sweat soaked long sleeve white t-shirt outlining each one of his hard muscles. I force myself into the bathroom, then find a locker for my stuff, and have to talk myself into actually going to work out.

Working on my mental toughness, I open the door with my ear buds already in and playlist ready to go. The gal at the check-in desk stops me, so I pull out one ear bud.

"Some of the starters are here for the team. It may be crowded."

"Thanks." I try to be polite, but really want to respond with, "No shit, Sherlock."

Only focusing on my phone and the lifting workout displayed on the screen, I get right to work. I asked Trainer Jay to set up something for me to keep me nice and toned. I had to beg, plead, and kiss his ass for it. He's always worried about me pushing myself too hard. Thank the lord he doesn't know I run at night as well. He'd die and then kick my ass for being out after dark.

It's an arm day, and I cringe when I see that's the part of the gym Tuck and his teammates are occupying, so I decide to skip arm day and go for the leg machines. I'm here dressed and ready to go, so there's no way I'm about to leave now. I catch a glimpse of Tuck spotting Noah out of the corner of my eye, but see his attention is more on me than Noah. I smile at him and shake my head. My knees buckle when he actually grins back at me.

Noah has become one of my best friends. Sad, but true, I know. The gorgeous quarterback, and he's just a friend. We study together when we have time and have made a few more trips to the beach. Not one romantic exchange, and I am fine with that, and Noah seems okay with it as well.

I begin a quick warm-up jog on the treadmill and groan when I see Captain Asshat walk into the gym. I have no idea who the guy is, but he's a dick and I've always distanced myself from him. I think he's a soccer player, but he's a puke, and of course he heads my way to start his workout, probably avoiding the mass of football players.

I'm not sure what it is about him that intimidates me. Maybe it's the glares he sends other females training in the gym, or that one time he bitched out another person for not placing the weights back where they belong. He gives me tingles, and they're not the right type of tingles. More like stranger danger tingles.

I've got this. Avoid staring at Tuck and ignore asshat, do your forty-five minute workout, and then head back to the dorm. I turn up my Kid Rock and go about killing it. Finishing my warm-up, I make my way to each leg machine, doing my sets and pushing the limits on the weights I add. When I stand from the leg press bench, sweat rolls off me, I get light-heated for popping up so quickly, and my legs feel like rubber.

It's pure satisfaction knowing I'm pushing my body to be better. Before I have the chance to grab the towel and spray bottle to wipe down the machine, I'm shoved from the back, sailing me into a stand of free weights. My face slams down into them and I feel the sting of the unforgiving iron.

"Watch where the fuck you're going." I hear a voice, but my head is still adjusting to what the hell just happened. "You think you can just pop your pretty blonde ass up anywhere?"

A warm liquid runs down the side of my chin and I immediately taste blood in my mouth. When I'm finally able to stand up and turn around, the last thing I see is a blur of Tuck and flash of Noah chasing behind him. Chaos breaks out in the gym as Tuck has the man pinned to the ground and hammers him in the face while growling every single foul word as he lets his fist fly.

Noah and a couple other teammates try pulling Tuck off the man, but their attempt is useless. The back of my heels hit the rack behind me while my palms spread across the same iron weights my face smacked into earlier as I stare.

"Tuck," I scream. "Tuck, stop."

My voice finally catches his attention and he looks up in my direction.

"Stop," I plead again, and it knocks Tuck off guard and gives Noah and another man the opportunity they need to pull Tuck off of the man, and to no surprise it's asshat. Campus security rushes in along with some football coaches, and shortly followed by Jay. They surround the man on the ground and listen to the manager of the gym, and it all still seems hazy to me. My body has remained frozen on the weights trying to process everything that just happened.

Was I in his way? Did he push me? Did I pass out again?

"Blue."

I look up into midnight black eyes as Tuck rests his forehead on mine and places a hand on the small of back and tugs me into him. I feel the pad of his thumb try to brush away the blood, then he just holds it there to stop the bleeding. His touch and his voice cause me to cry, and it shocks me, but I can't help it, and then my body begins to tremble.

"What happened?" I ask.

"Do you know him?"

"I've been working out here and I've seen him, but avoid him."

"He came up right behind you and shoved you."

"Why?"

Tuck places his lips on my forehead, leaving a light and sweet kiss on my skin.

"I don't know." He shakes his head and I relish the feel of his lips.

"Blue." Jay breaks between us with no apologies. "God damn, child, you're always pushing the limits and your damn body." He guides me to a bench to sit down. "We're going to the hospital."

"No." I sit up and look at my face in the mirror. "It's a split lip and a bruised cheek. I'm fine."

"Hospital," Tuck barks out behind Jay.

"Tuck, over here now." I look in the direction of the voice to see a mean-ass guy who seems to be extremely pissed off.

"At least your coach is nicer than his. That boy's gonna get his ass ripped." Jay examines my face further; I can feel his breath on my cheeks as he talks.

"Who?" I ask.

"That guy friend of yours who was all up in your

business when I got here."

"Tuck?"

"Yeah, Tuck."

"But why?"

"He has bloody knuckles and that guy on the ground has a bloody face."

"But that guy pushed me and he's a dick." My voice is shaky but comes out louder than I intended, and it catches the attention of Tuck's coach.

I bolt upright and feel the pain in my cheek tingle and the side of my lip swell. Jay tries to hold me back, but can't.

"Excuse me, Tuck helped me. He shouldn't be in trouble."

The man tugs down on his visor and stares me down, but he has no idea that mean coach face does nothing to me or my courage.

"What happened to your face, young lady?" he asks with his intimidating stare.

"That man pushed me to the ground for no reason, and my face caught the iron rack." Then I find a little courage and place my hands on my hips. "And my name is not young lady, for your information. It's Blue Williams, head cheerleader for squad C. Tuck saved me and shouldn't be in trouble."

The last part may be a teeny-tiny white lie, because I think the asshole wasn't going to do anything besides push me, but oh well. The gym manager breaks into the crowd.

"She's right. I'll handle the situation from here with Dominic." He points to the ground where the man with a bloody face is now sitting up. Both of his eyes are already swollen shut. "Coaches, do what you need to."

"You're going to the hospital."

My head swings back to Tuck's coach.

"Excuse me?" I counter.

"You're going to the hospital to get checked out." He doesn't back down on the tough guy act. "Your face is swollen and you're still bleeding from your lip."

I take a step in. "My father is the top plastic surgeon in Colorado, and as soon as my ass ends up in an ER he'll be on the prowl. I may be a cheerleader," I use my hands to air quote cheerleader, "but I'm not fragile nor a victim."

I don't wait for his response, Jay's, or Tucks before I spin on my heels and head straight back to the locker room on my now rubbery, shaking legs. An odd combination of adrenaline, anger, and admiration swirl around my head, and I surrender to a full meltdown as I let my body sink down the chilled slate gray lockers until I'm curled up on the ground. The tears roll down my knees as I pull my body tighter into a ball and cry, allowing all my frustration to leave my body. I'm not sure how long I'm on the floor sobbing before all my tears dry up and I'm just left with swollen eyes and a severe headache from the freak-out.

"Blue."

I recognize Tuck's voice from the entrance of the locker room, but I don't answer him.

"I'm coming in."

If I had the energy to roll my eyes I would, but I don't. The next thing I hear is footsteps, and when I look up he's towering above me and the butterflies spark up in my belly. Even in the lowest part of my life, the man seems to be able to turn me on somehow.

I hear the cracking of his knees as he squats down to come face to face with me.

"Your trainer is worried about you. Says you're pushing yourself too hard."

He stares at me and I want more than anything to

light the motherfucker up and let him know it's all because of him. If Tuck would just give me an evening or two to satisfy the hunger I have for him, I might not be so hell-bent on working him out of my system. But instead I shrug, not willing to share with the man who will give me nothing in return.

"He said no practice tonight. I'm taking you home."

I watch as he eyes the open locker next to me, then grabs my bag and throws my water bottle in it.

"I can walk. I just need a few minutes." Digging my heels into the speckled tile floor, I slide my body back up the lockers and don't miss the fact Tuck's eyes seem to drink in my every move.

"You're not walking home."

I step right up into Tuck's face and tap his chest with my finger. "You do not have the right to tell me anything when you have done nothing but treat me like dirt."

I get even more pissed off when my tears come back. I know it's a surefire sign that I'm beyond pissed, but it's also a sign of weakness. Tuck ignores my words as he throws me over his shoulder. I begin to panic and beat on his back, calling him all sorts of colorful words, but when he steps out into the gym I see a crowd. Instantly I shut my mouth, not wanting to cause a scene. A stout running back packing a girl over his shoulder while carrying her gym bag is scene enough. I don't need my added screaming.

The outside air runs over my sweat-dampened body.

"Are you ready to fucking listen?"

God, I want to punch this guy in the balls.

"Yes," I spit.

Tuck gently sets me back to the ground, and soon as my sneakers feel the solid pavement below them I'm ready to bolt, but he's able to catch my wrist first and begins dragging me toward the parking lot. I dig my feet in but have no other option but to walk or my knees will be kissing the asphalt.

"Tuck, I'm fine. Let go of me."

He comes to an abrupt stop before a tan Dodge truck, places both of his hands on my shoulders, and turns me to face the driver's side mirror.

"Look." His fingers dig into the top of my shoulders. "You call that fine?"

My red, swollen eyes stare back at me in the mirror, and I notice the dried blood around the corner of my mouth and the deep blue bruise forming high on my cheekbone.

"Get your fucking ass in my truck."

His voice isn't even a growl this time. It's harsher and way more forceful, so I don't question him. I slide behind the wheel and try to scoot to the passenger seat, but his hand catches my thigh, stopping me in the middle of the bench. He climbs in and I notice a long scar on the back on his neck that I never noticed before. It's a serious scar, but I'm distracted as he slides something on my face.

When I perch up to look in the rear view mirror, I see he put his aviators on my face. I go to protest the action and finally give the fucker everything I have when I see Stephie and her clan waltz in front of the truck, waving. I turn slightly toward Tuck to hide the injured side of my face and do my best job of smiling and waving back.

"Thank you," I whisper and lay my head on his shoulder. As soon as I relax into him I realize how fully exhausted I really am. The sound of the engine and the slight moves of his shoulder as he drives calm me a bit. My eyes get heavy as the silence in the cab combined with the lull of outside noises soothe me, while the breeze refreshes my heated skin.

The truck comes to a stop and I slowly lift my head to see Tuck's house and Noah sitting on the front steps with a grocery sack between his legs. He smiles when he sees the two of us, and that damn thing is so contagious I can't help but shoot back a pitiful grin.

He's on his feet and opening the passenger side door before I grasp what's going on.

"Damn, Blue, what's the other guy look like?"

He reaches his hand out to me, and I take it and without thought, like it's second nature. Looking over my shoulder, I watch Tuck do what he does the best, slink back into the background.

"What are you doing here, Noah?"

Noah and Tuck both laugh, and it's obvious the joke is on me.

"I live here."

My heart sinks so low in my chest it slams into my stomach as I feel the sting of their punch line.

"Don't look so surprised, Blue. It's not like we're a lot of serial killers or something." Noah guides me up the steps and into the familiar living room.

"Who else lives here?"

"Just the two of us." A deeper voice answers, and I see Tuck leaning back on the counter in his open kitchen with legs crossed at the ankles.

"I managed to steal some clothes from your dorm room. I think Sophie and Lane were in the shower."

A disgusted moan escapes me. "Let me bet, our door was left open and you pilfered through my underwear drawer like a creeper?"

"Damn, Blue, you have me nailed." Noah chuckles as he tosses the bag in my lap. "I also picked up some first aid shit at the store. Us football men just rub some mud on that shit and get on with it."

"Oh my god. You sound like my dad." I laugh hard at

Noah and his ridiculous statement. "Going to have to avoid FaceTime with my mom tonight. She'll freak."

I hear a can of pop open in the kitchen and turn to see Tuck in the same position, but tipping back a beer.

"Fucking healthy, Tuck." Noah shakes his head and strides down the long hallway, leaving me sitting on the couch.

Well, hell, this is a wee bit awkward-ish...in the most awkward of ways.

I hear my ring tone and know it's my mom. Tuck holds my phone out from his stance in the kitchen, not making a move toward me. Pulling myself from the couch, my face throbs with pain, and know I need to get some ibuprofen down the hatch sooner than later. With the plastic bag gripped in my hands, I walk toward him and take the phone and let out a breath when I see it's just a call and not FaceTime.

I let my belly lean on the counter next to Tuck, so that our shoulders and arms rub each other, flop the grocery sack down, and poke the green call button flashing on my screen.

"Hey, Mom." I force my voice to be chipper and just what she'd expect to hear.

"Blue, sorry no FaceTime today. I have a tee time at the country club, and by god if I'm going to let that bitch, Dianne, beat me today. I need my game face on."

"It's okay, Mom." I chuckle into the phone.

If anyone ever wonders where my competitive spirit comes from, they don't have to look too far. I feel a slight vibration rolling off of Tuck and know he can hear my mom's voice.

"How was school today?"

"Really good." It's all a lie, but I don't need her to worry at all. "The bike's holding up and I have everything down. Cheer practice was cancelled tonight, so I'm just going to settle in and catch up on some work."

"Oh, why was it cancelled?"

I panic and look toward Tuck, elbowing him in the bicep. I only get a shrug and a hell-if-I-know look from him, and then he points to the lights.

"What?" I mouth.

"Power out," he whispers.

"Blue, are you there?"

"Oh, yeah, I guess there's a power outage at the practice facility, so a day off for me."

I tear open the bottle of meds in the bag and pop three, and then I grab the beer from Tuck and wash them right down. I listen to my mom go on about how odd it is the power is out, and the more she talks, the worse I feel for lying to her, and the more of the beer I pound.

"Okay, Mom, I'll let you go. Go kick ass and take names. Text me your winning score."

We exchange our goodbyes, and I hang up the phone and bury my face in my hands.

"You suck at lying."

"I never lie to my parents, ever. That was just the cherry on the top of my fucking day."

Tuck turns me around and has me seated up on the counter before I know what's happening. My legs open for him as he steps in between them. I can't help but focus on his blood crusted knuckles. Reaching over, he turns on the faucet and dampens a paper towel and begins cleaning my lip. I place my palm on his forearm and try to grip onto his shirt. He flinches and becomes uncomfortable, but I don't care and refuse to lose the contact.

I let out a contented sigh as I watch him open a tube of antibacterial cream, and I shoot an eyebrow up in his direction. He melts my heart when he smiles back at me.

"I could use rubbing alcohol to clean you up."

I wedge one of my legs between his. "And I could knee you in the nuts."

A chuckle vibrates low in his chest as he uses his inner thighs to squeeze my leg. I let go of his arm and grab on to the back of his neck, dragging my hand up to his beanie.

"I won't take it off. Trust me."

Leaning forward, I'm shocked when he doesn't move. My lips brush his, and I inhale his scent. He pulls me to the edge of the counter and then relaxes, cupping my ass, and I smile at him.

"Why are you fighting this?" The question pours from me onto his lips.

"You're way too beautiful for me, Blue."

Cupping his face, his cheeks sting my palms.

"You don't feel this, do you? I've never wanted another person in my entire life, and you won't let me in, Tuck."

"I can't."

"You can."

"You won't like what you see, Blue. You're meant for a castle and king. I'm just the poor peasant."

"You have no idea what I'm meant for."

Before he has the chance to throw me another excuse, I seal my lips to his, and it's a short distance, considering we were lip to lip. I let go of his beanie, hoping he'll be comfortable with me if I leave it alone. I wrap my arms around his neck, pulling myself deeper into him. Our kiss turns passionate and heated as our lips attack each other. I'm the first to open my mouth, and Tuck doesn't hesitate to take full advantage, exploring it deeply with his tongue. He forces me back as he leans into me, and my head crashes into the cabinet behind me. The pain sears the back of my skull, but I don't let it stop me. Tuck winces as he hears the crashing sound, and I take advantage of his mouth, lapping up his taste and sinking my teeth into his bottom lip.

Noah's voice slices into our passion. "Tuck, Blue, I'll go grab us dinner."

We pull away and I peer over Tuck's shoulder as he buries his face in the crook of my neck. I focus on the smile pressing into my skin. Noah sends me a look, and there's no hiding what we were doing. It's written all over my swollen, love-struck lips.

"Pizza okay with you two?" A blush covers Noah's light skin.

"Yeah, sounds good," I reply.

"I'll be back in fifteen."

He shoots out of the kitchen as if his ass were on fire, and once I hear the front door slam shut, Tuck and I break down into fits of laughter.

Wiping the tears from my eyes, I say, "I feel like we've been busted by a father figure or something."

"Yeah, no shit." Tuck finally lifts his head and looks me in the eye. I love how soft his eyes are now. "I'm sorry if it comes across that I treat you poorly or whatever. You're too much, Blue. Too much beauty, life, and, shit…I don't know."

Tuck pulls away, placing his hands on the top his beanie, and for the first time I see real pain covering his face and don't push him any further.

"I need to shower." My fingers grip the yellow countertop until my knuckles go white. It's the only way I won't reach out for him.

"Follow me."

"Hey."

He stops in mid-step, turning back to me. "What?"

I hold up the tube of medicine he was going to put on

me.

"After your shower."

"Now."

It only takes him three long strides before we are back in the same position, but this time it's only business as he applies the medicine and then helps me off the counter, gently setting me back on the ground.

"See, you know how to treat a princess, Tuck." I slap him on the ass as he walks me down the hall to the bathroom. He doesn't respond, only shaking his head.

We enter the small bathroom, and it's so clearly a man's place. I watch as he kicks together a pile of towels and boxers into the corner.

"This shower is a tricky bastard. I'll get it going for you."

I let Tuck fiddle with the shower and gaze in the mirror at the impressive bruise forming on my face. It's going to take a whole hell of a lot of concealer to hide this one.

"Okay, it's ready. My room is right across the hall if you need me."

Tuck left himself open for so many comebacks on that one, but I let it go. As he passes, I snag his wrist to stop him. Bringing his hand to my lips, I plant a light kiss on each blood crusted knuckle.

"Thank you, Tuck."

He throws his head back and stares up at the ceiling. "You're going to ruin me, Blue."

I hear Noah walk in the front door, so I let Tuck go and lock the bathroom door behind him. If the man wanted to take this further, he could have me in this damn steaming shower, but he doesn't. I hear the deep voices of the two men down the hall and let my curiosity get the best of me.

Cracking the door a bit, I try to listen to their

conversation, but with the noise of the shower and the distance to the voices, I can only make out Noah's enthusiastic tone. After several minutes, I give up and climb in the shower, remembering Tuck's soft brown eyes, gentle touch, and the words he spoke. I've been pissed and intrigued by the man, but nothing has hit me as hard as when I saw the pain covering his face. It was deep and real. It almost seemed as if he wanted to reach out to me as well, but forced himself to hold back.

I growl at the man soap and two-in-one shampoo and conditioner in the tub. Since there's not much of a choice, I use it and rinse off quickly. Turning off the shower and sliding across the smiley face shower curtain, I see someone left me two fresh towels and a brush on the counter. I could've sworn I locked the door. Well, whoever it was, I hope they enjoyed my rendition of *Everybody* by the Backstreet Boys.

I open the bag and take one look at my clothes and holler Noah's name out the cracked door.

"What?"

"Are you fucking kidding me?"

I throw on the clothes he packed and twist my hair into a quick side-braid and walk out into the living room. Both men instantly crack up laughing when they see me dressed in short spandex volleyball shorts and a sequined cheer top which is basically a glorified bra.

"Really, Noah?"

He shrugs, takes a bite from his slice of pizza, and talks through his food. "I felt like a fucking weirdo going through your drawers."

"Yeah, you're even more of a weirdo for picking this, you sicko."

"Here, I'm going to shower." Tuck gets up from the couch and puts his empty pizza box to the side. "I'll get you a t-shirt."

I follow him back to his room and watch him dig around his drawer. He pulls out a long sleeve black shirt and silently seeks approval.

"Thanks." I snatch it from his hands, and of course make sure to make contact with his flesh.

"Go eat while I shower."

I wait in his room, hoping like hell he will pull his shirt over his head and I can finally see those defined abs, but he just walks into the bathroom and comes back with the grocery sack and my gym bag.

"Thank you."

I hear the bathroom door shut and the shower turn on, so I go to the living room.

"Noah, I'm going to kick your ass."

"Blue." His laughter fills the room again. "I'm sorry."

"You look so sorry. Did you pigs leave any food for me?"

"On the counter."

Noah took me to his favorite pizzeria two times for lunch, so he knows exactly what I like on my pizza and ordered me a whole one. I'm sure with the intentions of him and Tuck polishing it off. I throw a slice on a paper towel while still talking to Noah. Their living room and kitchen are pretty much one big room with no barriers besides a low bar.

"Why didn't you ever tell me you lived with Tuck?" I flip open every cupboard and finally find one filled with plastic tumblers from the dollar store.

"You never asked."

"Is your water safe to drink?"

I can't see Noah's face, but can hear his chuckles.

"In the fridge."

"Thanks, jerk."

It takes me a few minutes to get settled on the couch

on the opposite side of the living room from Noah with my pizza on my lap and glass of water by my side. We sit staring at each other for a long time before either of us is willing to talk. The sound of the shower fills the room. I have questions and want them answered now.

"Tell me about him." My words are the first to break the silence.

"I've told you. He's a good guy."

"Noah." This time my voice comes out a bit too whiny.

"Tuck is closed off. A shut book. A simple guy. He goes to school, plays football, and goes home for the holidays." Noah leans forward on the tattered red fabric recliner. "Want to know how many girls I've seen him talk to in three years?"

"How many?"

"One. Want to know who?'

"Me." I take a bite of pizza. "Well, is he gay then?"

"Tuck, gay?" His laughter this time is uncontrollable.

"I mean, I have great tits." I set my pizza on the couch and cup them for emphasis. "And I've all but thrown myself at the man."

"Blue, if you really like him, you have no idea how much he's already given you."

"Then why is he so quiet and reserved? And scared of me?"

"Not my story to…"

I cut him off and mimic the rest of what he's going to say. "…to tell. God, I can't stand your damn brotherhood of football."

"It's called best friends, Blue. I love him like a brother, and I can tell you're special to him. I just don't know."

"Don't know what?"

The bathroom door opens and our conversation is

over. I try to peer down the dim hallway in hopes of getting a view of Tuck, but he's too swift.

Chapter 11

"That was a bullshit call."

A loud voice jolts me from my sleep. Looking around, I see football film still streaming through Tuck's MacBook to their television. I fell asleep listening to Noah and Tuck talk football after I filled my stomach with pizza and drank a couple of beers. A total no-no, diet-wise, but my give a fuck button is busted.

Somehow I managed to curl up in a ball on the couch using Tuck's thigh as a pillow. Mentally, I curse myself for startling awake, because this is a position I don't want to leave.

"Sorry." Tuck pats my hip.

"What time is it?"

"Past ten."

Noah's lean body stands up and points at the paused screen. "See that son of a bitch right there? That's who you need to get by in our game opener and you'll be racking up the yards."

"Yeah, if your greedy ass isn't passing the ball all over the field."

"Fuck off." Noah turns the TV off. "Blue, your phone has been going crazy."

"Where is it?" I mumble, half asleep.

I feel my head being mashed between his thigh and rock hard abs and again can't complain.

"Here." My phone is placed in my hands and roll onto my back to see my screen filled with frantic texts from Sophie.

"Everything okay?" he asks.

"Yeah, just my roommate freaking out. Funny she even knew I was gone. She's never home, and I mean never. She's always out fucking Lane somewhere."

"So, you sit in your dorm alone?"

"No, I have my stuffed animals."

"Funny, Blue."

Tilting my head back on his thigh, I look up into his face and don't break eye contact. "No, I go to class, work out at the gym, spend three hours at cheer practice, eat dinner and do homework, and then I go on a glorious nightly run. I only sleep there."

I want to add *and pine over you and our shared kiss.*

"Jay's worried about you."

"I know," I say, rolling my eyes and typing out a quick message to Sophie.

"You need to slow down a bit."

"Whatever. I bet your day is the same as mine. I could tell you the same thing, Tuck."

"You're a stubborn shit."

"Not as stubborn as you."

Another cellphone goes off in the quiet, dimly-lit living room, and I look back up to him.

"It's mine," he replies while digging into his pocket.

"You can answer it."

"Nah, it's fine."

I give him a moment to silence the call.

"Hey, Tuck."

"Yeah," he answers, and I can tell he's distracted by whoever is calling him.

"Ask me what my favorite part of my day is."

He looks down at me with a crooked eyebrow.

"Blue Williams, tell me your favorite part of your day."

"My nightly runs. I feel free and optimistic and it's the only time in the day when a sense of completeness fills me." I raise my palm to cover his cheek. "It's you, Tuck."

"Blue, I…"

I push my finger into his lip and shake my head, not wanting to hear his excuses, and then get up from the couch.

"Thanks for feeding me tonight, and, well, kicking that guy's ass."

I shove my feet into my tennis shoes and look for my bag, then finally spot it at the end of the couch. Walking over, I don't look back at Tuck as I bend over and grab it. My hand grips the brass doorknob and I still don't have the urge to look back. The creak of the door as I open it is deafening in the small house.

I'm pulled back into Tuck's hard chest as a low growl fills my ear. My body gives in to him and allows him to drag me about the house. My bag is thrown on the couch as I follow the gravity. I'm so attracted to Tuck. He spins me into his room and I back up as he flips off the lights. The backs of my legs hit the edge of his mattress as he pushes me all the way back onto it, and I hear Ed Sheeran fill the room, and the words couldn't fit this situation more perfectly.

"Don't break my heart, Tuck."

"It'll be your fault if I do. I told you to stay away, Blue."

Propped up on my elbows, I can barely make out his figure as he walks about his room, but the moment his body covers mine, I lose sight of everything. My cheerleading, school, goals, and everything possibly close to my heart vanishes with his touch. When his lips meet mine, I pour every ounce of gratitude into him as we kiss and know there's no threat to being caught.

My eager hands roam up his back as my lips soak up his taste. I feel Tuck push into my center and moan into his mouth as I feel his excitement too.

"No hands and no touching, Blue."

He grabs me by my biceps and pushes them up and over my head, pressing them down into the mattress.

"Why?"

"Want this or not?"

I breathlessly try to say, "Yes."

I feel his hungry mouth back on mine, devouring me. My hips buck up into him, pleading for more. A kiss is almost torture. I need more, want more, have to have more to survive.

"Tuck." I feel a flush run through my cheeks as my simple word comes out as a yell.

He buries his face in the crook of my neck, sucking and licking every inch of my flesh. His hands rip my oversized t-shirt off in one fell swoop, and then my bra is gone before I can blink.

He pins my hands above my head again with one of his large palms. When his teeth sink into my perked up nipple, I scream. His other hand covers my mouth as he sucks harder, teasing me with his mouth. My hips writhe up and down, trying to get to more of him.

"You touch me once, Blue, and this is over."

I couldn't care less what his demands are in this moment, as long as his lips don't leave my body. Clenching my eyes, I focus on the sensation he's sending through every single part of my body and hum in appreciation. His lips make a trail down between my breasts to my belly button, and I giggle when he swirls it with his tongue. In the next moment he has me naked, ripping off my shorts and underwear in one motion.

The sound of the rest of my clothes being tossed off makes me smile, but when he gets up from the bed, I groan, already missing his contact.

"Tuck."

I'm not a whiny person, but right now I'm the biggest whiner on the planet.

He hooks his arms around the back of my thighs, dragging me to the edge of the bed, and then his lips begin to wander up the inside of my thigh. I have to cover my own mouth to muffle my screams. It takes every ounce of willpower not to reach down, rip off his stupid-ass beanie, and tug his hair.

He leaves his sweet taste behind as he drags his tongue the entire length of my inner thigh, and then he hits the sweet spot. I can't help but let my moans of pleasure out as my hands fist into his blanket on the bed. Just one sweep of his tongue threatens to send me into a burst of pleasure. I try to slow things down by concentrating on something else…fuck, bunnies or stuffed animals or some shit like that. I don't want to go before he even does anything spectacular.

But the moment he grips my ass, nearing the point of pain, and buries his face deeper in me, adding his fingers to the mix, I let my body move along with him.

"Tuck."

I repeat his name over and over until I can no longer hold in any of the pleasure about to blossom in me. When he scrapes his teeth along my skin, I explode and stars fill my vision, and I break Tuck's rule and grip onto his forearms holding my legs. My hips writhe, riding out each flick of aftershock of my orgasm.

"Holy shit." I run my hands through my hair and rest them on top of my head. "How the hell am I going to pay you back for that?"

"Just sleep here with me tonight and kiss me one more time."

"Are you asking for a goodnight kiss, Tuck?"

His fully clothed body covers mine again, and it reminds me how completely exposed I am.

"I'm naked. You're not."

Tuck puts his lips on mine and smiles. "You're

fucking gorgeous, Blue. I need to stay away from you."

"Just kiss me."

He begins kissing me passionately again and it's the sweetest thing ever with both of our tastes mingled together. Tuck keeps it short this time as he picks me up, cradling my naked body as he walks around the bed. He flicks on a little night lamp.

"Tuck."

He just shoots me a crooked grin.

"I'm naked. You're fully clothed and off limits. So, either turn the lights off or give me my clothes."

He's such a gentle giant as he lays me down on the bed and then grabs my clothes and tosses them toward me.

"I'll be right back. Need anything?"

I shake my head as I struggle to get back in his black shirt, trying to give him minimal view of my tits. I have to have something on the man that he hasn't already had.

Moments later, Tuck comes back in and shuts the door with a smile covering his face and two bottles of water in his hand. "Here, grabbed it just in case."

"Thank you."

He doesn't waste time turning off all the lights, climbing in behind me, scooping me up in his arms, and pressing me into his chest.

"Why won't you let me touch you?"

My words dissipate in the dark air and I can't muster up the energy to ask again before sleep takes over.

Chapter 12

The ceiling lights whirl around in my vision as my back slams into the mat.

"Williams, that's going to hurt like a bitch when you do that on the track in front of a home crowd."

It's the fifth time I've landed on my ass during a rolling back handspring. It's very typical for me to do six of them and stick it every single time, and I know it's something very popular at football games, but it's been nine days and no sight of Tuck. Not even at night during my runs.

I finally broke down and told Sophie everything and made her promise not to judge or mother hen my ass. She told me my pussy was probably poisonous and killed the guy off. Noah finally gave up the details last night when he came over to the dorms with Lane.

Tuck's ass had been handed to him by his running back coach for the scuffle in the gym, and he was put on suspension with the threat of not starting the first game of the season. I guess he was given a hefty list of things he had to complete before he'd be eligible, and even then it was going to be iffy. Noah went on, explaining the soccer player, AKA Captain Asshat, was kicked off his team. It was a third strike kind of thing, so basically I ruined two men's careers by stepping in the gym that day. But it seems my ugly, selfish tendencies have taken over once again, because I just want Tuck back.

Noah refused to give me Tuck's number even after I threw a fit and offered him money. I know deep down it's because of Tuck's privacy issues, but in Noah's defense, he probably wants his star player focusing on the game and not me. Noah didn't miss his chance to mercilessly tease me over the last nine days every single time he saw me. He calls my name out in a very steamy voice similar to the way I called Tuck's out.

"Again, Blue." Coach Lindsey stretches a hand out to me, and I spring up again.

After three more attempts, I land a continuing seven back handsprings down the royal blue mats of the gym, and then do it five more times to keep the actions memorized in my muscles.

"Huddle up." Coach stands on her stack of red mats in her ready position. "Football and volleyball seasons are coming up. Home and away games will all have cheerleaders. We will also be visible at soccer games, so this is one of the last practices we will all be together." She pulls a stack of papers from behind her back. "Here are the schedules. If you can't attend or become ill, you report to your team captain, and then they'll report to an assistant or myself. No excuses."

I stand back and let the swarm of girls grab theirs and run off to shower. Most of them have places to be and things to do, but I, on the other hand…nada. When the crowd clears and it's just Coach, I step up and take mine.

"What's bothering you?"

"Is it that obvious, Coach?"

"Written all over you."

I shrug. "I guess I'm just stressed. Promise to have my head screwed on straight from here on out."

"I have no worries."

She walks away, and I admire how cut and dry she is as a coach. No bullshit or gray areas with that lady, just straight business, and boy, how I wish I could've kept my college life that way.

"Blue, want to go to dinner?"

Sophie has her bag slung over her shoulder and is

running out of the gym. She's made an effort to be around a bit more the last nine days, and I've really appreciated it.

"Sure, but I'm going stinky."

"Me, too. Lane loves my smell."

"God, you two are disgusting."

"You know you love us." Sophie's tan arm pulls me into her as we walk outside into the sunshine.

Lane's truck is easy to spot as he waits for Sophie in the first parking spot. It does stick out among all the small cars.

"There's my girls." He jumps from the driver's side of the truck, letting his phone drop to the seat. He opens the door for us, and I let Sophie slide to middle and then get in after her. Before he shuts the door, Lane gives my thigh a light squeeze and sends me a comforting wink, and I know Sophie told him everything.

When he rounds the front of the truck, I elbow her in the ribs.

"Sorry, I thought he might have more info on Tuck."

"And?" I ask, slapping her leg.

"He wouldn't budge. I even swallowed."

"Sophie," I scream and give her another elbow.

As Lane hops up in the driver's seat, he asks, "What has she done now?"

"Nothing. Absolutely nothing," I say, leaving no room for further inquiry.

I listen as Lane goes on about football practice and how hard the coaches have been on them, while I pretend to be more interested in my phone than listening to him. I'm on high alert for any Tuck info, or even the mention of number thirty-two, but nothing. All I get is the information I already know. The first game of the season is an away game, and I will not be cheering, even though I'll be at every other fucking football game.

Coach Lindsey is letting all the seniors go. I guess it's tradition or some shit like that.

So, in five days when Tuck gets on a plane and flies east to play his first game of his junior year, I'll be at an all-day volleyball match cheering and passing around a damn coffee can for money for our national cheer competition this spring. *Oh, the life.*

We pull up to the greasy burger joint where I ate the first day on campus, and the whole cab of the truck hears my stomach growl with delight.

"What can I say?" I shrug as I get out and try to contain my giddiness over a greasy bacon cheeseburger. "I'm going to even splurge on cheesy fries, bitches."

"You'll run it off, Blue." Sophie grabs my hand and we portray a very odd happy threesome as we walk in.

"You're still running at night?" Lane cranes his neck to look at me, his eyes wide with shock.

"Yeah, why?"

"Blue, you shouldn't be out after dark with all the fucking crimes that've been going down."

"None on campus, so no worries."

"Yeah, but Tuck hasn't been with you."

His last words cause my eyebrows to shoot straight up. "Excuse me?"

Our conversation is broken up as we enter the crammed diner with clattering noises surrounding us. I want to push him for information, and need to know how he knows that Tuck used to run with me, but I don't. Instead I head to the counter and order, not giving Lane the chance to buy my food, which he always tries to do.

"I'll find a table."

I turn to scope out a place for the three of us and leave the lovebirds at the counter to order. I roam the corner where the football players usually are and find their long table vacant, then settle for a cozy booth on the opposite side of the diner. I sip on my cold water as I wait for the rest of my party. Lane and Sophie climb in the booth and tangle their bodies together.

"I'm so bummed I won't see your first game, Lane."

"It will probably be for the best." He slumps over as her elbow connects straight to his ribs. "Less distraction is what I meant. Ohio is going to be one of the toughest opponents of the year. This game will be setting the pace for the whole season."

"Nice cover up, lover boy." I roll my eyes in his direction.

Sophie perks up and perches her elbows on the table. "So, Blue, tonight is the last official party before football season."

I try to keep up with her conversation between her eye rolls and finger quotes, but find the surrounding noise distracting.

"Sure." I shrug as a waitress sets my food in front of me. The melted cheese on the golden fries dances with delight before me, and I can't help but plop one of the delicious bitches in my mouth.

"Are you serious?"

"Why not?" I answer around a mouthful of cheese.

"Well, fuck me running, I thought I was going to have to drag you."

"Nope, I need a distraction from…"

My words are cut off by a loud ruckus, and I see a large crowd of players enter the diner. Lane props himself up, giving some of them high fives and slaps on the ass as they walk by. I turn my head just in time to see Noah and Tuck walk in. In typical fashion, Tuck's eyes dart away from me quickly and he heads for the back table while Noah offers up a feeble smile, but that's it.

"I guess your pussy didn't kill him," Sophie whispers.

Those motherfuckers.

Noah orders and heads straight back to the corner, not making any effort at all to acknowledge me.

"Blue, you might want to shut your mouth and wipe the cheese sauce from the corner of your lips."

Sophie is right. I place my hand under my jaw to keep my mouth firmly locked shut, and then use the back of my other hand to smear off the cheese sauce and then dart my tongue out to finish the job.

"Wow, that was all sorts of manners," Sophie adds.

I keep my mouth closed, mostly to keep all the words ready to spew from me hidden away.

"Take it easy, Blue." Lane ruffles his hair. "Tuck got in deep shit for beating that guy up, and when we are days away from a big game, we stick together with no distractions."

And my seal breaks.

"Distractions?" I draw the word out, putting emphasis on each syllable, and point between the two of them.

"She's my girl. It's like my get out of jail free card. I'll release frustrations and then band together with them."

"Fuck your band. Fuck you." I pick up my hamburger and slam it back down. "Fuck this food, and fuck everything football."

"Blue." I hear Sophie's voice, but I'm too far gone.

I slide from the booth and continue on my rant. The noise level doesn't break as I continue.

"And fuck motherfucking weak assholes who have no fucking manners." I pluck my cheesy fries from the table. "And don't forget to pick me up tonight."

"Blue, stop."

"Sophie, I'm walking back to the dorms, and don't try to stop me."

My left shoulder is dragged back as someone runs into me.

"Watch where the fuck you're walking." I turn to see a group of giddy bitches making their way back to the football team.

"Are you talking to me?"

"Does it look like I'm fucking talking to you?"

This has gone from bad to worse and I have no intention of stopping it. My cheese fries go flying back onto the table as I step right up into the bitch's face, ready to hammer her. Before I get the chance, Lane drags me outside and probably saves me from being kicked off the cheer team. Through the front window, I watch as she walks her way back to the football team, and then I catch sight of Noah and Tuck and feel all that anger boil right back up.

Lane spins me around in his arms and begins shaking me like a ragdoll.

"Get a grip, Blue."

"Fine." I pull back, throwing my hands up in the air. "I'm fine."

"Seriously, Tuck is not a bad guy, nor is Noah."

"Yep, they're fucking heroes," I shout over my shoulder as I walk away from the whole fucked-up scene.

My phone goes off in my pocket, and when I pluck it out, I see Noah's name.

Noah: Are you okay?

Me: Fuck you

I type out a quick message to my mom telling her I will be gone the rest of the day and then turn off my phone to avoid any further distractions. I need to clear my mind and get my head right. *Holy shit*, I've never blown up like that in my life, not in public, nor have I ever let that many f-bombs fly. I'm on the road straight to disaster if I can't get a grip on it. I might as well catch the next flight back to Colorado.

When I pass a little boutique with bikinis displayed in the front window, I stop in and find one of the cheapest two pieces and decide to walk to the beach. It's not the same one Noah has taken me to, but I do know of one about a half mile away.

The beach is quiet, with hardly anyone loitering around. I don't even worry about not having a towel or the sand getting in my crack as I slide down my workout shorts and peel off my tank top. The lady in the boutique was nice enough to let me change before I left. The sun pounds down onto my skin, tingling it with its heat. I let the waves entertain all my senses as I focus on my breathing and trying to let everything go.

I don't want to be angry, needy, desperate, or in love. I just want the old Blue back, but have a feeling deep down that Tuck has placed an invisible curse on me.

"Is this you, god? Playing a nasty trick?" My voice is weak compared to the roar of the ocean.

"What do you expect from me?" My voice is louder this time as I raise my hands up to the heavens, waiting for the answer.

"Fuck me in the goat ass," I growl as I flop back on the sand and close my eyes. I'm pretty sure the higher powers didn't appreciate that last part.

Between the sound of the ocean pounding the beach and the tingle of the sun, my eyes close, and my problems slip away one by one as I drift off.

Time isn't a factor, and Tuck doesn't touch even one thought while I'm out. When I roll over, a stinging sensation shocks my skin, and when I sit up, my whole body is stiff and burned. Reaching in my bag, I grab my phone and wait for it to power on. I skip the several missed text messages and look at the time. I'm stunned to see that two hours passed.

Crawling up to my feet, I stretch out my kinked body and cringe when I feel the sting of the burn. But it's almost a delicious, welcomed pain. My phone starts to go off, and I take a quick look at all the texts. I ignore Noah's and a weird number, but respond to Sophie. I'd hate to mess up their lovemaking schedule since Lane is using his get out of free jail card, after all.

Me: I'm okay. I'll be ready to go by 7. Pick me up at dorms?

Sophie: KK. Noah came and asked about you.

Me: They are now a hard limit to me…no more talk of them.

Sophie: KK

I can't count how many times I've told her that the use of "KK" in speech and text is annoying and absolutely unnecessary, but I guess some habits are hard to break. Nothing drives me more nuts than that use. Ignoring the stupid-ass two letters put together, I make my way out to the water for a quick dip to cool my skin.

The waves crash into my shins, and it's a quick eye opener of how ice-cold the water is. I just keep walking deeper and deeper into the ocean, letting the waves threaten to knock me off balance. I fight forward, struggling to stand straight up. By the time I go under, I don't have the panicked sensation or envision anyone's face…I'm numb.

Chapter 13

Counting Stars blares in the dorm room as I wiggle my lotion-slick body into a tiny black dress from Sophie's closet. The bastard is tight as hell and hugs every curve, while showcasing my lean, long legs. I'm thankful my lobster red burn has simmered down into a glowing olive tan. The one factor that may talk me out of this dress is the boob region. Man, the girls are perked up and plenty luscious for the viewing.

It's the third dress of Sophie's I've tried, and I think it's the one. I strap on a pair of her blinged out sandals, and by blinged out, I mean they could blind someone in the sun. They're flats, because with how short this dress is, I don't need to add any more attention to my legs.

My platinum blonde curls fall over my shoulders, hiding some skin, so I decide to pin them back, letting my shoulders be visible. I'm not sure if listening to Miranda Lambert's latest hit, *Little Red Wagon,* was the best idea while getting ready, but it sure makes my badass come out.

I touch up my light make-up and let my sun-kissed tan shine through, then send Sophie a quick text telling her I'll meet her out front. As I step in the elevator and check out my reflection in the mirror, it may be the first time I feel like a college freshman with no cares in the world.

"Hot damn."

Sophie's not shy or quiet about her excitement as I step out of the lobby into the parking lot. Lane even lets out a low whistle, causing me to blush.

"Shut up, you guys." The backs of my legs stick to the leather interior as I try to slide in beside Sophie.

Climbing up into a monster truck in a short dress is damn near impossible to do without flashing a shot of my beaver to the world.

"You're going to show him."

I elbow Sophie with all my might and don't even feel bad when I hear her let out an *umph* of pain. "Hard limit, and I'm not kidding."

It takes everything to not add the f-bomb in there somewhere.

"Are those my shoes?"

"Maybe." I grin in her direction.

"Is that my dress?"

I just shrug.

"Let me see your panties."

Sophie grabs the hem of the dress, trying to rip it up, and I let my head fly back and roll into a fit of laughter.

"Stop." I swat her hand. "I'm wearing my own. Thank you very much."

"Good, keep your poisonous coochie out of my panties."

We both crack up at that. Poor Lane has no choice but to listen, but he's a smart man, not laughing at any of the jokes. Even Sophie knows they're borderline, but hey, if you can't laugh at yourself, as they say.

When Lane pulls up to the party, my body truly goes into overdrive. It's a similar scene as the first one, but on steroids. I spot other cheerleaders, soccer players, the cross-country team, and several other students. Bodies fill the yard, barely leaving a tiny path up to the house.

"Everyone have their phone?"

I know the question is directed at me and shake my head. "I'll be fine."

"Blue, you won't be fine dressed like that and with your attitude."

"Afraid I'll get lucky tonight, Lane?" I shoot a high

arched eyebrow in his direction.

I slide from the truck and look back at my worried friends and then grab my crotch and give them a little hip thrust. “It’s poison, remember?”

“Do you have your phone, Blue?”

“No, I don’t, Lane. I am a big girl.” I enunciate every word like an immature, childish asshole. I don’t want to be a royal bitch to my only two friends left on campus who will actually talk to me, but I don’t want to be protected either.

“Stay close.”

“Fine. Let’s go.”

I make my way through the crowd and check over my shoulder every once in a while to see if Lane and Sophie are following. Not only are they following, but they’re right on my heels.

Sophie puts her hand on my shoulder then yells in my ear, “Go inside.”

I nod and continue walking, not missing the stares I’m getting from appreciative eyes. It actually feels exhilarating to be noticed when all I thought I wanted was to blend in. A high rushes through me like it used to in high school, and for once I feel as if I fit in.

When I enter the living room, it’s less crowded than outside.

“Blue,” a group of female voices scream, and I turn to see my cheer squad.

I rush to the girls and envelop them in one big hug. Looking around, we are all here…well, except for Stephie.

“Oh my god, I didn’t think you’d come, so we didn’t ask,” Sara says as she flips back her long red hair.

“You’re always so serious. You scare the shit out of us sometimes.” Brandi’s comment catches me by surprise and almost hurts my feelings, but I brush it off quickly.

"I love you. You're my girls." And that wasn't a lie. I spend more time with them than anyone else, including Sophie, even if she were to keep her ass in the dorm room.

"Want to meet some boys?" Sarah asks, waggling her eyebrows.

"I'd love to. Lead the way, ladies."

I keep my eyes plastered to the girls and refuse to let my vision wander, but when we round a corner, a dark hoodie and sexy brown hair are impossible to miss. Tuck and Noah. Seems the band of brothers are enjoying their last party before the season as well.

I let out a sigh when we move in the opposite direction, and I refuse to make eye contact with either of the dickheads. Sarah and Brandi bookend me on each side, linking me with their arms, and begin introducing me to an array of men. My head swims while I try to brand their names with their faces, and I actually enjoy it because they're not all football players, and several of them are dazzlingly gorgeous.

A tall and tan man steps up and takes interest in me, and I even lean in a couple times to hear what he has to say, even though he's talking to the crowd. Our group is standing in the middle of a walkway, and I seem to be a roadblock. Everyone keeps bumping into me. Soon Sarah is off my side, and the tall, hunky gentleman is there with his arms wrapped low and resting on my waist.

I melt into him, tired of being bumped into and knocked around, and find it easier to listen to the conversation. The men in the group are trying to talk the women into a game of beer ping-pong. It's just not going their way, but is a hoot to listen to.

"Are you thirsty?"

"Jay, right?" I look up into his piercing blue eyes.

He nods down at me.

"Do I have to play ping-pong?" I smile.

"Nah, I got the hook-up."

"Yes, please, then."

"I kind of like this spot, so save it for me." The vibration of his voice tickles my ear.

"Sure thing."

As he steps back, I slide my legs out as if going into the splits, but stop before I hit the guy who was standing on the other side of Jay.

"How's that?" I ask over my shoulder.

He just sends me a wink as he takes off, and before I turn back to the group, I catch Tuck staring at me, and I can't help but laugh. I'd be a fool to say the seething look on his face isn't a bit scary, but he can fuck off.

I sure in the hell didn't come here to piss Tuck off, but I won't pass up on the opportunity either. And if I thought my skin burned before in the California sun, it's nothing now to the holes I feel Tuck boring into me.

This group's conversation is light and very entertaining, nothing too deep, and no brooding athletes.

"Blue."

I turn to see Sophie waving to me from the corner filled with football players, which happens to be the same place Tuck is. I give her a thumbs up and a huge, genuine smile and avoid eye contact with anyone else. She mouths they'll be there for a bit. I send her another thumbs up, then I feel a tap on my shoulder.

Jay is holding two red Solo cups with a genuine smile of his own. I'm pretty good at reading energy, and he seems super nice.

He bends down and asks loudly, "Are you a beer girl?"

I reach up and nuzzle his ear with my nose. I know

I'm being extra flirty and it feels good. I'm not sure if it feels good to be doing it in front of Tuck, or because I'm just acting careless for once.

"I love beer, Jay."

"Here you go."

The plastic cup is chilled and feels refreshing on my palm as the sweet scent of beer fills the space between us, but it's snatched out of my hands before the frothy golden liquid has a chance to hit my lips.

"Blue." I look up to Noah, who has weaseled his way in between us. He replaces the beer with a new one and whispers in my ear, "Do not take anything from anyone besides Tuck and myself. Do you hear me?"

"Fuck off, Noah."

"I mean it, Blue. I know you're hurt and pissed right now, but we are just looking out for you."

I see red for the second time in the same day, and I'm pretty sure it's from his use of the pronoun *we*. The red sparks to into large flames when I look over at Tuck and see several girls surrounding him. Before Noah can react, I snatch the beer from Jay's hand and shotgun that bitch. Then I pound the one he handed me.

"Now you can give Jay that beer and leave us alone."

I pluck the beer from Noah's hand and give it to Jay, and then I turn back to the group.

"Do you know who that was?"

"Yeah."

"He's the quarterback."

"So?"

"Are you his girl?"

"Nope."

Jay holds his hands up in the air. "You seem like a nice girl, but I'm not getting involved in that."

Jay doesn't wait for an explanation before he leaves me, so I shotgun the third beer in mere moments and let the magic golden liquid induce a hazy effect.

"He's an ass and doesn't know what he's missing." Brandi hooks her arm around mine and tugs me back toward the living room.

I catch sight of Noah holding yet another red plastic cup, so I stall our progress and snatch it from his hand.

"Thanks, fucker."

Brandi lets out a little giggle, and I'm not sure if it's from me snatching his drink or calling him a fucker. I know I should share this drink with her, but don't. When the liquid hits my tummy it burns like a motherfucker, and since all my senses are thrown off, I'm guessing he wasn't nursing a beer.

We are thrust into a mass of sticky, sweaty people moving to the pumping music. My body finds its rhythm easily, and in my mind I'm dancing like a fucking star, but I can tell my movements are loose and sloppy. The same DJ seems to recognize us again and makes a big deal about cheerleaders being at the party.

We once again hop up on a table and bust out some of our best moves, and against my better judgment I slam two more cups of liquid back to quench my thirst and overheated body. At one point, we dance more like we are strippers at some high class club. No clothes come off, but we do leave very little to the imagination. I don't recognize any of the songs, but I keep up easily with the jamming beat pouring through the speakers.

The crowd gathers closer around the table as the beat turns sexier, and then hands begin groping at thighs, and I watch as Brandi is pulled from the table. Her smile is evidence that she freely wants whoever just snagged her. Different palms try to pull me, and I don't want any of it, so I move toward the other side of the table and feel the same skin on skin action. Then I hear all the vulgar calls through the music. I don't want to be touched or called these nasty things.

My head swims through the alcohol, heat, and pouring music. Panic or passing out threaten me as I'm completely dragged from the table in strong arms that I have no chance of fighting. An elbow or two flies back into the solid chest, but I don't budge, nor does his grip. I flail, my feet trying to connect with a shin, but nothing is keeping this man from taking me wherever he wants. I try to scream, but everything is stuck in my throat as tears flow down my cheeks.

When I'm pushed through the front door onto the porch, I feel his mouth near my ear.

"It's Lane. Stop fighting me."

My vision comes into focus and I see Sophie standing next to Lane's truck beyond the fence. Every muscle is tensed up and ready for fight or flight, but his voice causes me to melt in his arms. Lane readjusts me in his grasp, and my sight is filled with a majestic black sky with twinkling stars blinking back at me. Their brightness and subtle flashing make my stomach lurch, so I close my eyes. The movement of walking and not seeing anything makes my stomach spin even harder.

"Thank you," I whisper as he sets me down on my feet.

It takes a few minutes for me to gather composure enough to walk the three steps to the back door and grip the handle. Without having to look up, I know several people are gathered around, and whether or not they're staring, it sure in the hell feels like all eyes are on me. I strap on my courage and dig up all my steadiness and go to climb in the truck. And if the last few weeks of my life haven't been torture enough, I catch sight of Tuck leaning on a chipped white pillar on the porch watching my every move with a little blonde hanging off of his arm.

With steadier legs than I thought I would ever be able to muster, I step up on the chrome bar and my middle finger goes up without thought or hesitation before I land a belly flop on the smooth leather back seat. A seatbelt digs sharply into my left hip, but it doesn't faze the hysterical fit of laughter I spiral into.

"Blue, are you okay?"

With a cheek pressed to the cool leather, I look up into Sophie's concerned eyes and feel like an even bigger ass than I already did. I just nod, dragging my cheek up and down the seat. I try to sober myself up, but it seems as the seconds tick by and the further Lane drives, the drunker my limbs become.

A cellphone rings. It's not any of my ring tones, and even if it was, I don't even fucking know where my little shoulder purse is.

"Hey." Lane's voice is a bit muted, but obviously it was his phone. "I've got her. She's pretty fucked up."

Silence for a bit, and I strain to hear.

"No, didn't say anything about you. I'm pretty sure she's over you."

An acidic taste begins climbing up my throat, and when Lane whips the truck in what feels like a 180-degree turn, that taste escapes me. My stomach acts as if it's trying to burst from me through my throat. I make horrid gagging sounds as the burning fluid tumbles to the ground. Vomit splashes back up, spattering me in the face. The harder I fight the urge to cease the puking, the more retching and god-awful sounds come out.

"Shit. Got to go." I barely hear the sound of Lane's phone being tossed on the dash over the roar of my severe vomiting.

"Get back to the dorms now, Lane."

Then my world goes black as I pass out in a pool of puke on the leather seat.

Chapter 14

I swear the dizziness of being hung over and beyond fucked up still lingers throughout my body five days later. I'm sure the loud gym filled with volleyball players and an eager crowd doesn't help. Sophie damn near rushed me to the hospital to get my stomach pumped the night I got so drunk, but Lane came to my rescue, even after I puked all over in his truck.

He nursed me back to health and kept Sophie calm through all of it. The man needs a gold medal for putting up with us. When I was able to walk, the first thing I did was head to his truck to clean up my mess, but it was already sparkling clean.

I know the last few days without him have been miserable for Sophie, but deep down I was grateful not to have to see him. My skin heats with embarrassment when I think about my actions that night.

Volleyball matches suck ass. I'm eager to feel the excitement at a home football game while cheering and shining, but for now I'm stuck here and take the three shifts of walking around passing the can down for donations. It feels better on my still pounding head instead of cheering near courtside. We do have one performance between matches and then only an hour left.

The football game just started back east, and the crowd goes nuts every time the commentator updates us on the score. My hearts jumps in delight when Tuck's number is announced as making the first touchdown. It's what the team needed on their opening drive. And as much as I hate Noah and Tuck in this moment, I can't help but smile for them and imagine them celebrating in the end zone.

Sophie runs up to me as we are walking out of the gymnasium. It was one hell of a long day. The football game is in the third quarter, and she has it streaming on her phone. Tuck set the pace for the game, but unfortunately the other offense answered back every time.

"Blue," Sophie squeals as she watches Lane catch an interception and run it in for a touchdown, putting the boys up by seven. "Please sit and watch this with me."

I'd never admit it to her, but I only want to watch it and be there in the moment with Tuck. The last five days have revealed one thing to me as I analyzed and reanalyzed my massive fuck-up at the party. Tuck Jones has captured my heart and destroyed it.

"I'm going to grab some food and be right back." I point to the food trucks lining the sidewalk.

"Get me something." She doesn't pry her eyes from the screen as she intently stares at the game unfolding.

I pull out my own phone and bring up the message from the strange number that texted me the day I was at the beach cooling down from my raging fit. The line is long to the taco truck, so I rub my thumb over his message he sent me.

Blue, you'll never understand my reasons, but I'm sorry for pulling away and what I did. You deserve better, and that's why I'm staying away.

It took every single ounce of willpower I had to not text back or run to his front steps and beg to be back in his life. Message after message I've typed up to send back to him, but then always talk myself out of it. I've tried to focus on nothing but cheer the last five days through my foggy-ass frame of mind.

When I head back with two plates full of street tacos, I see Sophie toss her phone to the ground and know that can't be good.

"They just scored back to back. Noah threw an interception, and now we're down six points with a minute to go."

Sophie flops back onto the grass with her phone held up toward the sky, still intent on the game.

"Was I gone that long?" I ask with a crooked eyebrow.

"Like a whole freaking quarter."

I've found myself losing track of time a lot lately when I get thrown into a Tuck tailspin. Focusing on the tacos and my growling stomach, I enjoy them while listening to the game pour from Sophie's phone. Nothing but timeouts and lots of commercial breaks happen, but then it's time, and I hear Noah and Tuck's names being talked about by the commentators, and the wide receiver's name is thrown in there too. It's the last play of the game and all in their hands.

"With seventy yards to go, what will the head coach call?" A short silence goes by, and then the commentator goes wild. "It's a handoff to number thirty-two. He's wrapped up…wait, no, he breaks loose and is ten yards out with a defender coming at him. He leaps over him. He's at the fifty, the forty, the thirty, the ten. Touchdown."

The man's voice is a joyous roar as he narrates each one of Tuck's moves.

"Please don't be a flag. Please don't be a flag," Sophie chants as she jumps to her feet with her hand covering her mouth.

There's no flag, the extra point is good, and I focus back down on my plate and can't help the smile that forms on my face. He did it. He just won the game for his team. Digging into my purse, I find my phone and send back a message, but it's not the one I've wanted to send to him.

Nice job, Tuck.

Before I know what happens, I'm thrown back onto the grass, with Sophie pouncing on top of me cheering and screaming her lungs out. I look to her beaming face and giggle at her reaction to the win. Whether it be school pride or Lane or the fact her man will be on his way home very shortly, I join in on the celebration with her.

"You do realize you are dry humping me?"

Her legs straddle my mid-section and she just laughs even harder and then rolls off of me. "Oh my god, Blue, they did it. They had to have that win."

"Yeah, yeah."

I know all of this and try to not care.

"Why don't you try to call him, Blue?"

It's the first time she's brought him up since the disastrous day at the diner.

"He's made it clear that he doesn't want me."

"Yeah, I know, but Lane says it's more complicated than that, and Tuck just needs a woman to push him, and Noah said he thinks Tuck will really fall for you."

Rolling up onto my side, I face Sophie's profile. "Why in the hell would I want to keep fighting for a person who does nothing but turn me on and then turn me down? I don't deserve to be hurt time after time. Problems or not, I deserve better."

"True." She pauses for a moment. "But I know you fell for him too."

"I did. I have. I am. I'm over it."

"It's okay to fight for love, Blue."

"I know." My head falls down on her shoulder, and I watch the after game interviews with her. The coach's proud and humble face, Noah's dazzling white smile and damn sexier than sin blonde damp hair, all front and center answering questions, while Tuck remains in the background even though he was the true hero of the game. Not even one sports broadcaster approaches him. With his running back coach by his side, and then the head coach and Noah shielding him from being seen, I realize it's not just me. Tuck doesn't want the world to see him, and something about that soothes my broken heart a tick.

Chapter 15

It's the third home game before fall break, and I'm still a bundle of nerves as I roll out of bed. The alarm clock on my nightstand blinks back 4:32 a.m. and I know it's worthless to even try to nuzzle back down in my blankets. Sleep has done escaped me, and I know it's because of a curious mixture of nerves and excitement.

There's not any greater high than cheering at a hometown football game, especially in the huge, roaring stadium. The energy is something I can't even begin to explain.

Mom and Dad were supposed to be at the first home game, but Mom took a header on an icy patch, and Dad basically had to tie her down in bed. And then while she was strapped down with a fractured ankle, he broke the news to her that I wouldn't be able to attend the scheduled family vacation to the Bahamas for Thanksgiving.

You'd have thought Dad broke her other ankle when the news hit her, but I've reassured her that I have several open invitations to spend the holiday with my coaches and teammates, which is the truth, but it still didn't help her. I think finally last night she came to grips with a romantic getaway with Dad.

My feet hit the cold floor and I tiptoe toward the door. I decide on an early hot shower and don't want to wake Sophie. The poor girl has been put number two on Lane's list behind football, and we've hung out more the last month than the total combined since meeting. And it's been nice. Actually it's been perfect and has given Sophie and me a chance to get to know each other. Between her, cheer, and school, they've been the ideal distraction from my screaming, aching heart.

The communal bathroom is perfect this early in the morning. The scent of fresh lemon cleaner fills the air, and the water is soothingly hot in a matter of minutes. I allow the scalding water to wash away my worries and some of my nerves. I hear my phone go off as I turn off the shower. I grab my towel quickly to dry off before I pick it up, because I know exactly who it is. Tuck texts me every single game day. He never responded when I sent him a text after his first game, but has sent me one every game morning since then, and it still comes up as a random number.

Like I said, my heart still screams out in pain at odd moments, and most of them happen at night when I run. Some say time heals all, but going on nine weeks of mourning Tuck's denial, I'm not sure it will ever get easier. When I'm finally dry enough, I snatch the phone from the bench.

Game day. Thinking of you, Blue.

If their winning streak continues, I'll send him the same text I've always sent him. It's beyond fucked up, but I need that crumb of hope. As far as I know, not even Sophie knows we text those simple lines on game days.

A shiver races up my spine, causing my body temperature to drop and chills to spread. I race back to the dorm room, remembering to actually shut and lock the door behind me. Sophie's light snoring fills the dark room. I quickly braid my hair and throw it over my shoulder as I climb back in bed and reread Tuck's text over and over. I realize as the weeks have played out without him in my life, that each day I become weaker and weaker.

My fingers are hungry to type a message back to him, and it doesn't consist of anything about the game, but my heart can't handle another rejection from the man of my dreams. The one who has placed the most wicked curse he could've on a heart and doesn't even know it. The saddest part of the whole story is I'd let Tuck take me to bed in an instant.

Fuck this. I need my head on straight and have fought to keep it that way the last months. Creeping back out of bed, I throw on my sleek black running pants and a hoodie, then lace up my running sneakers. I can't sleep and need to release some endorphins to clear my mind. I still run every single night, and knowing me, I'll run again tonight while Sophie has her usual fuck frenzy with Lane.

It's dark when I make it outside, and the brisk air feels refreshing as I take off on the trail. I've often wondered what time Tuck runs now, or where he runs, because it's never with me. Stuffing in my ear buds, I turn on a low-key running playlist, knowing I need a laid back workout this morning. When the first bead of sweat rolls down my forehead, I realize I'm going to have to shower again. I really need to look into applying for the poster child for "hot mess."

***

My fingers itch to text Tuck. We've blown out the opponent, and it's homecoming, so the crowd is especially wild and rambunctious. The student section is spackled with bare-chested students with painted letters on their skin. They've made the job of cheering simple and electrifying. My eyes remained glued to the big screen watching replays, since the field is impossible to see from the sidelines.

And thanks to Tuck, my arms burn and my abs are screaming at me, since we have to do push-ups every time our team scores, and it's not just seven each time.

It's the total score, and the asshole has racked up thirty-five points alone, and the final score is fifty-six.

"Blue." Sophie's face beams brightly as she runs over and hugs me. "Man, that was amazing."

Stephie quit the squad a month ago and hasn't been seen since. Word on campus is she was knocked up and it wasn't Ethan's baby, so instead of facing her mistake, she ran. Seems pretty typical of someone that shallow, and I can't say I miss her. She did her best to be a royal bitch while she was cheering at the few home games with us, but she'd never know my broken heart trumped all of her cruelty toward me.

"We have to go out tonight, Blue." She squeezes the top of my arm tightly. "Lane said if they win, the whole team was going to meet up. We have to go."

"We're in."

I see Brandi and Sarah with shit-eating grins plastering their face and know the two of them would love something like that. They are just two gigantic flirts out for a good time.

"Go ahead girls." I wave them off. "It's late, and I have to study."

It wasn't all a lie. It is late, but I don't have even a shred of homework to do. When I reach my bag, I send out a quick text to Tuck and then head back to the dorms. When I get to the parking lot, I hear someone call my name…or at least I think I heard something.

"Blue."

Turning around, I see the black beanie first and then his dark eyes. It's something I haven't seen in months, and I nearly fall down in a melting puddle of goo. I try to speak, but everything catches in my throat.

He takes three long strides and is in touching distance. All it would take is one stretch of an arm and I'd have him on me. Instead I arch an eyebrow and force myself to employ all defensive tactics.

"I need you tonight."

Those four words are probably the most beautiful words I've ever heard. I tilt my head and stare at him, unable to speak.

"I need you and want you. Please."

"What happens after tonight?" My voice is steady and serious.

"Blue, you know I can't."

"Tuck Jones, then you don't need me tonight. Go round up one of the other blonde bitches who love to hang all over you."

I turn to stomp off, but he wraps his hand around my upper arm, dragging me back toward him. My back slams into his hard chest as he bends down and whispers in my ear.

"I'm sorry I can't give more."

Everything inside me boils with rage, and I feel another one of those hissy fits coming on, but this time my brain is in the game and I know it's useless. Jerking my arm from his grasp, I square up and stare him down.

"Don't ever touch me again, Tuck."

"It's over?"

His question actually causes me to giggle, which turns into a loud laughter.

"It never started, and that was your choice, Tuck, not mine."

My voice is laced with hostility and passion, a dangerous combination to have lingering around this man. In the next moment he pulls me into his chest, and my body easily falls into the force called Tuck.

"Just give me one night."

My forehead flops down on his chest, and I bang it lightly there and know it would be so easy to give in to him and let him take me. He might even give me more, all of him, and make me feel on top of the world for one single night, but then the days of agony will follow.

I push away from him. "I deserve better."

Pain sparks in his eyes and they grow darker, if that's even possible.

"I deserve all of you, Tuck, and that's what I mean by better."

This time when I walk away he doesn't stop me, and I don't hesitate as my feet pound on the sidewalk, furthering the distance between us. My phone dings in my pocket, and I can't curb my curiosity.

You're right. You deserve better and it's not me. Sorry.

The fucking guy doesn't get it. I want him…all of him. I type out a quick text back to him.

I WANT YOU. ALL OF YOU. AND YOU CAN'T GIVE THAT.

I hold down the button until my phone powers off, then walk quickly back to the dorms. And just like I predicted, I need to release steam, and my body aches with the desire to run. Without hesitation, I throw on my workout gear from this morning. Yes, gross, but I'm beyond the point of caring. Tuck's scent still lingers on me and is enough to push me over the edge of crazy town. I need a release, and not one involving him.

Within minutes, I'm on the trail, pounding it hard and with purpose. The music from my ear buds screams into my ears and begins to drown out my other senses that are still reeling from all things Tuck. The more he fades, the more pissed off I get, the harder and faster I run.

The two-mile marker comes up into view, and I decide on the longer loop that leads around the back side of the campus. It's a beautiful view in the day, with large palm trees lining the path and gorgeous flowerbeds all up and down it. It's the furthest away from the campus and the place where I feel the freest. I let the night air fill my lungs and then let it all out, allowing bits of pent-up stress to leave as well.

The last bit of moonlight is shadowed behind the row of trees as my eyes focus on the trail ahead. Sweat beads form and roll down my forehead and then onto the front of my shirt, and I just push myself harder. In the next moment, I feel a hand on my shoulder and don't jump and scream like my first stunt in front of Tuck.

I simply turn my head to see my hooded prince who's cast a love spell on my entire soul. When my eyes connect with his, I flinch, but it's too late. Brown eyes stare back at me…and they're not Tuck's. The man's face is masked, and before I can react, he sends my body spiraling in one swift movement to the ground. My arms shield my face the best they can, but do nothing when my face smacks into the asphalt of the running trail. The skin from my elbows pulls away as they rub against the hard surface, and my hands scramble to grip the trail to pull myself up and run away from my attacker.

My feet find the pavement, and I spring forward and try to run again, but something catches my ankle. The skin is sliced away from my kneecaps as I fight, but I feel the tug of the back of my hair and then my face is slammed into the pavement, and everything goes black.

Chapter 16

Tuck

"Blue?"

Her phone has dialed me twice and there's only been rustling on the other end. Fuck, she's never even dialed this number and now twice in a night. Our living room is way too loud with all of our teammates loitering and celebrating.

"Sophie, follow me."

My deep voice shuts the entire living room up, and Sophie moves without question. I know panic paints my face and is evident in my voice, but I know something is fucking wrong.

"What, Tuck?"

Lane's on her ass and I signal them to shut the door.

"Blue has called me twice now and I don't think it's on purpose. Something is wrong."

"What? How?"

Sophie's words are cut off as my phone interrupts our conversation with another call from Blue. I quickly answer and turn on the speakerphone.

"Blue," I roar into the phone.

The next sounds I hear are far worse than my most vicious nightmares—Blue is screaming for help. Sophie throws her hands to her mouth and screams Blue's name. Lane grabs her, trying to silence her. After a few seconds that feel like hours, it's clear Blue has no idea she's dialed my number.

"She has to be running." I tuck my phone to my ear and bolt out the door without thinking. "Lane, help now."

I catch Noah's attention and nod to him as well, and they both follow. Lane takes off in his truck as Sophie fumbles with his phone.

"What the hell is going on?"

I can't answer him, but hear Lane's. Blue's phone goes dead again.

"Her call ended."

"Someone call the fucking cops," Noah roars. "I don't have my phone."

I keep mine gripped in my hands in case it rings again.

"Fucking Sophie, call the cops." Noah's hand slams into the back of the passenger seat.

"I got it. I got it." Sophie whirls around to face me. "She's on the running trail."

I snag the phone from her hands. "What the fuck is this?"

"Find My iPhone. We are on the same iTunes account. Just go. That's where her phone is."

The truck lurches to a stop in the dorm parking lot, and I take off, watching the location of her phone and mine. It only takes a few moments to realize where she is. *Fuck, the furthest place she could possibly be.*

My thighs burn as I run faster than I've ever run in my life. I don't hear her screams the closer I get, and that nearly freezes my whole body. Hot pink sneakers lie in the middle of the path and her long, white legs come into view. Blue's body is twisted with her blonde hair covering her face.

"Blue."

My voice startles her and she screams and begins to scramble.

"It's me, Tuck."

I go down to my knees and place my hands on her hips, trying to roll her over to see me, but she fights me off like a wild beast.

"Hey. Hey, now, it's me, Tuck. Look at me, Blue.

Look at me."

Her eyes dart up to mine, and when we she connects with me, the amount of pain filling her is like nothing I've ever experienced, and it takes me back to my own living hell.

"Where is he?"

"Gone."

Her sobs start, and I try for more information while carefully cradling her to my chest. I feel like a dickhead, but totally relieved when I noticed her panties are still on and not torn.

"Blue, help is coming."

"No, take me home."

"You need to go to the hospital."

"No."

Her instinct to fight me kicks back in as she tries to scramble from me. In her weakened state, there's no way she'll ever be able to escape, but I don't want her to hurt herself any further.

Holding her securely with one arm, I dial Noah and give him our location, and explain the situation as quickly as possible.

"Okay, Blue, we'll go to my house. You can't fight me. You're hurt."

She settles easily back into me when I remove the threat of the hospital, and I know it's because she doesn't want her parents to know. It's just something Blue would do, but she's going to the hospital.

I hear the roar of Lane's truck on the opposite side of the row of trees.

"Blue, I'm going to pick you up and take you to my house."

It kills me to lie to her. I didn't think anything would be worse than pushing her away these last few months, but I just found it. She cringes as I stand with her and then wails from sheer pain. My fists clench and I see red, ready to fucking kill whoever did this to her.

With each steps she cries out, and I know she has to go to a hospital. She doesn't have a choice. Her body goes limp as I near the fence and the truck comes into view.

"Fucking Noah, be careful."

It takes every single ounce of willpower I have to let go of her.

"Is she alive?" Noah asks, his eyes wide with horror.

"She just passed out."

I leap the fence in one swoop and jump in the back seat.

"Give her here."

Noah passes Blue's lifeless body to me. Leaning down, I let her breathing tickle my ear and rub the side of her jaw that's uninjured.

"She refused to go to the hospital and panicked when I brought it up." I look up into the other three worried faces. "She has to go."

Sophie crawls over into the back seat and lays Blue's head in her lap and begins crying and kissing her delicate skin.

"She doesn't want her parents to know. They just flew out a day ago."

"She has to go to the hospital," I repeat mindlessly.

"They'll call the cops."

"I don't fucking care." It comes out as a roar. "She needs help."

Blue jumps at my face, throwing her arms around my neck while wincing in pain. Sophie rubs her back and talks to her.

"Your parents won't find out. We are going to the hospital, Blue."

Chapter 17

Blue

"For the tenth time he didn't rape me."

The nurse glares, and I know she's had it with me.

"It's protocol."

"I'm not an idiot. No."

She leaves the room, and I hear Sophie let out a loud breath in the corner chair.

"You shouldn't be so damn stubborn, Blue. They're just trying to help you."

"He didn't rape me." I sit up in the bed while a sharp pain attacks my right side. "It's just like I told the cops. He threw me down. I blacked out for a bit, and then got my pepper spray."

I don't even want to know what would've happened if I didn't wake up. Actually, I know exactly what he would've done. The curtain rustles and Tuck and Lane rush to my bedside. And in the oddest of moments as time stands still, I still can't make eye contact with Tuck. His voice saved me from my demise. I heard him and then fought, and somehow I associate it with the attack. It should be in a good way like the king on the white horse who saves the kingdom, but for the moment it's the complete opposite.

I turned to see my attacker, anticipating his face, and then my world turns upside down. I've managed to keep the hospital from calling my parents and coaches. Being eighteen and protected by privacy acts have been my only allies. Looking down at my wrapped knees and then rubbing the pad of my finger over the road rash on my jaw, I feel ashamed and embarrassed.

"Blue Williams." I look up into the face of a doctor with an officer behind him. "We are ready to discharge you. It looks like no broken bones, just a slight fracture in your right rib. You'll need lots of rest and no strenuous activity for a couple weeks."

I twist my fists into the sheets, and Tuck must notice, because he steps up and untangles my hand from the bedding and holds it in his.

"I'll send you home with some painkillers and ointment for your skin." He pauses and gestures to the officer behind him. "Blue, you really need to file a report."

I gently shake my head, and the doctor opens his mouth to argue, but Tuck interrupts him.

"I have all the information and will be taking care of her over fall break," Tuck says while rising to his feet, but not letting go of my hand.

"You have my card." The officer nods and leaves the room.

The doctor begins speaking again. "Your discharge nurse will be with you in a minute."

"I'm not going home with you, Tuck."

I don't wait until the curtain is swept shut to blurt out my words and make eye contact with him, and strangely, it doesn't sting as badly as I thought it would. He doesn't talk to me, but stares down at me with his relentless glare.

"Take me to the dorms, Tuck."

"Your bags are packed and you have no choice, Blue." He lowers his large frame to the edge of the bed. "I'll drag your bratty ass out of here screaming and kicking. I'm not leaving you. I should've been there with you."

"Tuck, you hate me. I disgust you, and you only use me to get your rocks off."

My fingers are squeezed to near pain in his large palm. "Blue, you have two choices. Go quietly, or fight it the whole way."

"Transport here." A doughy-faced young man walks around the curtain, pushing a wheelchair.

"Perfect. My truck is waiting in the u-drive out front."

Tuck stands and gathers a couple bags that I hadn't noticed sitting on the edge of the bed, and when I think about it, I don't remember much since being checked in here, or what day it even is.

"What day is it?" I ask as I sit up in the bed.

"Sunday afternoon."

"I've been here…" I try to wrack my brain.

"We brought you in last night around eleven. They've been running tests."

My feet grace the cold hospital tile floor, and Tuck's on his knees slipping on my sandals. I hate that he's the one doing all of this.

"Where's Sophie?" I want her helping me, not Tuck.

"She and Lane just left."

"To where?" I ask with a raised eyebrow.

"He's taking her home for break."

"She just left me?" A pang of hurt hits me hard, and it's worse than the sharp pains in my side.

"I made her leave."

"Uh?" I look down into his dark eyes.

"I see the hurt on your face. I made her leave."

"Why, Jones?" As his last name slips from my tongue, it sounds odd. I hear his teammates call him by it all the time.

His palm runs up my calf, caressing uninjured skin. "Because, Blue, it's time you meet the real Tuck."

After all the hurt, denial, and longing for this man, he just spiraled my lust over the edge for him into straight and pure love.

"Fine." I place my hand on his and remove it from

my skin. He can think what he wants of it, but the truth is it was burning a hole in my flesh, and I'm not ready for that yet.

I push up off the mattress, but before I'm able to stand, Tuck scoops me up in his arms and gently sets me in the wheelchair. His touch is so opposite from his mean look and hard muscles, and it sends shivers down my bruised body.

Everything inside of me wants to tell him off, but my body is pulled to him. I watch my hand reach to his, and he walks by my side as the nurse rolls me down the hallway. We reach the sliding glass doors, and I see he's not kidding about Lane and Sophie being gone. I scan the parking lot for Lane's monster truck, but it's nowhere in sight.

Tuck's older truck sits in the u-shaped driveway, and I'm almost knocked back into a blackout where I don't want to believe or feel anything.

"Tuck."

"Yeah, Blue." His breath is on my ear as he bends down to hear my whisper.

"Don't break me again."

"I won't."

"If you do, I won't recover."

"It's your choice from here, Blue Williams. I'm about to open up more to you than I ever have to Noah."

The melody of his voice and the sweet nothings he pours into my soul soothe an aching part of me, but that little devil on my shoulder doesn't want to believe a word he has to say.

He lifts me from my wheelchair to his truck effortlessly, and again I'm pressed between the sweetest spot of my life and the hardest brick of chest I've ever experienced. His scent fills the single cab of the truck, and every single one of my tensed up muscles unwinds.

It's the scent I've clung to for months…the one urge I've fought over and over to not devour, and now it's surrounding me and I find myself relaxing. When I hear the driver's door shut, I look up into his still, midnight eyes with his hoodie covering his beanie. But this time his arm and hand are outstretched to me, and it's one offer I don't hesitate to accept.

"Careful, Blue, your right side hurts."

I hear each word, but don't take the time to process them. I'm a strong, fighting, athletic individual, and this man makes me melt into him every single time.

Tuck Jones, what have you done to me?

Chapter 18

"Tuck."

"Yeah, Blue, only two more hours."

"I just wanted to tell you." Lifting my head, I focus in on his beautifully etched face. "Pissing matches aren't my style. I prefer to drown out the competition."

"Oh yeah?" His smirk fills my vision.

I don't know if it's the pills he has been feeding me or his fucking charm, but I reply, "Be prepared to drown."

Then my eyes rest again, finding everything black and safe in their path. Over the past few months at college, black and safe seems to be my polarizing force, which I prefer to bask in.

***

In grade school you learned how to tuck, duck, and roll, but this seems like the earthquake drill they taught you. Hide under your desk and pray your ass doesn't get shaken into a deep crevice of the Earth and trapped until you rot…

"Blue."

My eyes shoot open at the familiar baritone voice, and flashbacks hit me. I turn my head to see him, and it's not him. It's another person attacking me, beating my face into the asphalt and ripping clothes from my body. Then I hear his voice when I should've seen his face.

My eyes clench while I hear his voice hollering my name, but hands are assaulting parts they should never explore. But it's his voice, and I scream a little louder and then fight a bit harder.

"It's Tuck, I'm here."

His voice is soothing and dangerous all mixed together, and I freeze. I'm sick of the tug of war or teeter or totter I've been riding. I need safety.

"You don't love me, Tuck, or want me."

"I told you." Strong palms grasp my cheeks. "I'm taking you home and showing you everything." His gaze burns holes into me, while I'm used to him peering away or backing off. "It's all yours, Blue. Now let's see if you are up to it."

I'm not sure if it's the sound of his voice or him finally giving over, but a drowsy haze hits me and I succumb to darkness once again. Cheer, goals, and GPA fly out the passenger window as I fight to see and hear Tuck for the first time.

Chapter 19

It may be the meds or willing myself to unconsciousness, but it sucks when I wake up in waves of awareness and then float back to sweet dreams. Words like beef jerky or diet Pepsi float in my vision, or were they really in my face? Sometimes strong and sturdy lips attack mine and I mimic them back like a playful kitten, relishing each taste as my tongue reaches deeper inside to soak up the sexy taste. Then just like a bad dream, my shoulders begin shaking and sounds invade the peace and reality sets in. A sweet voice similar to Tuck's but much less agonized fills my dreamy haze.

"You're home."

Every muscle in my body focuses on opening my eyes to see just where this wonderful sound comes from. And when I focus on the so much sweeter version of Tuck, who is also years younger and toothless, I almost smile until that sharp pain in my right side reminds me of all my mistakes and past fouls in the game of life.

"Uncle Tuck."

"Shhhh, Ruger. Go on in. I'll be there in a second."

"You have a girlfriend."

I watch as the younger Tuck's eyebrows waggle up and down and his toothless grin mirrors back at me.

"Run inside and let your mom know I'm home."

"Roger, Dodger," the little Tuck replies before he peels off toward a porch light.

My voice is a squeak in the night air. "Leave me alone, Tuck. Why are you pushing me?"

The tighter I shut my eyes, the quicker I spiral out of control once again, letting pain dictate every part of my life.

"I'm going to pack you to my bedroom."

"Were you kissing me?" I pry my eyes open to see his face and the little smile that spreads across it.

"No, but I can." His lips run over mine as he leans in the cab of the truck. "I think you were dreaming about me kissing you, though."

"I don't want to wonder anymore or remember what you feel like on my lips."

Tuck doesn't waste a moment before he lays his lips on mine, his kiss hard and full of passion. And it's just as sweet as my dreams remembered. He grabs my hips and tugs on them. It takes everything in me not to squeal in pain.

"Okay, she knows." The sweet voice is back, and Tuck pulls away and twists just enough to see the little boy standing behind us.

I wasn't dreaming when I thought he looked like Tuck. He's a miniature version of him, posture and all. I look closer and notice the football tucked under his arm, and I immediately know I've already taken too much of Tuck's time in the boy's eyes. The slamming of a door startles me, and I see a beautiful brunette standing on the porch of the smaller home.

It's a simple ranch style home with a white fence and the perfect scattering of flowers. Nothing super fancy, but just the right size and look for something Tuck would come home to. When I see the way the woman looks at Tuck, my stomach sinks and the pain in my right side is nothing compared to what just hit me. My focus shoots back to the toothy boy, and then Tuck and the woman walking toward us. It's his secret. The reason he'd never get close to me. He has a kid.

"Tuck," the woman squeals.

He leaves me and wraps the woman up in a hug and

spins her around. Her laughter sends chills down my spine as bile begins to rise up my throat.

"About time you got your ass home. We've missed you." She pulls back and gazes at him with love covering every inch of her face. "Never stay gone that long again."

"Mom, please," the little boy says.

"Okay, Ruger, you can play catch now."

Tuck turns to me, and I focus on the strange woman. Her eyes are full of kindness, and she even steps up to me, pushing past Tuck.

"Welcome. Tuck's talked so much about you."

"Let me get her settled and I'll be right back, Ruger."

"You ass, aren't you going to introduce me?" She slaps Tuck hard on the back of the head.

I cringe at the sight and wait for Tuck to blow.

"Goddamn, sis, you pack a punch." He rubs his head while still smiling. "Blue, this is my older and very annoying sister. Her name is Joe."

I nod, not sure how to respond, and feel embarrassed with the bruises and road rash covering one side of my jaw. Tentatively I reach out to shake her hand.

"No, no. Give me a hug now." She wraps me up in a massive hug.

"Careful, Joe, she's hurt."

"Shut the hell up, Tuck, I know this." Her voice rings in my ears, and then it falls to a whisper so only I can hear her. "He's never brought a girl home. You must be special."

"Okay, out of the way." Tuck shoves in, nudging his sister back. "You okay, Blue?"

I nod, speechless. It's like time has been warp speed since the football game.

"I'll take you to my room, but I have to play catch with Ruger or he'll have me by the balls all day."

He lifts me easily from the cab and knows just how to hold me without causing any further pain.

"I want to sit on the porch in the sun, please."

He looks down with raised eyebrows. "Are you sure?"

"Yeah, it seems I've been knocked out the whole drive here."

"Pills."

"I think I'm good."

Tuck sits down on a long, padded porch swing with me in his lap.

"You have a game waiting on you," I say with a grin.

"I don't want to let go of you, Blue."

Agony and regret speak volumes as they dance on his rugged features.

"It's not your fault, Tuck." I place my palm on his jaw and let his thick stubble tickle my skin. "I chose to run."

"Blue." Tuck's hands wrap into my thick side braid. "I love you, and it scares the shit out of me."

"I…" Before I can finish my thoughts, I have to ask, just to be sure. "Is that your kid?"

His low, deep chuckle makes me wince in pain.

"No." He ducks his head around me and hollers for the boy.

"Ruger, this is my girlfriend Blue, and Blue, this is my nephew Ruger."

"Okay, can we play now?"

I finally laugh and let the worry escape me.

"Yes, go play now."

"Are you going to watch, Blue?"

I nod at the boy, who can't be over the ripe age of eight years old.

"I've heard Mom talk about you. You're a cheerleader, and Tuck says you've got the sexiest legs he's ever seen."

Tuck slides out from under me and ruffles the boy's hair.

"What else has he said?" I lean forward as far as I can without wincing.

"Oh, that you're a queen and—"

"Enough," Tuck growls as he wraps an arm around the boy's shoulder.

Before Tuck walks too far away, I grab his hand and make him turn back to me.

"I want all of you, Tuck Jones."

A smile I've never seen on him before shines back at me, and then I watch his amazingly taut ass and thick thighs walk down the steps and imagine if only those damn gym pants weren't in the way.

I let the sun soak into my skin as the two begin to warm up by tossing the pigskin around, and then it eventually turns into Ruger doing some play calling and Tuck acting along with the kid. It makes me smile to see Tuck so relaxed and not hiding in a dark corner. The sun shines brightly on him as he fools around with his nephew, and I think how similar the two look with their ball caps on backward.

"This is Mabie."

I peer up to see Joe with a baby propped on her hip. The chunky little girl dressed all in pink smiles back at me through her chubby cheeks with one tooth showing. She's adorable and I can't help but smile back at her.

"She's so stinkin' cute."

"And a living terror. Ruger was nothing compared to this diva."

A light laugh escapes me as Joe sits next to me on the swing. Her legs automatically start a rhythmic rocking motion as the little girl reaches up to tug on my long braid.

"Hi, sweetie." My fingers run along the pleat of her dress.

Being an only child, I've always wondered what it was like to be around other siblings.

"Doing okay, hun?" Joe's eyes are caring and nurturing.

I offer up a grin and nod.

"So, you suck at lying. That's good." She plops the baby in my lap and stands. "Where are your pills?"

I shrug, realizing I don't know. Am I taking pills? What pills?

"Tuck." Holy hell, Joe has the mother scream down pat. "Where's Blue's stuff?"

He jogs back up to the porch with Ruger on his heels, and my fucking ovaries melt as he smiles up at me in all his sexy glory. This is the feeling I fought so hard for Noah to give me, but nope, it's Tuck.

"Why? You okay, Blue?"

"Fine."

The word is on repeat as it flies out of my mouth.

"Bullshit. She's in pain, and I need to see her meds."

"Truck. My backpack."

Joe storms off the porch, and the baby squeals in delight as Tuck nears us. Her pudgy little arms reach up to him as her squeals become louder.

"Okay. Okay." Tuck plucks her from my lap and begins talking to her as she slaps his cheeks in joy.

"Well, shit." I feel someone take a seat next to me and look at the little boy, stunned.

"What?"

"Well, shit, game over. I'm pretty much screwed now." Disappointment covers Ruger's face.

I glance at him and then up to Tuck who is mesmerized by the baby, and for a minute I wonder what fucking planet I'm on. "What?"

"The baby, my bossy nurse of a mom, and now my game is lost. I need these skills for my own game tomorrow," Ruger says.

I don't get the chance to respond as Joe interrupts and I officially meet the bossy nurse.

"Holy shit, you have a fractured rib? Thank god all your tests came back normal. This looks bad, Blue." She stretches her hand out with a pile of pills in the middle of her palm.

"Thanks," I manage to squeak out. Ruger elbows me lightly in the side and I almost scream, but don't want to get him in trouble. When I look down he has an 'I told you so' face.

"Tuck." I snag the hem of his long sleeve University shirt. He looks down at me with concern. I nod to the side where Ruger is with his pouting face. I pick up a bottle of water on a little glass table in front of me and down the pills, then hold my arms up for the baby.

"Don't worry. I read the log and know what she needs." Joe pulls Ruger up by the collar and sits next to me.

Tuck gently places the baby in my lap and then kisses my forehead. Using a combination of my eyebrows and nodding gestures, I send him back out to play with Ruger.

Joe slides the baby between us and begins rocking the swing again in a lullaby motion, which I find soothing. It's like she can read the pain on my face.

"Are you really a nurse?"

"Used to be before I had her." She points to the baby who is now chewing on the hem of her dress. "Tuck's told you nothing, has he?"

I bristle at her question, even though the pain meds are doing the opposite to my body. We're in a good place right now, or I'm high as a fucking kite and think we are. The last thing I want to do is break Tuck's trust, so I just shrug.

"I could beat his ass." Joe blows out a long breath, ruffling her loose bangs. "He's a good boy."

"I know that. He's pushed me away." I pause, knowing I shouldn't be talking right now. "He kind of captured my heart the first time I met him."

"He's a little shit like that."

We sit in silence for the next hour, and I keep dozing off and on in the sun. A loud, roaring engine pulls up in the driveway, startling me awake and sending me into a panic attack.

"Just my hubs, Blue, it's okay." Joe pats the top of my thigh reassuringly.

Ruger takes off to the black truck, allowing Tuck to walk up the stairs to me. I stand to meet him and feel shocked when no pain hits me. He cocks an eyebrow in my direction and I smile back at him.

"Easy, tiger." Tuck pulls me in on my left side. It's as if he has memorized every one of my injuries and avoids them at all cost.

"Whatever you gave me, Joe, has really helped my side." I turn back to see her smiling face.

Tuck's palm covers my good cheek and forces me to look back at him, and before I realize what's happening, his tongue is down my throat. And like a love struck fool, I let him. With each swipe of it I feel memories of the attack dissolve a bit.

Chapter 20

Well, I sure know where the cussing comes from in this family. All of them. They talk like sailors and wrestle like barbarians. Joe's even been flipped on her back a time or two by Tuck and had to scream uncle to escape, but the feisty little shit brought it on herself.

Joe's husband, Austin, barbecued dinner for us. And of course the nurse in Joe wouldn't let me help set the table or anything. I've just sat back and watched the family dynamics play out in front of me.

Joe helped me shower, and it made me feel like a new person. As I dry off, I examine my wounds and realize the pain on the inside is far worse than any one of them on the outside. The long patch of road rash on my jawline will heal quickly with a cream my dad gave me. It's a magic healer, and I guess it helps that my dad is a plastic surgeon. Everything else can be covered up with clothing.

"Blue," Tuck says from the other side of the door, followed by some light knocking.

I unclick the lock and crack the door a bit. Tuck pushes his way into the room and I cover up my bare boobies and thank god I had just slid on my panties.

"What are you doing?" I hiss.

"Coming to help." I don't miss his devilishly sly grin.

His lips attack the side of my neck, and I enjoy him nibbling on my flesh way too much.

"How are you feeling?" he mumbles on my skin.

"Not as sore. Look like hell, though."

He lifts his head, cupping one side of my face. "You look like my gorgeous Blue to me."

Something in the air kills the mood and Tuck goes to

his serious dark place.

"Don't," I plead.

"Don't what?" he asks.

"Don't turn yourself off."

"I'm not, Blue." He leans back on the wall opposite from me, crossing his legs at the ankle. "I do need to apologize to you. I was a dick and handled everything wrong. I know Noah told you about the trouble I got into, but there's more. I never should've gone after you. I knew it was all or nothing, but I couldn't resist you. My coaches all told me to stay away and focus."

His words hit me hard as I realize he's about to open up to me for the first time. I remain frozen like a statue, still covering my breasts.

"Your texts were the only thing that helped soothe the pain I caused. And when your number called me that night and I heard you screaming and struggling, I died, Blue."

"I called you?" I whisper.

"Somehow your phone rang mine, and I kept screaming for you, but I just heard rustling. Sophie used some damn app to find your location." Tuck drops his head, rubbing his hands over his ball cap. "When I found you, you thought I was him. You were scared and refused to go to the hospital."

"Stop. Please stop."

All the blood rushes from my face and my head goes dizzy as the awful thoughts from that night begin to invade my mind.

"You remember it, don't you?"

"Tuck." I look up into his eyes with tears streaming down my face. "I do remember it, but do you want to know how I came to in time to get my pepper spray?"

He doesn't respond, but only steps forward.

"I heard your voice."

Tuck drops his head onto my shoulder and lets out a pent-up breath. "Blue, I'm fucking scared that after you see the real me, you'll run."

"Show me."

"When I was—"

"Hello." There's a loud banging on the door. "I need to pee, and Dad said you guys were probably making babies in there."

I grab the sides of Tuck's face, horrified.

"Are you almost done?" Ruger calls out.

I panic and send a punch into Tuck's rock hard abs.

"Get out," I hiss between my teeth.

"You afraid of a little seven year old?"

"Now. Go entertain him." I point to the door.

"Just one more kiss."

His lips are on mine before I can refuse, and god dammit, I melt into him. I wrap my arms around his neck as he cradles my injured side to his body acting as a brace. He lifts me to the counter, setting me down, while still kissing my lips. His hands leave my skin and I can hear him fumbling around on the counter for something. Within moments, he's clasping my bra on me, only pulling back when necessary to snap it, and then sealing himself to me again.

I giggle into his mouth when he pulls a jersey of his over my head, which drowns me.

"Really?" I mumble into his lips.

"Noah packed for you, and I think the clothes are too skimpy. I think he got into your costume drawer."

I laugh, then wince, pulling back and holding my side. "I don't have a costume drawer."

"Well, this looks damn hot on you."

His lips go back to work on mine as his fingers run up and down the front of my belly, and goose bumps form behind his touch. His fingers dip below my panties, and I pull back from his mesmerizing kiss.

"Um, no. I get all of you before you get that again." I push back on his chest.

I don't miss his loud and very deep grumble as he tries for it a second time.

"I'm serious, Tuck." I tap my finger on his chest with each word I speak.

"Okay, I might pee my pants out here. Are you done making babies?"

"Holy shit," I mouth to Tuck. "Does he really know what making babies is?"

Tuck only laughs as I try to put on my shorts with no luck, and his hands glide up my legs to tug them on. Before his delicious fingers have a chance to play with anything down there in that department, I bolt for the door.

"All done."

Ruger grins toothlessly at me as he does the potty dance.

I step out into the hall and hold the door open for him.

"Where's the baby you made?" he asks.

"Um, ask your Uncle Tuck."

I don't even feel bad when I head for the guest bedroom, giggling the whole way. When I enter, I notice the stack of pills on the nightstand and know it was Joe. I grab the bottle of water by them and chug the whole pile in one swallow and hope we eat soon, so I have a fighting chance of not passing out.

I don't wait for Tuck before I head outside, following the aroma of the barbecued ribs. The whole family is seated around the picnic table chatting away, and it warms my heart to see Tuck so relaxed. I hear Joe's husband give me hell about the number I'm wearing, and I just fire back with a smartass comment.

"It was on clearance at the bookstore. Some overrated player." I shrug and take the seat next to Tuck.

"Eat." Joe shoves a plate my way filled with a gorgeous green salad and a steaming pile of sweet beans.

"Thank you."

Tuck reaches over to snag a crouton off of my plate, but Joe slaps him hard before he has the chance to get it.

"She needs to eat with all the medicine she's on."

The scent of the food sends my senses into overdrive, and suddenly I'm scarfing down the meal like it's my last one. Tuck laughs at me as I shovel it in my mouth at a steady pace. It's not long before his sister provides him with his own piping plate of food, but his has ribs stacked on it. I pluck one off of his plate and cringe mid-movement, wondering if I'll get the same hand smack, but the burning slap never comes.

With a full tummy and relaxed muscles with the slightest numbing sensation, I watch as the three boys fool around with the football.

"Ruger has a game tomorrow that he's dying for Tuck to go to."

"I can't wait."

"He wanted you to cheer for him in that skirt Tuck told him about, but I told him you were hurt."

I giggle at the thought of Tuck actually telling his family things about me. Mabie is trying to chew on her big toe without tipping over on the grass, and I laugh even harder at the sight.

"Thank you for all of this, Joe."

She places her hand on mine. "You are so welcome, and I know it's none of my business, but you should really tell your parents and file that report."

"I know. The thing is, my dad is a plastic surgeon and my mother a worrywart. I'm their only child and shit will hit the fan. I just want to pretend it never happened."

"Shit like this doesn't just disappear. You need a support team."

"She has me and needs nothing else." Tuck's deep voice breaks into our conversation. "Enough, Joe."

"It's fine." I shrug. "I think I need to lie down now."

Standing up, I give Joe a hug and thank her once again.

"Oh, hey, when do I get to meet you guys' parents? Do they live around here?"

As soon as the words are spoken, I know I never should've asked. I see the painful look blanketing Joe's face, and then my gaze focuses in on Tuck's clenched jaw.

"They passed away several years ago," Joe finally says.

My hands fly to my chest. "I didn't know. I'm so sorry."

Joes waves me off, and in typical Tuck fashion, he scoops me up from the picnic bench and carries me to the house. I've lost the fun, carefree Tuck.

"I'm so sorry, Tuck." I place my hand on his chest. "You know I can walk."

"It's a good workout." The stairs creak below his feet as he takes them one by one. "It's fine, Blue. I should've told you. It's just a hard topic."

"You can tell me anything, Tuck, and I do mean anything. Well, besides to leave." My finger traces a swirl pattern on his chest through his shirt.

Tuck lays me in the bed and gently slides down my shorts, and then undoes my bra. I wait for his playful fingers to try some funny business, but they don't. He nestle me up in his blankets, and his scent captivates me. I've never been so immersed in Tuck. My eyelids win the war as I fall instantly asleep wrapped in his musk.

Chapter 21

Watching Tuck pace back and forth at Ruger's game is comical and bordering on the edge of panty melting. He's clearly a hometown hero. This morning when I woke up, it dawned on me that I had no idea where we were, and Tuck's response was small town, Arizona.

He was up and out of bed before I had the chance to cuddle with him. He'd already hit the gym and made the whole family breakfast. Seeing him sweaty and in his workout clothes made me sad, and I instantly longed for the gym, and then remembered everything that had happened. The face of the man who attacked is still muddy in my memory, but pieces of it haunt me when I sleep. More and more of the attack is coming back to me, like hearing Tuck's voice on the phone and then fighting to get to my pepper spray. I even remember ripping off the man's ski mask.

A chill runs up the length of my spine, and I focus back on the game and the peace surrounding me. Just like his uncle, Ruger is the running back, among other positions. He constantly keeps looking over to Tuck for his approval.

"Here." Joe hands me Mabie. "Can you hold her while I grab the snacks for the team?"

"Yeah." The pads of my fingers brush over her sweet little cheeks.

"Are you sure that doesn't hurt you?"

"Not at all. Whatever is in that one pill has really helped my side."

"It's a strong-ass ibuprofen and probably helped relieve some pain."

"Go, we are fine." I wave her off.

Mabie does cause a tiny bit of pain to my side, but it's well worth holding the perfect little girl who is decked out in a pink cheerleading outfit with her chubby legs sticking out. She's very intrigued with my baseball cap and aviators, trying to pull both of them off. I really didn't want to go out in public looking like I'd just had my ass kicked, but Tuck left me no choice.

He's been overprotective since the attack, and I know deep down he stills feel guilty. It's a good thing I'm quite the pro with working miracles with make-up. The long, nasty bruise lining my jaw is barely visible. Even though it's tank-top weather, my arms are covered in a long sleeve t-shirt and my legs with a pair of blue jeans to hide scrapes and bruises.

"Here, sissy." Tuck pulls the baby from my hands and props her on his hip.

She's immediately content with him as she lays her head on his broad shoulder.

"Come here. There are some people I want you to meet." He holds his other hand out to me, and I've never seen anything that looks and feels more like home to me. "What's that grin for, Blue?"

Looking up to him through my aviators, I clutch his hand with confidence, and simply say, "Because I'm happy."

I snuggle into his side as we walk, and he leans over and kisses me on the top of the head. "I am too. For now."

And there's the reluctant Tuck.

We spend the next hour talking to his old teachers and coaches, and it's even more evident how everyone in his hometown adores him. I don't miss the stares of concern when eyes float my way and know they are only worried about me breaking Tuck's heart. If only they knew the truth of the situation and how this man could crush me in a matter of seconds.

"Tuck, go with them." I wrap my arms around his waist, laying my head on his chest.

"Nah, I'll go home with you guys."

"Take Ruger and go have lunch with your friends. I need a nap anyway and will ride home with Joe."

His large palms cover my cheeks, forcing me to look up at him. "Are you sure, Blue?"

"Yeah."

"Have I ever told you that you are gorgeous?"

"Stop."

His lips lightly graze mine.

"I'm serious, Blue, like you're more than I deserve."

"Stop." I pound on his chest. "Not that slippery slope."

He kisses me again, and it's light and quick. We both know anything else leads to nothing but trouble and overheated actions.

"Go, Tuck." It takes all my willpower to shove down my pent-up horniness and walk away from him. I send him a quick wave over my shoulder as I head toward Joe's minivan.

"I'm impressed," Joe says with raised eyebrows as I shut the door behind me.

"What?" I flip down the visor to check out my bruise.

"That you got him peeled away from you."

"I'm not going to lie, me too." A light laugh escapes me.

"He's so in love with you."

I whip my gaze in her direction, and I expect to see a joking expression covering her face, but I don't find it.

"It's no joke, Blue. That boy is head over heels for you."

"Joe." I pause to readjust myself in the seat to face her. "He won't open up to me. I mean, he's practically treated me like I was nothing until this. I knew he wanted me, but he kept pushing me away."

"Tuck has issues."

"I'm scared, Joe." Mabie's bottle flies into the front seat, startling me. Leaning over, I pick it up and hand it back to her. "I'm afraid when we get back to campus and I'm healed up that he'll put his walls back up around him."

"Like I said, Blue, he has his issues and I've encouraged him to tell you, but he is Tuck, and Tuck has always been a stubborn ass."

"He is that." I run my fingers up and down the tan interior of the door. "I just hope he takes a chance on me."

Mabie decides to throw her bottle again and serenade us with her screams. The girl is clearly over football and the car ride home. Quickly, I unbuckle my seatbelt and climb into the back.

"Ow, ow, ow," I howl as I contort into a small enough ball to get over the console.

By the time I'm settled next to her, she's quit crying and stares up at me in shock. I do my best to keep her calm and love on her to soothe her cries for the remainder of the drive.

"Thank you, Blue." Joe glides open the van door, and Mabie squeals when she sees her face. "You need something to eat and take your meds."

"Okay."

My phone dings in my pocket.

Tuck: You okay?

Me: Yep, just got home.

Tuck: The boys want to go hang out at Coach's house.

Me: Go for it. I'm so tired and want to lay down.

Tuck: Okay. Dream of me.

Me: Seems I've been doing that the past few months.

Tuck: Sweet dreams, Blue.

Joe whips up a couple sandwiches for us, and I inhale one and then have pills shoved in my direction.

"You're the best, Joe."

"Get your ass to bed and let that gorgeous body of yours heal up."

"Thank you." I wrap my arms around her and pull her into a tight hug. "For everything."

She slaps my ass, and I laugh at her. "Get to bed."

"Yes, Momma Joe."

The house is extremely quiet with the boys gone, making the creaking of Tuck's door deafening as I shut it behind me. His room is filled with his scent, and I become drunk on it, allowing it to overtake my senses. My pants slide to the ground, as does my shirt. I glide between his sheets and love the feel of my skin on his bedding.

I decide to send one final text before dozing off, but this time it's a picture text with some extra body parts in it to ensure Tuck knows I'm safely snuggled into bed. I'm not sure if it's the effect of the medicine or sheer exhaustion, but I fall deeply asleep before I get the chance to see how he responds…or if he responds.

Chapter 22

My eyes are open, but darkness fills the room instead of sunshine. I search for my phone in the sheets as I force myself to wake up. Holy shit, it's past seven o'clock at night. I've been asleep for over five hours. Tuck did end up texting me back hours ago.

Tuck: Damn

I giggle at his simple response. It takes a few moments for me to crawl from the bed and gain my bearings. I stretch lightly from side to side, and then crack my neck. A loud ruckus roars in the living room, and it's a sure fire sign the boys are back. Using the flashlight on my cellphone, I locate my clothes and pull them on.

As soon as I open his door, a strong aroma of fresh tomato sauce fills my senses and my belly growls. I walk across the small hall to the bathroom and freshen up before going out to see everyone. And when I look in the mirror, I'm thankful I did. My hair is plastered to the side of my face, along with wrinkles from being pressed into the sheets. It's obvious I didn't move a muscle while sleeping.

The hallway is dimly lit with the kitchen light shining brightly ahead, and I spot Joe cleaning up the kitchen.

"Hey." My hand glides along the dark mahogany dining table.

"You're up."

"Man, I was out."

"How do you feel?"

"Good, actually. Really good."

"Hungry?" Joe holds up a plate piled with pasta, green salad, and a fresh breadstick.

"You sure know the way to a girl's ass." I grab the fork and dig in, taking a few quick bites. "I want to go say hi to the boys."

"Careful, I think its WrestleMania in there."

"I can only imagine." I snag the ice-cold glass of milk in front of me and down it.

When I round the corner, she was right. It's like all hell has rained down on the poor living room with bodies intermingled and all sorts of elbow drops falling down. Ruger soars off the couch, landing on Tuck's back, and then does his best to wrap him up in a headlock. Mabie squeals and claps from the couch as she sits on her daddy's lap. Austin is more interested in what's on television than the wrestling match while he swigs on a beer.

A holler from Ruger catches my attention, and I look back to the wrestling match on the floor. He stands with his arms flexed and hollering in victory. He has Tuck's shirt pulled up and over his head like they do in hockey, exposing all of Tuck's back. A loud gasp bursts from my lungs, but is drowned out by all of the other ruckus filling the small living room. The scars cover the entire surface of his skin, and they aren't just scars—his skin is marred and barely recognizable.

I cover my mouth as I fight to hold back the tears. Joe comes up behind me and places her hand on the small of my back. When I look down at her, she just offers me a feeble smile.

"I don't think you have to worry about him running. It's you he's afraid will run after you see all of him."

Thought after thought races through my mind, making me dizzy and nauseated. Here for months I thought I wasn't good enough for him, he was a manwhore, an asshole, and so many other off the wall theories to answer why he was being so reserved and running from me.

“Blue, watch me kick Tuck’s trash.”

Ruger waltzes up and lands a kick right on Tuck’s ass. The tension in Tuck’s back is visible when Ruger speaks, and I watch as he slowly raises up on his knees and pulls down his shirt.

“Play time over, buddy, I need to go make a call.”

Tuck doesn’t make eye contact as he storms out the back door.

“Tuck.” My voice is weak and barely audible to my own ears.

He doesn’t stop, and I’m in motion before I realize it. My feet move quicker than my brain.

“Tuck,” I holler.

His hunched silhouette shines in a sliver of moonlight on the picnic table, and I walk closer without thinking about any of the consequences and grab his clutched hands from his lap. I make sure each knuckle brushes over my lips, and then I drop them back down into his lap and make the boldest move of my life and grab the hem of his shirt, pulling it up and over his head. It’s as if he’s lifeless, allowing me to expose him. The front of his chest mirrors the back, with burnt flesh covering every surface. Some spots are deeper than others, and when he flexes back down on his knees, resting his elbows there, I spot the scars running down his arms.

“Tuck,” I whisper.

He refuses to look up or answer me back, so I place my hands on his back and feel my palms collide with the ridges and waves of his skin. He shudders at my touch, and then I hear him sob. I refuse to let go of this. I begin exploring every part of his skin until he’s breathing out of control and ready to explode. My lips brush along the tortured skin and place delicate kisses on him.

“Look at me, Tuck. You told me I could have all of

you. Did you lie?"

He remains silent, and I put my lips on his skin and feel his shame on them. I don't back down and push him even harder.

"Talk to me." This time my voice comes out as a desperate plea.

He raises his head slowly, glaring at me. "You wanted all of me, so here it is."

Tuck raises his arms to the heaven, exposing all of his scars covering every single part of him. A long incision line runs from one of his armpits down his entire ribcage, dipping into his pants.

"You lied, Blue, you so fucking lied."

My brain tries to keep up, processing all the pain this man had to have once suffered, and it's also trying to figure out why he's calling me a liar. Before I have the chance to ask, he is up on his feet and glaring down at me.

"I saw the horror in your face when you saw my back. The disappointment and disgust was written all over your face."

"Fuck you, Tuck." Without thought I shove hard into his chest. "I've done nothing but worship the ground you walk on since meeting you. I fell in love with you, and you've been nothing but a dickhead to me."

"You are just like everyone else. All the doctors and surgeons who want to fix me or make me halfway human looking," he interrupts.

I land my palm across his cheek as hard as I can, and it's the best sting I've ever felt. "I love you, Tuck. I want all of you, and if you can't accept that, then that's your issue. I'm done. I've given everything to you."

When I spin away from him, he catches my wrist and tugs me back to him.

"Kissing your back was the sweetest thing I've ever

done."

With a hard jerk, I pull away from him. He lets go, and I'm not sure if it's because he's given up the fight or if my words stun him. Even though I'm barefoot, I head for the gate and walk down the sidewalk. I have no clue where I'm going, I just need to be away from the asshole. I hear his footsteps behind me, but ignore each one as it pounds the pavement. I'd give anything to be able to run away from him. Open up in a sprint and get as far away as possible.

If only I had my shoes, purse, and phone, then I'd walk to the nearest motel and book a flight for tomorrow. Strong hands wrap around my waist, and it startles me even though I know it's Tuck. I thought it was him the other night tugging on my shoulder.

"Blue." I'm spun around in his arms, looking up into his face. "When I was younger, there was a house fire. Killed my parents, and I made it out alive. Joe was already at college. She came home and raised me."

He drops his forehead to mine. "I'm trying here, Blue."

"I don't think you're disgusting." I cup his cheeks and force him to look at me. "But I do think you're an asshole."

"Uncle Tuck."

We both look back to Joe's house to see Ruger hollering from the lit porch. Tuck clasps both of my hands in his.

"Please come back with me, Blue."

"Don't ever push me away again. I won't come back, Tuck."

"I'm a fucking mess, Blue, I can't promise anything."

"Push me away one time—just one more fucking time—and I'm gone. I can promise that."

I follow the tug of his hand as he pulls me back

toward Joe's, and we walk in silence.

"Mom said it's bedtime. Will you tuck me in, Tuck?" Ruger giggles after he asks the silly question.

"Sure, buddy."

We all follow the little guy into the house and see the married couple studying us with worried eyes.

"I'll meet you in bed," I whisper to Tuck.

"Blue, you need your pills." Joe jumps up from the couch.

"Not tonight."

I don't give her the chance to push them down my throat. I need to be wide awake for what's about to go down between Tuck and me, because I have every intention of pushing him to his limits, and if he pulls back even the least bit, I'll just accept my fate of living with a cursed, broken heart.

"Goodnight." I don't make eye contact before I head down the hall and enter Tuck's room. I want to cry. No, I take that back, I want to collapse into the fetal position and sob for his pain. I keep it all inside because I sure as hell don't want to scare him off now, or ever again. All elements of emotions for the man who has been burned must vanish, and I can only look into those eyes of his.

The door creaks open and I turn to see Tuck standing there frozen with no dark or pissed look on his face. He's devoid of all emotion. It takes only three long strides across the room to shut the door behind him, and then I take his hand and guide him to the bed like he did to me at his house. When the back of his legs hit the bed, I stop him and go for the damn beanie on his head and toss it to the side.

I have every intention of stripping this man to his core and proving to him that I'm not running. My fingers nab the hem of his t-shirt and begin tugging it up and over his head, and then I push down his gym pants. I don't let my gaze linger too long on his scarred body because I can't help but feel for him.

Taking two steps back, I look up and down Tuck clothed only in his boxers. If I thought the scars would shatter me and make me melt for the man, then the pained look on his face just broke me. I strip before him, exposing every single part of me to him in the light of the room and then close the distance between us.

The moment my skin hits his bare chest I know beyond a shadow of a doubt the curse is real with all the zinging tension bouncing between us. I spiral out of control with love and need, finally feeling Tuck on me. I place my palms on the most damaged part of his chest and look straight into his eyes.

"I love you, Tuck. You saved me, now let me save you."

I feel the strongest man I've ever met tremble under my touch. He holds college records and takes on the best defenses in the nation, but with my touch he collapses back on the bed, and I have no intention of stopping. I'll push him to his limits just to make him feel me.

"Blue." Tuck relaxes further back on the bed with his forearms covering his eyes. "I've never—"

I plant my palms on either side of his head and crawl up on him, covering him once again, and there's something about our skin contact that's oddly addicting.

"You've never what, Tuck?" I ask, placing a light kiss on his lips. "You've never driven a woman wild with just a look or pleasured her until she fell apart?"

"No, Blue." Tension and a hint of anger fills his voice, but I continue to push.

"If you love me, you'll open your eyes and watch me love every single part of your gorgeous body, Tuck."

Seconds pass, then moments pass, and what feels like an eternity passes, but I don't give in or remove my palms from his chest. Feeling the burn marks underneath them pushes me harder to make the man open his eyes. My fingertips dig into his flesh, and I see his dark gaze and those eyes that have haunted my dreams.

"Watch me, Tuck, watch me make love to you."

My lips touch down on his chest, and it's as if he were stung by a wasp with the sharp intake of breath he inhales. My tongue runs down the rippled and scarred flesh all the way to his belly button. He's hidden all of this from everyone. As my tongue continues to trail over his hard ridges of muscle, he squirms under my touch.

"Eyes open, Tuck."

His abs relax a bit while I continue to swirl my tongue around his muscles and run my hands up to his shoulders. He grabs onto the back of my hands, clutching them with desperation. I'm pulled up to face level with him by his powerful force. Eye to eye, I wait for him to tell me to leave. It's clear there's something messing with him.

"Blue."

"Tuck."

"I've never done this, and you are scaring me. I need a moment."

"So, you're saying we can't do this?" My body goes into safety mode and I pull away from him. Before I'm able to get away from him, he flips me over on my back and glares down at me with his stormiest eyes yet.

"If you'd listen to me, I was going to tell you that I've never had sex, or even let anyone besides Joe, Ruger, and Austin see the real me. Joe came home and fucking saved me and nursed me back to health while continuing to go to the community college to finish her degree." Tuck rests his elbows on the sides of my head, and I turn my head and place a light kiss on a part of his marred skin. "I've never even been into a girl until you,

Blue, and I fought to keep you away."

My hands run up and down Tuck's back, caressing and memorizing each contour of his burns. My fingertips gently pay careful attention to them while falling even fucking harder for the man. I'm thirsty to taste each of his wounds, helping him heal one at a time.

"But I want you, Tuck. Does it look like I care?" My hands work harder to portray even more conviction.

"You should." His eyes squeeze shut. "You're fucking gorgeous. Flawless, Blue, and I'm a monster of evil emotions and tainted skin."

"No one is perfect." I reach up and place a light kiss on his lips. "Be my scars and flaws, Tuck, be mine."

Something unleashes inside of Tuck as he forces himself into me without any warning, and I scream.

"Shhh…you want me, so here it is."

I know we are being loud in the small house and shouldn't be, but neither of us can control our yelps and growls of pleasure. His skin rubs up and down mine as he works himself in and out of me. I hike my heels up and over his lower back, allowing him to drive harder and deeper. Tuck handles me like a ragdoll as he rolls me over to my belly and enters me again.

His palm covers the back of my head as he presses my face harder down into his mattress. He's being aggressive and controlling, but the only important part is…he's letting me feel and see him for the first time. The pain from my side nearly threatens to knock my ass out, but the overwhelming pleasure keeps me from surrendering to it. Tuck slides his hand down to the nape of my neck, squeezing it even harder, and I spiral out of control. Ripping my head away, I bury my face and let the pillows drown out my screams.

Tuck doesn't stop as he continues to relentlessly drive in and out of me, and I feel that pleasure begin to build and bury my face again to muffle the sounds. The lack of oxygen threatens to knock me out, but when I feel him grow harder inside me, I explode and feel the earth move then scream out in pleasure. Let everything out that's been building for months.

Tuck's quick to cover my mouth with his hand as he finishes up with his own release. His warmth spreads inside of me with each thrust of his hips, and it's something I've never felt before. He rolls over, taking me with him, my naked back pressed against his sweaty chest. I run my hands up and down his sides, following the scar on his side all the way down his hip as far as I can reach. It doesn't take long before he's tensed up again with my touch.

"Tuck."

I only get a light growl from him.

"Was that the first time, like, ever?"

"Yeah." His hands cover the backs of mine, stopping them from running up and down his skin.

"You did good." I'm thankful he can't see the stupid smile on my face right now.

"I don't like your skin on mine."

I try to roll off of him to look at his face.

"No, Blue. I don't want to look at you."

"What the fuck?"

"You have to have some patience here, Blue. You're flawless, laying on my burns and touching me, and I don't know how to react."

"Do you like it?" I ask, clenching my eyes shut.

"I more than like it, and that fucking scares me, but it also makes my skin crawl with the thought of you seeing me."

Sitting straight up, I go for the lights and turn them off. Then I make my way straight back to Tuck. Starting at mid-calf where his burns begin, I caress every part of them and then trail kisses along them. Slowly I work my way up his thighs and then glide my tongue across his delicious hips, stopping to appreciate his v-muscle.

"Blue."

His heart is thundering in his chest, and I know his anxiety has to be sky high.

"Tuck, I'm not looking at you. I'm just trying to love you." I push up into a sitting position and straddle him. "Are you going to let me do that?"

"Fuck, I hate this," he growls and slams his fists into the mattress.

"Hate what?" I push him harder.

"That I'm this and you're that." I feel his hands wave around in the air, but don't see them.

"I don't see your scars, Tuck." I trail my finger down his chest, letting it bump and glide over him. "I see the man I want so bad. I see the man who has dark eyes and the most gorgeous face I've ever seen. I see you."

My need for him to give in or break grows stronger as I bend down and gently place kisses all over his chest and then trail slowly up his neck. From burnt skin to perfect skin, my tongue licks across him, and I moan in pleasure, soaking up everything Tuck. I just have no idea how to show this man I want all of him.

My lips rest on his as I mumble into them. "It's your choice, Tuck. I'm begging to be with you, and if you can't believe that, then we need to stop this now."

"I want you and love you, but, Blue, you're going to have to be patient with me."

His lips attack mine without warning as he kisses the ever loving shit out of me. Tuck's words are not convincing at all, but the passion he pours into kissing me is my guarantee he's in this to try. I kiss him back, and it shocks him to life, and his hands begin exploring my body. His hands grip my ass, squeezing to a near point of pain, and making me yelp in his mouth.

He pulls back with a devilish grin on his face. "I think you've created a monster in this beast. I'm never going to get enough of you, Blue."

Something very large and extremely hard pokes between us, and I squirm against it.

"My turn, Tuck."

My hips easily find him, and he has me so ready I slip down on him with ease. I splay my palms out over his chest and push myself up into a sitting position and begin to rock back and forth. My fingers dig into his skin as my pleasure builds. The electrifying sensation feels so amazing I try to slow it down to feel all of it before I burst, but I don't have the chance before Tucks grips my hips and forces me. He controls the speed with his deathly grip pounding me up and down on him.

He growls, and then I feel him harden and it's all over for me as I tumble into ecstasy with him and go limp on his chest. He tenses right back up after his sensations wear off, but I refuse to move.

"This is the most comfortable I've been in a long time, Tuck."

He brushes my hair from my face while his other hand rubs up and down my back. He never quits playing with my hair, which eventually lulls me to sleep.

Chapter 23

I feel his hand on my shoulder again and turn, expecting to see Tuck, but it's not him. All the feelings flood back, and I scramble to safety, but am being held down by a stronger power. Panic sets in and I fight harder and try to scream, but my voice is stuck in my throat.

"Blue."

My shoulders begin to shake, then I hear my name being called again.

"I have you. It was a dream."

I pull my face from Tuck's chest and look into his eyes and immediately relax into him.

"Oh fuck," I gasp.

"It's okay, baby."

His hands are on me again, rubbing everywhere.

"I need a drink."

"Okay, let me get up."

He tries to gently set me on the bed next to him, but I yelp and he freezes.

"Let me, Tuck."

"Fuck, are you in that much pain? We shouldn't have."

I grip his face with both hands and force him to look up at me. I can barely make out his features in the dimly lit room. I kiss him softly.

"We should do that every night of our life. Just give me a sec. I'm a little stiff."

I wince as I roll off him and realize it probably wasn't the smartest idea to sleep on the brick wall known as Tuck in my condition.

"Where are you going?" I ask as he gets up from the

bed and throws on his boxers.

"To start a bath."

"You'll wake the whole house. No."

"Fine." He grabs the doorknob. "I'll get the hot tub ready and find your pills."

Somehow I have to fight through my pain and sore muscles, because there's no way I'll let him know how badly I'm hurting. I wouldn't change last night for anything. I brush my feet on the dark hardwood floor, remembering everything that went down, and pray that Tuck won't scare. He's the most beautiful man I've ever seen, been with, and touched. I just have to make him feel the way I see him.

Creaks and squeaks from the hall fill the silent room and I know he's on his way back in. I do my best to stand and move around the room, slowly gaining my bearings. One of Tuck's large shirts lays on the ground, and I snag it and pull it over my head.

"Ready?" He pops his head back in the door, and I see he's fully clothed.

Walking over to him, I tug his shirt off. "Am now."

He growls, but doesn't take too long to protest as I hug him from the back and begin walking with him, trying not to clip his heels.

"I didn't know your sister had a hot tub," I whisper.

"It's back in the corner. She's paranoid about one of the kids getting in it. It's just a small one."

"Nice." I kiss his back as I follow him through the kitchen. I relax even more into him as he doesn't growl or tense up this time.

"They call it their personal soak and poke."

"Ewww." I slap his shoulder. "Tuck, that's gross."

"Don't worry, I'm sure Joe has it well cleaned with chemicals, but I'm pretty sure they made a baby or two in it."

"Stop." I pull back to walk down the stairs.

His laughter soothes my heart, and I know in this moment that is a sound I want to hear the rest of my life. Before I know what's going on, he sweeps me off my feet and wraps me in his arms.

"Jones broke the line, he's at the thirty, now the twenty, and he jumps over a defender." He calls the plays out as he jogs to the hot tub, carrying me. "One defender left. Can Jones go all the way?"

He drags his voice out just like a commentator would, and I laugh the whole way. The damn laughter causes my side to hurt worse than his jogging and juke moves.

"Touchdown," he roars as he places my bottom on the edge of the hot tub.

I wrap my legs around his torso and tug him closer into me.

"I think we've both scored. You do know I'm your biggest fan, right, Tuck Jones?"

"I'm starting to realize it."

He pulls my shirt off, and I sit bare before him in the moonlight. I use my toes to dig into the waistline of his gym shorts and inch them down.

"God, you have a huge ass, Tuck." My toes struggle to get his shorts over his big ol' booty.

"I work out." A sly smile dances on his face, and I lean forward and kiss it.

When he's completely stripped, I pull him in as close as possible and wrap my arms under his, cupping the back of his shoulders.

"This is us, Tuck. Nothing between us ever again."

"This is us," he repeats as he bends over and kisses me lightly on the lips. "You're nipping out."

We both enter a fit of laughter as the night chills my body and goose bumps attack my skin.

"It's cold." I turn in his grip and swing my legs over into the hot water. It's a welcoming feeling compared to the cool air. Slowly, I sink lower into the hot tub. Tuck was correct about it being a small one; it's probably a three person hot tub at best. And I try my best to avoid all thoughts of Joe and Austin baby-making in here.

"Here." Tuck's outstretched hand holds all my pills. "Take them, and no arguing."

"But…"

"No damn buts. I can see the pain all over your face."

I know it's a losing battle and the last thing I want to do is fight with this stubborn ass.

"Fine." I snag the bottle of water from his hands and down the pills. "But get your ass in here so we can have some fun before the meds knock me out."

He sets the bottle on the ledge. "I never said I gave you the strong painkiller."

He winks at me and then hops in, not caring that he sent gallons of water splashing over the edge. I crawl into his lap and straddle him, facing him, and it's like an automatic trigger neither of us can control. His lips meet mine hard and fast, not hesitating as I run my hands all over his back and shoulders, gripping down tightly into his flesh when he bites my lower lip. My hips begin to grind into him and find him hard and ready.

"Again?" I pull back with a questioning look.

"I told you that you've released something vicious inside of me."

"By all means, I'm not complaining, lover boy."

It only takes one swift movement of my hips and I slowly sink down on him. Just like everything Tuck, he's hard and huge down in the boy department. It takes several moments for my body to adjust to him, and I relish every single second of it. He lays his head back on the ledge, then puts his hands on my hips, guiding me up and down.

We start out slow, but within moments we're rocking against each other at a rapid pace.

"Tuck, slow down," I beg.

The friction is so delicious I'm being pushed to my limits before I'm ready. I wind my hands in his hair and tug him up to me, pulling hard as I contain my screams of pleasure when I fall apart on the man who has captured my heart.

I melt into him, limp and unable to move from sheer exhaustion and the ecstasy coursing through my veins. Tuck moves me about in the deliciously hot water. My knees are propped up on the edge with my nipples now rubbing on the same ledge his head was just resting on, and then I feel him enter me from behind and can't hold back a loud moan. Our bodies meld, twist, and contort together until he finds the perfect position. His palms splay across my abdomen as both of my arms are wrapped back around his head, and with each thrust I feel him move closer and closer to letting go.

He tugs on my hair, pulling me as close to him as possible, then nips my ear, and I feel him let go. It's a sensation I'll never get tired of. We swirl and twirl until we are back in the same position we started out in.

"Thank you, Tuck."

He quirks up one questioning eyebrow.

"For letting me in." I splash water up in his beautiful face, trying to lighten the mood. "And for a virgin, you have some moves, boy."

"I never said I haven't watched porn and used my hand."

"You're full of surprises, Tuck Jones."

I rest my head on his shoulder and let him rub my back up and down in the soothing water. There's no doubt in my mind that I'd give everything up for this man, and I don't mean like 'the girl lost her way, hopeless heroine.' I mean in the way where I'll fight like a strong woman for this man who deserves to be loved in every way possible.

"Blue?"

"Yeah?" My eyes were shut, and I had every intent of drifting off to sleep.

"Did we just make a baby?"

"No, your sperm was blocked."

"Uh…"

"I'm on birth control."

I feel his muscles relax, and his hands go back to rubbing my back.

Chapter 24

Leaving Joe's house is harder than I thought it would be. Tuck and I spent the last three nights in the hot tub lit by the moonlight, exploring each other into the wee hours. We won't have this back at campus with both of our rigorous schedules, and that sucks. I want to stay here with him forever.

My jawline has healed amazingly well, with only light bruising left behind, but nothing my make-up can't handle. It's the bruises all up and down my legs that will be hard to conceal. There are five days until the next home game, and I can only hope they magically disappear by then. I'll cover them up with long spandex pants at practice, and I know my secret is safe with Sophie, Lane, and Noah. It doesn't make the fact I was brutally attack any easier to digest. I've kept it bottled up inside, hoping the lingering fear will dissipate one day. Tuck has brought it up several times and won't let it go. I know I should tell my parents, and I know I should tell campus security, but call me greedy—I just want to go on with my life.

"Buckle up and give me another hug."

Joe wraps Tuck up into a hug and hangs from his body. It's hard not to cry seeing the two of them together and knowing what they've gone through. Tuck opened up the other night and told me everything about the house fire. I fought to hold my tears back, but when he told me it was because of his mother who cradled him in her arms until the firefighters got to him, I lost it. In fact, I lost every single ounce of pain I thought I'd ever experienced in my life. It's the reason his face and other parts weren't burned. And then hearing about the countless surgeries he's been through shattered me.

I've taken advantage of every opportunity to tell him how perfect I think he is. I know he doesn't believe me, but one day he will.

Joe pulls me into a hug. "I love you like a little sister already, Blue. Can't wait to see you again."

I squeeze her right back. "Thank you for everything, and I promise you I'll never quit loving your brother."

"I know," she whispers. "Mom and Dad would've loved you."

Tuck's voice interrupts us. "Let's go, ladies. We have a long drive ahead of us, and we both have to get settled back into college life."

Joe slugs his shoulder, shaking her head at him, and then says the most embarrassing thing that has ever happened to me.

"Don't worry, little brother, I'll get all your man juice cleaned out the hot tub before my next dip."

I hide behind Tuck to conceal my giggles and the red blush I'm certain is covering my face.

"Oh my god." I slide into the middle position on the bench seat. "That was a bit horrifying."

Tuck just chuckles and continues to shake his head at his sister. Little Ruger stands on the front porch waving frantically at us with his football tucked under his other arm. I have no idea how Tuck has the willpower to drive away from this perfect family.

I lay my head on Tuck's wide shoulder, pull my aviators down, rest my hand on his thick thigh, and let out a sigh of contentment.

"How long is the drive?" I ask, realizing I have no clue. I've literally been in la-la land the last few days.

"Five hours."

"Mmmmm. Five hours in a truck alone with you. What shall I do?"

I run my hand up his inner thigh, creeping so very close to his most favorite part of his body.

"Behave, Blue."

"What fun would that be? Plus, I need to work on stretching for cheer practice."

I free him from his pants before he has the chance to argue. The bonus to doing an athlete is they're always dressed in elastic waistband pants. And then I do something I haven't done yet. My lips kiss the tip of him, and he jerks and takes a sharp breath. And I go for it, licking him from the base all the way to the tip, and then taking all of him in my mouth.

"Son of a bitch." The truck comes to an abrupt stop, but I don't.

My tongue and teeth invade and relish every scent and sensation. I help him along, working him hard at the base.

"Fuck, Blue. Oh fuck."

He grips onto my hair and tugs gently, trying to pop me from him, but I resist him and enjoy the twinge of pain he sends through me. It doesn't take long before I feel him spill into my mouth. My tongue laps it all up and takes a few more glides along his still rock hard shaft before I come up face to face with him.

"And?" I crook an eyebrow up in question at his sated face.

"You are going to be the death of me." He adjusts himself back in his pants and pulls from the parking lot we landed in. "And I'm going to love every second of it."

I lie back down on his lap with a very large smile on my face.

"Oh, and Blue, anytime, anywhere you feel the urge to do that again, just get on it."

I giggle at his response.

"Your turn."

I pop up and look him at him, confused.

"I've spilled a lot of details the last couple of days. I want to know about your childhood."

I sink back into him and focus on the road.

"Not much. I'm an only child. My mom was determined I'd be a beauty queen or some shit like that, hence the odd name Blue to stick out. I was in every single sport and activity growing up. My mom pushed me hard, but in the end I loved basketball and cheer. But I chose cheer, and it drives my dad nuts."

"I can only imagine. I mean, if you were my girl, there's no way in hell you'd be in those short skirts. I don't even like it."

"Wait. What?" I push up off of his shoulder and turn to face him.

"It drives me fucking wild seeing you in that tiny outfit at games. I want to cover you up in a burlap bag, for Christ's sake."

I lie back, leaning my head on the door and laughing hard. "Hell, I didn't think you even noticed me, Tuck."

I send my flip-flops flying to the floor and nestle my feet into his lap.

"Blue, you've haunted me."

"Well, maybe if you mark me and make me yours, others won't look. You know that night at the party when I tried talking to that guy?"

"You mean grinding on him and making me blow my fuse?"

"Yeah, that too. Well, when he found out that Noah and you were eyeing me, he backed off and went running for the hills."

"Good." He shifts his gaze to me quickly and then focuses back on the road. "What do your parents do career-wise?"

"Mom is a stay at home freak, and Dad is a plastic surgeon."

Tuck's jaw immediately tenses, and it dawns on me what has him so uptight. "He'll love you, Tuck. He's into sports and hates that I'm a cheerleader. You two will get along perfectly."

"He'll want to fix me."

The words are hollow and full of anger.

"Do you trust me?"

Tuck doesn't answer, so I push him.

I sit back up and invade his space. "Do you trust me?"

"Yes, you know I do."

"He won't want to fix you, I'll promise you that." I creep up his gym shorts and begin to stroke burned parts of his thighs. "He will want to fix me, though. I swear he hates cheer."

I change the subject back to me and carry on about my dad's odd sense of humor and how he'd cut off one of his legs if I would play college ball. Tuck seems to relax the more I talk about my dad and his personality. I know deep down in my heart my dad would never push more surgeries on Tuck, but he'd also be the first one to step up and help him if that's what Tuck wished.

***

"Blue, we are thirty minutes out. You can hold it."

"Tuck, I had to piss, and like ten minutes ago."

"For the love of Christ."

He pulls over to a gas station. I smile, place a quick kiss on his cheek, and dart for the bathroom before I piss down both legs. I really tried to hold it this time, but I drank way too much water trying to keep myself awake the whole way home so I didn't miss out on any conversation with him.

After relieving myself, I snag a diet Pepsi and some licorice for the dorms, and his face is priceless when he sees me packing the loot back to the truck.

"Are you serious, Blue? I'm not stopping again."

"You will if I ask." I slide across the bench and snuggle back up to him.

"You're probably right." He flips his ball cap on backward and continues to drive.

"I want you to stay with me tonight until I can find out more about your attack."

"But Sophie has been dying for me to get back and hang out."

"I'll drop you off at the dorms, go work out, and then come get you."

I try to talk, but he cuts me off.

"One, you're not working out tonight, and two, you don't have an option about staying with me."

It's as if he can now magically read my mind. I decide not to argue with him, but instead crack open the soda and give him an evil grin.

"You really need to talk to your coach about the attack."

"Okay, grandpa, get off my case."

"I think it was deliberate, Blue. Whoever it was had been watching you. No way in hell did they randomly find you that late at night running and attack you the furthest from safety."

It's nothing new. I've run it over and over in my mind a thousand times.

"You won't be out of anyone's sight until I find out who in the hell did this."

"What are you going to do about it?" I pop a piece of licorice in his mouth.

"Kill the motherfucker."

"Well, I don't think that's the best idea, Tuck. Can't

we just forget about it? I'll be extra cautious."

He doesn't answer me, and I know that's a no to him, but I try to convince myself it's a yes. I'll do everything I can to ease his mind about this topic, because he needs to be focusing on football and no other drama surrounding him.

The dorms come into sight, and I feel a twinge of excitement shoot through me. I've actually missed my Sophie over the past few days and have so much to catch her up on. I don't have the chance to ponder long, because I see her bounding from the front doors with Lane trying to keep up with her. I bolt from the truck and tackle-hug her ass.

"Oh my god, Blue, how are you doing?"

"I'm fine. I'm so fine."

When I pull back I can tell she notices my perma-grin and the new glow to my skin.

"Your face looks good. Not that you ever looked like shit, but you look amazing."

"Thanks, Sophie."

The two men gain our attention, or shall I say Tuck does, as he very clearly instructs Lane that he's not to leave my side.

"Baby, go work out. I'm fine." I wrap my arms around his waist and pull him into me, then stand up on my tiptoes to place a kiss on his lips.

"I don't want to leave you."

"I'm a big girl, and you better get used to it. We both are going in separate directions back here on campus. Cowboy up, cupcake."

He kisses me hard, leaving the sting of a bite on my bottom lip. "Oh, I'll be cowboying up tonight."

Lordy, the man makes my knees quake, even though we've been doing nothing but have sex the last couple days. I'm pretty sure we've beaten Lane and Sophie in the lovemaking department.

"Let's go. It's my turn with her, Tuck." Sophie drags me away from him by the waist. I offer a wave over my shoulder as I walk away.

It sucks walking away, but I do it just like ripping a Band-Aid off a wound.

"So, are you two dating?"

I don't have an answer to her question and stop dead in my tracks. When I turn around, I see Tuck standing by his truck watching us. He's at least a good fifty feet away.

"Tuck." I watch as he makes eye contact with me. "Are you my boyfriend?" I tilt my head to the side in anticipation of his answer.

He hollers back, never making anything simple. "Are you my girlfriend?"

"I asked first."

Sophie elbows me in the ribs. "Do you really need to be hollering this right now?"

"Yes, Blue, I'm your boyfriend."

I blow him a kiss and turn back toward the dorm. "So yeah, we are dating."

Lane busts out in laughter and Sophie just rolls her eyes as if our roles have been reversed. I'm now the giddy, love-struck friend with stars in my eyes.

"I want details, but not you screaming in the parking lot."

When we walk into the lobby, I see the security guard and give him a friendly wave.

"Hey, Blue, missed ya."

"Ahh, you're too sweet. My dad must have really paid you off well."

He chuckles as we pass and wait for an elevator. The ride is long and torturous as I'm dying to expel every detail to Sophie. My excitement is busting at the seams.

"Oh my god, shut the door, and Lane, get out." I flop on my bed and stare back at the couple.

"Did you not hear Tuck?"

"Are you serious?" Sophie asks Lane.

"I'm not leaving you."

"Well, you're about to hear a ton about sex." I shrug and climb under my blankets, wiggling out of my shorts and getting comfy. "Grab the ice cream from the freezer."

Sophie tosses me my favorite flavor of ice cream, and I dig in, waiting for the two of them to settle in.

"I'm not sure I'm comfortable telling you everything, because some of it's Tuck's story to tell."

Lane's eyebrows shoot up at me.

"I've seen him, Lane. All of him, and I'm completely heels over head for the man."

"Wait. What am I missing?"

I keep my gaze on Lane and watch the shock cover his face. "Blue, he doesn't even dress down in the locker room."

"I don't care. I love the man, and he's going to have to get over it."

"He's never had a girlfriend as long as I've known him. Hell, he only let a few girls hang on him at that party to piss you off."

Note to self, kick him in the shins for that.

Sophie jumps up on her bed. "Can someone fill me in?"

"Tuck has scars and doesn't like to be exposed."

Silence fills the room after the words leave my mouth. I trust Sophie to not publish any of this in the school newspaper.

"He opened up to me this weekend and…" I pause a second, giving Lane a chance to escape. "We had sex. Lots and lots of glorious sex."

Sophie leaps from her bed over to mine, wrapping me up in a hug and squealing, and then starts in on her twenty questions.

"Is he hung? I mean can he, like, go a long time? Tell me everything."

I skip the part about him being a virgin and go right into full details of our sexpcapades in his room, the shower, and the hot tub.

"Bitch, you're on birth control. How did it feel with nothing between you guys?"

I look over to Lane, who is clearly trying his best to check out of our conversation. He's spread across Sophie's bed with his forearms resting over his eyes.

"It was like nothing I've ever felt before."

"By the looks of it, I bet ol' Tuck could really entertain some meat curtains."

I look at her in question. "What the hell is a meat curtain?"

"You know." She nudges me with her elbow.

I try to process the two words, putting them together and pulling them apart, and still come up with nothing.

"Oh my god, you don't know what it is?" Lane pops into the conversation.

I toss a pillow at him. "Do you know, Lane?"

"It's like a puppet show. The balls are the curtain and the dick pops out."

Sophie howls in laughter and I try to speak over her. "I think she's talking about the female part."

After Sophie controls her fit of laughter, she sits upright and faces us. "Lips spread like a curtain." She uses her hands to gesture the sweeping motion of the movement.

Then laughter hits me and I can't control it. Poor Lane just shakes his head. Wiping tears from my eyes, I'm finally able to speak. "Clearly, your meat curtain isn't getting it hard enough."

"Fuck you." Sophie pushes into my shoulder.

Chapter 25

"Blue, why do you look so blue?"

I toss the nearest pillow with all my might toward Tuck's head. He knows I hate, hate that saying, and he makes sure to get it in whenever he can.

"I'm fucking exhausted, and I hate this math class and can't keep up with all of it."

Tuck takes a bite out of the slice of pizza he's currently making love to and raises an eyebrow at me.

"Then I have your sexy ass staring at me like that. I just want you to take me to bed and do all of my homework."

He stands, still eating the pizza, and walks toward me.

"Take your shirt off, Tuck."

The man still won't strip in front of me, even though it's been almost two weeks of us together every night at his house. I'm still constantly pushing him and pulling his clothes off every chance we get. I was shocked the day he walked down the hall shirtless in front of Noah, which proved just how close the two men really are. My dorm has basically become a ghost town with Sophie and me ditching it for our men.

In the sexiest of all sexy moves, he bites down on the slice of pizza. He lets it hang from his mouth and pulls his shirt off over his head, then covers me with his body, tossing my textbook to the side. Leaning up, I take a bite out of his pizza and smile back at him. He drops the slice on my chest, so I quickly pick it up and begin nibbling on it.

"I can take care of one your problems."

"Oh, you're such a sweet boyfriend to do my

homework." I lightly tap his nose.

"I'm not talking homework, Blue."

He pulls my shorts down in one quick motion and hikes my shirt up above my breasts, and I just watch him while eating my pizza and smirking down at him. Then my underwear are off, and he's dangerously close to a certain area where I love his mouth to be.

"Tuck, my homework," I whine.

Then his tongue flicks against my sensitive flesh, and I buck up into his mouth, wanting more. The pizza flies and any stress of homework vanishes. He nips at me, and I scream.

"Oh god, Tuck."

I feel a smile spread across his face, and he knows he has my undivided attention. When his fingers sink deep in me, his tongue goes into overdrive, and my hips work harder against him. It only takes seconds before I feel the lingering threats of an orgasm, and he pulls up and sits back on his heels.

"What the hell?" I pop up on my elbows.

He pushes down his pants, freeing himself, and slams into me without warning, and I cry out loud in pleasure and dig into his back. He grunts with each thrust into me. Tuck leans down and attacks my lips while keeping the same pace with his hips. I bite down on his bottom lip, letting him know my displeasure at his not finishing me off.

Pushing back up, Tuck brings my legs up in front of him, digging into the back of my thighs, and I finally give in, screaming as I hit the spot I've wanted. Every part of my body trembles in aftershock, and it doesn't help that Tuck still pounds away, searching for his release. When I look up into his face I know exactly what he's doing. He's pushing me to go again so he can go with me.

There's something I'll never be able to resist about this man, and I'm pretty sure it's the magnetic pull in those dark eyes of his. I don't break eye contact as I squeeze the flesh of his forearms and concentrate on the feel of him growing inside me as he fucks me. Before long I'm right there with him again.

"Tuck," I say breathlessly.

He grits his teeth and moans. With his second moan, I let go and feel him fall with me. The slick sensation between our connected bodies threatens to cause me to orgasm again. Tuck finally collapses on me, burying his face in the crook of my neck. His tongue darts out, lapping up and down my flesh, and then he nips at it every once in a while.

"Stop, that tickles."

He pins me down and does it even more, and I have no chance against the big brute. He knows it's my weak spot, and he loves teasing it.

"Tuck."

His phone goes off, saving me from any more torture. I watch his broad shoulders as he reaches over to the glass table and looks at it.

"It's Noah. Just checking to see if we are dressed."

It only took him one time walking in on us to learn to always check before coming home. Thank the good lord above, I didn't see his actual face since I was riding Tuck, but still embarrassing enough.

"Homework." I stick out my bottom lip.

He pulls me from the couch and slaps my ass. "Go clean up and get dressed."

"Homework." I point to the textbook on the floor.

"Get your ass dressed."

He slaps me harder and sends me squealing down the hall. I know what this always leads to. The man loves wrestling around, and then it turns into fooling around, and then we are fucking like animals. It's the one thing that's been constant since returning to campus.

I cringe when my gaze lands on the full body mirror in the bathroom. I've lost so much definition in my arms and legs it makes me sick. Tuck refuses to let me work out any more than one of my typical cheer practices. And I know he's right because my body has barely been able to function. I really should win an Academy Award for acting the part and playing off my injuries, even at the last home game. Sometimes I even impress myself.

Noah's already perched on the overstuffed chair, and both men are intently watching the television. I'm shocked to see it's the nightly news and not ESPN.

"What are you two watching?"

"They found him, Blue." Tuck grabs me by the waist and pulls me down into him.

"Found who?" I ask while still staring at the screen.

"The asshole who's been attacking girls all over town." Noah sits forward as he continues to explain. "He's the guy."

My attention slowly drifts back to the screen, and when I see him I feel nothing. No sheer terror like I experience every single night in my dreams. Not the spine-tingling chill when I feel like eyes are watching me, or an ounce of pain. There's nothing. When I gaze closer at his eyes, I know it's not my attacker.

"Fuck," Tuck growls. "I wish I could meet up with the asshole for a few minutes."

That's not my attacker. The words catch in my throat. I try again, but the same thing. Tuck and Noah go back and forth about the attacker and how their research and leads didn't point to this guy. I had no clue they were even looking into it. Again, how in the hell would they have time with practice, games, and, well…me?

"You were looking into my attack?" I look up to

Tuck.

"Yeah."

"When and how?"

"We put some people on it, and obviously some pretty shitty ones, because this guy wasn't even on our radar."

Again the words lodge in my throat, and there's no way in hell I'm letting them escape. I swallow them back down and feel each one of them cut like glass, but the pain is worth knowing Tuck won't be distracted with it anymore.

Me, I'll get through it and keep faking it until the pain dissipates. I've managed to keep most of the fear tucked away so far.

"Well, let's celebrate." I curl my toes in the shag carpet below my feet. "Let's call over Sophie and Lane."

"Fuck that," Tuck growls, and then pins me to the couch in a very familiar position. "Your parents are coming this weekend, which means I have to be on my best behavior."

Noah cuts in, "Yeah, back to porn and whacking it for a few days."

I giggle underneath Tuck.

"I forgot to tell you, my parents are coming the next weekend. Dad has some partner surgeon coming in for the weekend." I place my hands on his rock hard chest. "So, we have several days to fuck like bunnies."

"So romantic, little Blue."

"Wait," I squeal and wrap my arms around his neck. "You owe me homework. Homework first, then lots and lots of fucking like bunnies."

Chapter 26

Cheer practice sucked donkey balls. Every landing I could miss, I did, and every cheer I could fuck, I did. Coach didn't take it easy on me either, but I can't blame her since there's a home game Thursday night, and it will be broadcast on national television. The cameras always love zooming in on the student section and the cheerleaders, and that's me, the fuck-up.

I know exactly what this distraction is from, and it's not Tuck. He has been nothing but a gentle lover and his same beastly assholish self. The man has made love to me and fucked me thoroughly every single night, made me breakfast every morning, and then picked my ass up every day after practice. He's been spot on perfect, and quite honestly, I'm ready to marry the man after three amazing weeks of dating.

No, it's not him or the workload from school, or even practice. Hell, I've been able to hit the gym every night with him, so I'm working off all the extra stress and more. It's the letter. Yes, the letter that was slid so graciously underneath my dorm room door. I found it two nights ago when I ran up to my room to snag more clothes for Tuck's place.

The piece of paper only contained five dumb words, but they were strong enough to have me on edge. "I will finish the job." I've tried convincing myself it was delivered to the wrong room, and it was probably just a love letter to a girl from a guy who finished too early. But none of that has helped.

I let Steve, the friendly and probably overpaid by Dad guard, know when I left that night, and he reassured me he'd check the cameras and get back to me. I've really bonded with the guy, and knowing my dad padded his pockets a bit to watch over me might be the only ounce of sanity comforting me right now.

Tuck has backed off on the security detail since the city cops arrested the mad man on campus, but it's done nothing for me. I'm sure I'd recognize those eyes if I ever saw them again. The nasty glare is tattooed on my brain forever, and I see them every single night before I go to sleep.

"Blue."

"Yeah." A freshly showered Sophie is standing in front of her steel gray locker. "What's up?"

"I've been talking to you for the last five minutes. Did you hear anything I just said?"

"Yeah, sorry, I'm just hungry and fading out a bit."

"Well, the guys are out front, so move your ass."

I don't miss the look of concern on her face. Sophie is the one person who picks up on all my silent cues, but she never pushes for details. She just holds her arm out for support in a silent way, and I take it each and every time. It's like she sees the living nightmare play out on my face when no one else can.

"Burgers?" I ask.

"You know it. It's their night before one of the biggest games of the season."

"You say that every time…to you each game is a championship."

"Well, no shit. Don't you and Tuck talk football?"

"We don't talk much." I wait for her reaction, and it's everything I expected.

"I hate you, Blue. I picked the wrong one. I mean, Lane can screw, but he's not a double shooter and all-nighter like Tuck, AKA Mr. Fabulouso."

Her reaction is priceless, and every time I get the chance to rub it in, I do. It's actually a lie about us not talking. Some nights we've stayed up all night talking about the most random subjects. He's found out that he'll get kicked in the teeth if he ever gives me a foot massage, and I've discovered his phobia of bridges. It's the late night conversations that are my favorite because the dream never comes, and I always manage a couple hours of sleep snuggled up on him between our classes and practices.

It seems if I fall asleep during the day, the nightmare stays away. The black lines under my eyes are getting harder and harder to conceal with make-up, and I know I need to shut down the memories, but just don't know how.

My aviators will have to do the hiding as we walk out into the bright outdoors. Tuck and a group of men are gathered around his truck chatting, and I'm sure it's about football. We are both trained athletes and have fallen into an easy routine. I don't get jealous of his teammates or time he dedicates to the team, and the same goes for him with cheer and me. At this point, I'm my own worst enemy.

I hang back a bit and pretend to look at my phone, not wanting to interrupt their conversation. Booming voices fill the parking lot with lots of cheers and foul words. Someone for sure is getting the third degree for something. Just being around Noah and Tuck, listening to the stories they tell, it's clear it's part of the brotherhood to get the shit harassed out of you.

"Look, there's the little Hoover vacuum."

I recognize Noah's voice and look up to see the whole group staring back at me.

"Take it easy on my boy's neck. You're doing all sorts of damage to his game."

The crowd erupts again in laughter, and that's when I see several large hickies covering his neck. My hand flies over my mouth and embarrassment sets in. Holy shit, I was just fooling around. I had no intention of leaving behind love bites.

When I make eye contact with Tuck, I see a smile on his face as if he is proud of the marks, and it totally makes my embarrassment evaporate. This man has never believed in happily ever afters, or himself, for that fact, so seeing him smiling in a group of teammates over hickies makes me chipper. And in moments like these, all my nightmares vanish.

"So, this is the beauty who has our star player all flustered and dropping balls."

I don't see which teammate says it, but it encourages the rest to begin laughing again. Tuck must have really messed up today at practice. He's not even arguing or glowering at any of them. He just keeps shaking his head and then holds his hand out to me. Carefully, I step over the curbing and through a patch of woodchips until I reach him. Tuck spins me around, pulling my back into his chest.

"Paybacks are a bitch," he whispers, and then leaves a light kiss on my temple.

"Your dick must be magic to land someone as pretty as her with your ugly mug."

The men go on and on, and with every comment about Tuck and me, my skin begins to crawl. Noah plays along and it seems not to faze Tuck—on the outside, that is. I wonder just how much these guys know about him, but on the other hand, they are treating him just like any other player.

I relax back into him as the conversation turns to game day, and I realize this could go on forever. Turning into his cheek, I kiss him, and then fling one of my arms up behind his neck.

"I'm starving, Tuck."

"Me too," he mumbles back. "But not for dinner."

He reaches behind him and flings open his door as he whirls me into the front of the cab, laying me back on the seat and then covering my body. And if I thought the hoots and hollers were loud before, they are now deafening.

"What are you doing?" I try to ask between giggles.

"Pissing on what's mine. Those fucking pants show way too much."

"Stop." I push up on his chest. "You're being silly."

His mouth drowns out my plea as he assaults my lips, laying down the sexiest kiss I've ever tasted, and I feel him hard and ready to go.

"Tuck." I push my glasses back to glare at him. "Stop. We won't be able to stop."

"Jesus, Blue, you look like hell." The pad of his thumb brushes my cheek.

"I'm just tired and hungry."

One of his large palms cradles the back of my head, gently pulling me up to him, while his thumb still rubs soothing motions on my cheek. Either I'm doing a really good job of blocking out the outside noise, or they went on harassing someone else.

"Don't lie to me." He leans down and pecks the tip of my nose. "I know you're struggling, and you have to ask for help."

"I'm still scared, Tuck."

"I'm all in, if you haven't noticed."

"No, I'm scared of him." I regret the words as soon as they leave my mouth because of the growl Tuck produces.

"He can't hurt you, Blue."

"I'm just tired and hungry." I do my best to change the subject, and it's not a lie at all.

"Oh, I'll feed you." He pushes up off the bench seat.

"A big ol' sausage." He readjusts himself in his black gym pants.

"Ewww, you're gross," I squeal.

He only chuckles, pats his teammates on the shoulder, and rounds the front of the truck. But if truth was told, and if I wasn't so exhausted and hungry, I'd be blowing the hell out of him on the way to the diner. Tuck has turned me into a slut like that.

My phone rings as Tuck hops in the truck, and I see my mom's shining face trying to FaceTime me.

"Do you mind?" I ask him as the engine roars to life.

"No prob, Beauty."

He's FaceTimed with me several times, but has only met my mom, and they hit it off. Of course, Tuck was quiet at first, but my hyperactive mother had him talking up a storm in no time.

"Blue, you look like shit."

Her hair is done, and subtle make-up paints her face. She's always picture perfect. The way I used to be.

"Hi, Mom, love you too."

"Have you been eating? Are you sleeping? Are you taking those vitamins?"

She rambles off at least twenty more questions before taking a breath and letting me talk.

"Yes, Mom, I'm just living the college life."

"Is Tuck there?"

I flash the phone in his direction, giving her the perfect view of his silhouette as he focuses on the road.

"Hi, Mrs. Williams."

"Tuck," she gasps. "What's that on your neck?"

My heart drops out my butthole, and then I pull the phone from his face as fast as possible.

"Turf burn," I lie.

"Well, that looks just awful. Tell him if it burns to get some cream for it. Dad could call something in for him."

Tuck starts to chuckle, but then my elbow lands in his ribs. I do not need a lecture right now about giving a guy hickies, and the star player, at that.

"Well, in just a few days we'll be there with you, Blue."

I can practically hear the tears welling up in her voice. I've never been away from my mom this long and hope I can hold my shit together while she's here.

"Okay, we have everything planned out, and you have the hotel booked."

"Tuck, we can't wait to meet you." I center the phone in front of his face, avoiding his hicky patch. "You know Blue's never been in love before. Can't wait to meet the guy who captured her heart."

I glare at her, not allowing her to talk to Tuck any longer.

"Holy hell, Mom, want to tell him about the time I shit my pants in kindergarten too?"

"Oh, Blue, you are too sensitive. I'll let you kids get on with your day. Love you." I kiss the screen. "Oh, and your dad is missing you something fierce."

"I miss you guys, too." I send one final wave her way. "Bye, Mom."

Tuck rests his hand on my leg and begins rubbing it up and down while I flop my head down on his shoulder.

"You and your mom seem like quite the characters together."

"Yeah, you'll see soon enough, Tuck. We are like a hot circus on 'roids when we are together, and you can usually find my dad sitting back in the corner sipping on a longneck."

I don't have to look up at his face to tell he's worried about meeting my dad, because I can feel his whole body tense with just the mention of him. I've reassured him over and over again that my dad would never want to fix him.

"Tuck, he won't want to fix you, and do you know why?"

He pulls the truck to a stop at a stoplight and looks down at me.

I place my lips on his and talk into them. "You don't need to be fixed. You're perfect."

"I'll never believe it no matter how many times you tell me."

"Well, fuck you then. The light is green, and I'm hungry." I bite down on his bottom lip. "And I'm always right, never forget that."

"I hope you are, Blue."

His voice is deflated, and I know as much as I battle with the attack, he battles being with me and letting me all the way in.

"So, practice that bad?" I ask, changing the subject.

"The guys got a kick out of the marks you left on me." He looks down at me with a cute little smile on his face. "I'm pretty sure they're all still in shock I have a girl."

"Well, they shouldn't be. I'm pretty into you, and you've pissed all over me."

We don't have long to talk before Sophie and Lane are waving to us in the parking lot of the diner. It will be nice grabbing a quick meal with all of us together, since it seems we've all been locked in our rooms screwing the shit out of each other.

"I call Blue tonight, Tuck," Sophie hollers out.

"For dinner, but tonight she's mine," he growls back.

I grab for Sophie's forearm and whip her around to face the street. "Look, Sophie, look."

My voice is excited, but laced with confusion.

"What?" She looks into the sun and tries to shade her

eyes.

"It's Stephie."

"Where?"

"That blue car right there. I think she's with Ethan."

As soon as Sophie focuses, the car takes off down the road.

"Mmmm. I don't think that was her."

"It was," I insist. "Tuck, where's Ethan these days?"

He shrugs like he couldn't care less about it.

"He's been at practice. Just staying pretty quiet since Stephie ditched him," Lane adds.

"It was so her." I lock my arm in Sophie's. "I'd love to see her bloated and knocked up."

"You're so going to hell, Blue."

I laugh. "It'll be worth it."

I tug Sophie to the corner table, hoping for some privacy, finally ready to open up to her about the letter that's been haunting me.

"Sophie."

Her eyes are glued to the screen of her phone, clearly enchanted by something.

"Sophie, listen, I have to tell you something, and it's really important."

Her head flies up. "Oh my god, you're pregnant."

"Jesus, no, I'm not knocked up, but listen…"

Before I'm able to finish my sentence, she's sucked right back into the vortex of social media on her phone.

Tuck squeezes in next to me and our moment is over, but his comforting hands pull me into a hug, and the thought of that stupid-ass letter vanishes quickly. Lane follows suit shortly, with three teammates soon after him. It wouldn't be dinner without a crew.

"What were you trying to tell me, Blue?" Sophie sets her phone down and nuzzles into Lane.

I wave her off. "It was nothing, really."

As quickly as I dismiss her, she does the same to me, not prying for answers.

"So, Tuck, I hear you get to meet the parents this weekend." Sophie stares him down.

He only nods, but Sophie doesn't take it as any sort of clue.

"Are you nervous? I mean with Blue being an only child and perfection from head to toe, I bet her dad is a fierce poppa bear."

Everyone at the table erupts into laughter, and it's such a low blow to Tuck's confidence I want to kill Sophie. I understand she doesn't comprehend the whole situation, but she needs to back off.

"Actually, he's dying to meet Tuck. He said he's ready for me to be someone else's problem." I place a light kiss on Tuck's cheek and squeeze his hands, but I see it in his eyes that he's slipping away from me.

I give his hand an extra hard squeeze since that's the only reassurance I have to offer.

Chapter 27

Tuck managed to make love to me last night until I almost passed out, doing all sorts of dirty things to me, and then he was gone before I woke up. It's game day, and I understand that's part of it, but he made it clear he wasn't going to be joining my parents and me for breakfast. He also skipped out on picking them up at the airport last night with some excuse of a team meeting running late. Funny thing is Lane wasn't at that late meeting; I texted Sophie and asked.

He's putting up a barrier, and I have the sinking suspicion he won't even give my dad a chance, and that thought pisses me off. I'm already late to breakfast and have my cheer bag scattered all over Tuck's room. It's probably a good thing he's not here, because I'd be forced to karate chop him in the nuts for slowly morphing back into his guarded asshole persona.

I scramble to stuff everything back into my school-colored duffle bag, not giving two fucks what's wrinkled or not. The pad of my finger glides across the sharp edge of paper, slicing it open. I pull it up quickly to my lips to catch the drops of blood and dull the stinging throb.

"Fuck." My voice echoes in the quiet room.

Out of curiosity, I pull the paper from my bag and freeze in horror. It's the same writing and same message, only this time there's a photo of me taped to it. The rush of bile racing up my throat is not a threat, but rather a promise. I race to the bathroom and let it out in the toilet, dropping the note in the bowl with it. My stomach cramps as the convulsions don't let up, and all my air is lost between gut wrenching gags.

"Blue."

I barely hear a voice and know it's my mind playing a trick on me. I need to get out of this house and be with someone. The harder I fight to turn off the retches, the faster and harder they come out.

"Blue."

Turning my head, I see Tuck standing in the doorway. When we make eye contact he rushes to my side.

"What the fuck, baby?" He brushes my hair back from my face.

My sobs take over, and even if I wanted to tell him how scared I was, it would never happen.

"Here, baby." He lifts me up with his strong hands and sets me on the counter. He starts the water in the sink and begins cleaning me up, stopping every once in a while to shoot me a questioning stare, but I don't answer. When he brushes my teeth, I don't protest, I just open up.

"Did you forget something?" I ask.

"Aren't we going to breakfast?"

"I know there wasn't a team meeting last night." The words echo in the small bathroom, and they may be more painful than those words on that damn hate mail.

Tuck leans back against the door, running his hands through the back of his hair, not making eye contact with me. His hoodie rises just enough for the burnt piece of his abdomen to show.

"I'm trying, Blue, I'm fucking trying and don't know what else to do."

I pound my fists against the countertop. "Just fucking love me, be with me, and fucking protect me. Just love me."

My voice trails off, and raging emotion that I've never felt before leaves my body in tears and sobs. It's an attack I didn't see coming and try to hide from it by bringing my knees up to my chest and wrapping my arms around them. I rock back and forth.

"Stop."

He places his hands on each side of my face, and then his strong, gentle lips on the top of my head.

"You promised me, Tuck. You said you'd give me all of you."

"Stop, Blue."

He forces me to stop rocking, then picks me up from the counter.

"You're leaving me, aren't you, Tuck?"

He never answers my question as he places me in his truck, tosses my cheer bag in the back, and hands me my make-up bag. When I look in the mirror, I scramble to put some make-up on. The last thing I need is my parents riding my ass about my puffy eyes and tears. With everything I have, I suck it all back and focus on today. It's game day, televised, and my parents are here, and Tuck's here…for now.

By the time Tuck pulls up to the hotel, I have enough make-up slapped on to cover up any emotions that may be lingering on my face. Not one word is spoken between us on the drive over, but just like every single time I ride with him, he holds the door open for me, waiting on me to shuffle across the seat. He takes my hand, and for a moment everything feels like it will be all right in the world.

"Blue."

The screech pierces my ears before I even fully enter the hotel lobby. My mom is up and on her feet sprinting toward me. You'd think she hadn't seen me for months rather than last night.

"Momma." I nod and hug her back.

"Oh my heavens, this must be Tuck."

He stands frozen in place with his hands resting comfortably in his pockets. By no means did he dress up for the occasion in his black gym shorts, a long sleeve team shirt, and a ball cap, but then I look down to my warm-up suit, and I just shrug.

"Mom, this is Tuck, and Tuck, this is my mom."

He's wrapped up in a hug before he has a chance to even smile.

"Welcome to the family," I joke and look around for Dad. "Where's Dad, and where are we eating?"

I pull Mom off of Tuck and notice the tears forming in her eyes. The woman has been so damn emotional lately, and I know it's because she's homesick for me.

"He's on a call. He will meet us on the patio in a few."

I watch in awe as my mom loops her arm through Tuck's and begins leading the way. He snags my hand, and I follow the two. If you didn't know any better, we look like the picture of perfection. The eager, overzealous mom about to watch her only child cheer at a college game. The cheerleader with all the looks and zapped confidence. And then Tuck, the gorgeous, dreamy star player who is nothing but perfection. When in reality the two of us are nothing but a train wreck that's already crashed, and we're just trying to put the pieces together. The terrifying thing is the pieces will never go back.

Tuck pulls out a chair for my mom. He's playing her just like a fiddle, and she's eating up every second of it. I wait for him to sit by her and leave me standing and staring, but he doesn't. With his back to my mom, he whispers in my ear, "I'm here, Blue. You're not. You might want to wake up and enjoy this."

His words catch me off guard, and I pull back and look into his eyes, searching for the punch line to his joke.

"I'm doing my best. I love you, Blue, and that's the only reason I'm here."

"Sit, kids."

Peering over my shoulder, I see my mom's curious and beaming face. I place a quick kiss on his lips and repeat those three words back to him.

"I love you."

Tuck and my mom fall into an easy conversation, seriously distracting me from the worry of him running out on me, and leaving me to focus on the damn letter I found this morning. I rub the pad of my thumb over the loose skin of the paper cut and repeat the words of the letter over and over in my mind.

"Blue."

"Yeah." The sound of my name sucks me from the nasty vortex spiraling around in my mind. When I look up, I see my mom and Tuck both staring at me.

"Are you all right, honey?" Concern covers my mom's face, and I know she's just inches away from figuring out something is bothering me.

"Fine, why?" I shrug.

"I was talking to you, and you didn't even acknowledge me."

"Yeah, where are you, Blue?" Tuck elbows me and then pulls me into a tight side hug.

"Sorry." I slap his broad chest. "Just going over a routine in my head. A bit nervous for this televised game."

"Blue," says my mom in her 'don't feed me that line of bullshit' voice.

Someone grabs me from the back, tipping my chair, and then I feel my dad's whisker burns and hear his laughter. I fight to push him away just like I did when I was kid, but then laughter hits me and I can't get away.

The more he rubs his stubble on my cheeks, the harder I laugh. My mom hollers at him to stop, but it's not until she throws a croissant at his head that he does.

"Dad." I stand and turn into him, throwing myself into his chest and hugging him hard. "I love you."

Something about his presence comforts me when I'm the most vulnerable. He pulls away and goes straight to Mom, placing a kiss on her forehead, and then takes a seat. I don't realize the stare-down that's going on until my mom clears her throat.

"Honey, this is Tuck. Blue's boyfriend."

"Hello, sir." Tuck stretches his hand out over the table.

"Have you guys had sex yet?"

Holy shit, water spews from my mouth, sending ice cubes over the tablecloth, but it doesn't stop my dad.

"I hope you've been HIV tested, or I'll cut your nuts off."

"Dad," I squeal and then cover my face. "I told him you'd be nice."

"Well, if you so much as look at her in the least sexy way with those horndog lusty college boy eyes while I'm around, I'll kill you."

"Dad." My voice comes out muffled between my palms, and when I look up, Tuck's hand is no longer stretched out and he's turned off.

"Just shitting ya, kid." Dad's laughter fills the tiny café. "Please take her annoying ass off my hands, and my Visa will thank you."

I feel the blood rush back into my face and my jaw relax. "You asshole." I toss the croissant back in his direction, but he deflects, sending it into my mom's hair.

"Get over here, Tuck."

I watch as my dad rises to his feet and walks halfway to our side of the table. Tuck mimics his actions and is pulled into a tight hug. Dad pats his back, making a loud thumping sound as Tuck stands rigid.

"Sorry, can never pass up scaring the shit out of someone."

"Well, sir, you sure did." Tuck takes his seat next to me.

"Let's talk ball." Dad takes a long drink from his ice water. "Because god knows I've spent way too many years hearing about cheer and dance."

"Dad, you're an ass." I flick water in his direction.

"You know you love me, baby Blue."

The two men quickly and very easily fall into a conversation about college ball, and the sound of their voices mingling soothes me. The two men I need in my life…actually have to have in my life.

I have to cut them off so we can get to the stadium on time.

"Okay, we have to go, Dad. We will see you after the game, or at least I will."

I shoot Tuck a sideways glance.

"Oh, I'll meet up for dinner and keep arguing about the fact Emmett Smith is and always will be the best running back in the history of running backs."

"Boy, I have a lesson or two to teach you."

Tuck stands and gives my mom a long hug without hesitation, and then shakes my dad's hand, and even lets my dad wrap him up in a one-armed hug.

"Blue."

"What, Daddy-o?"

He steps away from Tuck and closes the distance between us. The pad of his thumb rubs along my jawline.

"When did you get this scar?"

"What?"

"This long scar on your jawline."

"Oh." I stall with terror and should've known my dad of all people would've noticed the fading scab. "I, uh, connected pretty hard with the mats one day at practice, but I've been using that cream."

"It's a nasty one, baby Blue. When you come home this summer, I can do some treatments on it."

"Nah, it's fine." I wave him off.

"Just keep your face from the mats from now on." He wraps me up into a full body hug and then whispers into my ear. "I expect the full damn story when your mother isn't here."

"Dad."

"Blue, I don't want to hear it."

"Fine." I push back off him. "We really need to get going, or our coaches will have our asses."

One final wave of hugs and goodbyes are exchanged before Tuck and I finally make it out into the parking lot.

"So?" I ask, clutching his hand.

"What?"

"You are such an ass, Tuck, I swear."

He scoops me up in his arms and throws me over his shoulder, and I break out in laughter. I swear the man knows when I start to get pissy and then breaks the mood. He begins jogging, dodging, and juking fake defenders.

"Stop." I helplessly beat at his back. My fingers find the waistband of his boxers and try tugging them up.

He gently slides me down the cab until I'm pinned between him and the truck with my feet barely touching the ground. His sweet lips brush against mine, but don't stop long enough to kiss me. Instead they trail down to my neck, and he begins and dragging his tongue along my skin, in between quick kisses. I shiver against him and practically moan, begging for more of him. He has this power, or maybe it's part of the curse—hell, I don't know—but he makes my knees quiver and heart race with the simplest of touches.

His lips move on my neck, and I try to comprehend each word he says. "I just wish you'd get help, Blue. I know you're still struggling with the attack, and you won't let anyone help. Meeting your family was the hardest thing I've ever done in my life, but I'd do it again just for you."

I wrap my arms around his neck and bury my head against his shoulder. "I'll be okay, Tuck, I just want to forget. I need to forget."

He forces me to look into his face. "You won't forget without help. You don't believe you're safe with me, and I don't know what else I can do."

"I don't think…"

The words stick in my throat, and no matter how hard I push, I can't get them out.

"You don't think what, Blue?

"I don't think I'm in danger with you."

Lying has to be the worst thing in the world. I just lied to my dad, and now to Tuck. It's wrong, so very wrong, but an addicting drug that I need to have to cover up the pain.

"Can we fuck tonight after dinner?" He thrusts up into me, letting me know how excited he is.

And we are back to our typical duck and weave tactic when hard topics arise.

"You could fuck me right now, right here, if you wanted, Tuck Jones."

A low growl rumbles in my ear as he swings open the truck door and throws me back on the bench seat and takes me.

Chapter 28

With football season over, Tuck has been driving me fucking nuts. I still have cheer practice, and now a strict schedule with basketball season and national cheer competition coming up. He still works out and does school work at lightning speed. I swear the man is borderline genius and the best athlete I've ever met. It took him weeks to bounce back from losing the national championship, but it seems he's more determined and driven to win it next year.

In the last three months, I've avoided the dorms as much as possible, only checking in with Steve and cycling out my clothes. I never let Tuck go in because I don't want him to stumble across a letter. They've been few and far between, but haven't left my memory. Last time I logged into Facebook, the same messages filled my inbox.

"Tuck, move your ass," I holler from the couch as I slam my math book. "You promised me."

"Calm your tits, Blue."

I've finally talked him into going to the beach with me. It's something I've wanted to do since spending time there with Noah. It's one thing Tuck doesn't do. He works out there running in the sand, but never spends leisure time bathing in the sun, and I get it.

"Hey, I've swallowed like ten times for this afternoon."

Tuck pulls me up from the couch and drags me into his solid chest.

"I thought the deal was eleven times." He smiles down on my lips.

I bite down on his lower lip until he winces in pain.

"Take me to the ocean right now, Tuck Jones. Spend a few hours there with me. Then bring me home and thoroughly make love to me, and then do my homework."

"Damn, I've really turned you into a princess, haven't I?"

"Only yours, Tuck." I clamp down on his lip again just to make him squirm. "And you're my prince."

"You mean Beast?"

I shoot him a dirty look. "You're either the asshole or my prince. Way too beautiful to be the beast of this story."

"I'd like to put it in your asshole."

"You're such a jerk." I slap his chest and grab the bag I packed. "Let's go."

On the drive, Tuck is quiet and reserved, but just like in the beginning, I push him because I never want him to think anything less of himself. I bought him a short-sleeved t-shirt that barely shows any of his burns, but he's still less than thrilled to be wearing it.

"Look," I squeal as we pull into the parking lot. "It's deserted like god reserved it just for us."

Tuck chuckles at me. "A bit overdramatic, there, Blue."

Before he has a chance to back out, I nudge him in his shoulder, urging him out the driver's side door, and then follow him.

"Grab the cooler. I've got the bag."

"Yes, boss." He pulls his shades down, and I see a twinge of hardness cover his face.

"Stop." I slap his ass as he hoists the cooler up on his shoulder, and he only growls back at me.

I could literally do cartwheels across the sand. First getting Tuck here was a battle, and then it being deserted is like the cherry on top of my dessert. I stop for a second and slip off my flip-flops, letting the sand tickle every single inch of my feet.

"Where to, Blue?"

I point off to an area around a slight bend with a mass of large rocks, thinking it would be the perfect spot even if someone did show up. Tuck would appreciate any sort of privacy.

"Damn, you're so hot." My gaze is locked on Tuck with that cooler perched on his shoulder and the barest slice of his abs peeking out through his t-shirt.

Every time I tell him how gorgeous or hot he is, he always has the same reaction. Nothing. I used to wonder if he even hears me, but that stopped the one night he wrote me a letter explaining why he can never accept my compliments. It was heart wrenching and made me hurt for him.

"You know what, Blue?"

His voice startles me. Peering up into his shaded eyes, I wait for his reaction.

"It feels really good to be loved." He leans down and places a quick peck on my cheek. Freezing cold water escapes from the cooler, landing on my shoulder and flowing right down the middle of my back.

Like a fool, I squeal and take off, trying to dance the cold liquid out of my swim top.

"Careful, toots, you might blow a tit," Tuck hollers.

He was less than pleased with my bikini top, claiming it left absolutely nothing to the imagination.

"Catch me, then you can put it back in for me."

I take off down the beach with our bag swinging behind my back and don't look back, because Tuck is one of the fastest men on the freaking planet, so if I have any chance of escaping him, I can't waste time seeing if he's coming or where he is. About thirty strides in, my body is lifted from the ground and cradled up into

Tuck's arms. The man's strength and power still shock the living hell out of me.

"Nice try, little bird."

"Ass," I holler.

The closer we get to the tide, the louder we have to talk.

"Call me that again and I'll punch you in the balls."

"Not much you can do about it, is there?"

"Oh, over there, Tuck, see that white sandy spot?" I point and try to kick free from his hold.

"Got it."

He doesn't put me down when we hit the place I want to camp out for the day. Instead, he drops the cooler to the sand and then flips me around, gripping my ass and forcing my legs to wrap around his mid-section. I drop the bag when my arms frantically grip around his neck.

"Tuck."

"I fucking love you, Blue. I hate the shit you make me do, but I fucking love you and want to remember how each second feels with you."

My lips break open to respond, but before they have a chance to, he claims them in the most aggressive kiss I've ever tasted. He's completely shocked me with his confession and powerful kiss. Tuck drops to his knees, still holding me above the sand, and I know things are about to get dirty. When he wants sex, nothing stops this determined train of a man.

I find the hem of his shirt and pull it up over his head, only breaking our kiss for a few seconds.

"I'm just loving you, so enjoy it." The words are lost on his lips as he continues to ravage mine.

He flips us around, so that he's sitting on the sand and I'm straddling his lap. Tuck's hands leave my face and begin fumbling with the button on my shorts. I'm afraid he'll rip them off in a second if they don't start cooperating. I rub up and down the rippled skin on his back. I've forced my palms to memorize every single one of his burn marks. They are what makes him who he is, and I never want to forget.

He grips my hips, raising me up and then slamming me back down onto him. A deep gasp of shock and pleasure escapes me. Tuck hypnotized me with his kiss and surprised me by entering me so quickly. I drop my head onto this forehead, pulling from his kiss and soaking up all the emotions running through me right now. He splays his hands on either side of him, digging into the sand.

"Watch me," I whisper.

I wait for Tuck's eyes to meet mine and then begin riding him. I find a steady rhythm that threatens to ruin our moment all too quickly. My hands lace in the back of his hair, knocking his hat to the sand. We've been completely exposed to each other before, but out in public like this is almost too much for me to handle. Every square inch of my skin is alert, reacting to any touch with overwhelming passion.

"Tuck," I moan, and then everything inside me tightens up and releases with painful, beautiful pleasure shooting from the tips of my toes all throughout my body. I feel Tuck go limp underneath me, falling back onto the sand. I giggle when I realize I hadn't even noticed he found his own release.

"That."

I place a kiss on his lips.

"The best."

Another kiss.

"Sex ever."

This time I don't pull up from the kiss, pouring everything I have into it. He rolls me over, pushing my back into the sand, and enters me again. And just like the first time, I gasp in shock and pleasure and send my hands flying over my head to rest in the sand. I let him take me and enjoy each stroke of it.

"I love you, Blue."

He grunts after my name leaves his lips and slams back into me one more time, filling me with the most delicious feeling in the world. I prop myself up on my elbows and kiss the tip of his nose.

"Thank you for this."

Tuck tilts his head to the side, not understanding me.

"You just gave me the world by coming here with me and doing this. I love you, Tuck Jones."

"Enough mushy shit, little girl. I'm going to dunk your ass."

And in Tuck fashion, he scoops me from the ground, snags my swim bottoms, and races toward the ocean. He has us both in the freezing cold water before I can protest, and this time when I go under, I'm holding onto him and staring straight into his dark eyes.

The eyes that've haunted me, broken me, and absolutely captured my heart from the beginning. I bring one hand up to his face and cup his cheek. Within moments, he paddles to the top of the water, still holding me.

"Damn, it's cold." Tuck flips the water out of his hair. "Wipe that goofy grin off your face, Blue."

"I can't help it." My fingers brush beads of water off his shoulder.

"So, what now?"

"We just relax. Do you know how to do that, Tuck?"

"No, I mean there's no weights or anything to lift."

I send a splash up into his face and then kick away from him, taking off into the water. I find it comical that I can swim faster than Mr. All-Star Jock. Hours pass as we play in the water, sunbathe, nap, eat, and then hop back in the ocean. And to our delight, nobody shows up to invade our slice of privacy.

"I need some real fucking food."

I roll up from my belly to see a disgruntled Tuck propped up on his elbow. "I packed food."

"No, like real fucking food that sticks in your belly."

Being an ass, I spread my legs wide open, and say, "Help yourself."

Tuck pounces on me, and I scream out in a fit of laughter.

"No." I pull him up by his hair.

"You can't taunt me like that, missy."

"Not here."

"Really?" He crooks an eyebrow at me. "Because I've taken you like four times here today."

"No, that's just too…"

"Too what?" His smile shines brightly while he waits for my answer.

"It's too intimate. My favorite thing you do, and I don't want anyone interrupting us."

"Good to know."

Tuck's stomach rumbles against mine.

"Burgers?" I ask.

"Please, for the love of all things fucking holy." The pitiful look and puppy dog eyes melt my heart.

"See if Lane and Sophie want to meet us there, and I'll pick up, big guy."

He rolls off of me without a second question, scrambling for his phone while I gather our few things and nibble on the remaining carrots in the cooler. This moment is bittersweet. It was the best day of my life, and I don't want it to end.

"They will meet us there. Ready?"

I look up into Tuck's excited face and can't help but smile back.

"Yeah, baby." I plop the last carrot into his mouth and then grab his hand as we make our way back to the truck.

For one of the first times in our relationship, I don't talk or bring up sore subjects. Instead I relish every second, branding each memory of our day on my heart.

"I don't care if they are here or not, we are fucking ordering food."

"Geez, Tuck, you act like I made you eat tofu and seaweed all day."

"You did, didn't you?"

He pulls me out of the truck, practically dragging me into the diner. If I wasn't on such a lust hangover, I'd be a little shit and drag my heels the whole way. He heads straight to the counter to order while I use the restroom to wash up.

I shake my head at my goofy face reflecting back at me as I soap up my hands. I've never in my life looked so ecstatic and overwhelmed by one person. It makes me giggle harder at the insane day I experienced with Tuck. A light squeak invades my happy moment, and I turn around to see a dark-haired stranger staring at me.

It's enough to spook spiral me back into reality where I have no idea who the enemy is. Quickly, I dry off my hands and rush back out into the main area of the restaurant and find Tuck, who is already eating. I fucking swear he has the waitresses and cooks wrapped around his little finger.

"Happy?" I ask, looking down at him.

"Now I am." He drags me into his lap as he chows down on his food.

He's so intent on eating, I'm afraid I may lose a finger if I snag a fry from his plate. Moments later, a server places a chef salad in front of me and I grin stupidly at it, realizing Tuck knew better.

"Thank you." I pet Tuck's thigh before digging in.

"What the hell?" Sophie stands before us with her hands perched on her hips.

I shrug. "You know that no one gets between Tuck and his food."

"Bitch." She plops down on the bench opposite of me.

I slide my plate over to the center of the table and let Sophie pick off her favorite parts.

"What did you guys do today?" I ask around a mouthful of food.

"You know."

"Okay, okay, shut up now."

Lane sits down, and Tuck doesn't share a damn lick of his food.

Chapter 29

"Three more. Blue, you said you wanted defined thighs. Deeper."

"Really, Tuck?"

Every muscle in my upper thighs quivers and quakes, but I settle lower into the squat each time. Even though this man can make it sound dirty as hell when he says deeper, I focus on the actual movement of the exercise. He's been working my ass over in the gym, prepping me for nationals, which is weeks away.

I'm pretty sure this is how Tuck entertains himself in the off-season, and now he has a victim to torture. I won't complain since we spend all of our free time together, and I've conned my way into him doing my homework ninety percent of the time.

"Leg press machine." Tuck adds weight after weight.

"Are you fucking kidding me?"

"Nope. Four sets, and then you can go home and ride me for your cardio." Tuck pulls me into his sweaty torso and kisses my lips.

"I hate you sometimes."

I know it's a losing battle to argue with the man, so I settle down onto the seat, and adjust my sticky skin against the red vinyl and dig in. I've learned to not dare cheat on a set, or he'll make my ass do it over. I power through each set, only resting seconds in between intervals, and even surprise him on the last, pushing myself to failure and easily exceeding twenty reps.

"Damn, someone must be very eager for their cardio." Tuck steps over, straddling me, while he stares down with a mischievous grin on his face.

"Maybe, but I don't think I can walk."

He reaches to pull me up and easily whips me into a standing position.

"Go get your stuff or I'll fuck you here."

I try to walk away from him and can barely keep my rubbery legs steady. My shorty short spandex shorts are riding up my ass, so I dig one side out as I hobble off to the locker room. I'm pretty sure everything about me right now gives a new definition to hot mess.

When I look up after I steady my sea legs, I come face to face with Captain Asshat. My heart stops and my legs shake harder, if that's even possible. I try to walk forward, but am halted when I find myself staring into his eyes. Fear grips my common sense, making it impossible to process if I know those eyes, but I keep staring straight into them. He's talking, but I don't listen as I stare.

In slow motion, I watch his hand raise to my shoulder and land on my bare skin. Chills run down my spine, and yet I keep staring into his eyes.

"Excuse me, Blue."

As quickly as he appeared, he's gone. My body was braced for the worst, but nothing came. I spin around looking for him, but the gym is empty. *Did I just imagine that whole thing?* My feet finally come to the party, and I scurry into the locker room, snatching my bag and heading for the checkout counter.

Tuck's in a heated argument with the clerk at the desk, immediately answering my question whether it was a dream or not.

"He's not allowed in here. I'll be calling management."

Tuck spots me, and I know a shit storm is about to ensue. If I thought I'd seen the man dark and upset before, then that was nothing. The veins running along his hairline are popped up, and his face is shades of deep red. He clutches my hand and drags me from the gym.

"We won't be fucking back," he hollers over his shoulder as he slams the glass door as hard as he can.

His fit of rage is doing nothing to calm me down or steady my legs. Tuck tugs on my hand one last time when he steps out into the parking lot and I fall to the pavement.

"Tuck," I scream, but it's too late as my skin is once again torn.

"Son of a bitch."

He picks me up and carries me the rest of the way to the truck. With each step I feel the blood trickle down the front of my shins. When he sets me on the passenger side, I don't attempt to slide to the middle, but stay put and go for my gym towel. I let it soak up the blood flowing from my kneecaps. When I hear his door shut, I don't look up at him.

"I'm sorry, Blue, I'm just fucking livid and didn't mean to make you trip."

"You pulled me fucking down, Tuck." My voice is shaky.

"I'm sorry." His arm wraps around my shoulder as I feel his body come closer to me.

"Don't touch me." I press the towel deeper into my wounds and face him. "Don't fucking touch me."

"Blue." The hurt look on his face doesn't even faze me as I completely fall off the cliff of sanity.

"That was him, Tuck. Fucking listen to me. That was the guy who attacked me. It was him. Are you fucking listening to me?"

"What?"

"Just fucking take me home."

"Blue, you have to talk to me."

"Oh, really?" I whip around to face him. "I need to talk to you. You, the man who just pulled me down on pavement and made me bleed again? I don't think so."

"Blue, are you serious right now?"

"Take me home."

Tuck tosses his hands up in the air in surrender, and then the next sound is the squealing of his tires zipping out of the parking lot.

"Tuck, stop driving like a fucking lunatic."

He doesn't respond or let up on the gas pedal.

"I'm sorry." My fist pounds into the dash. "I never had the courage to tell you the guy on the news wasn't the attacker. I wanted it all to go away, but it hasn't. It haunts me every fucking night and every second I'm not with you."

"Are you sure it was the guy at the gym?"

I shrug because now I don't feel sure about anything.

"Blue, fucking talk."

"I don't know." My scream is deafening and dangerous. "I just know it's not the guy you think it is, and…"

"And what, Blue?"

"Nothing." I collapse into a ball in the front seat, giving in to all the fucking emotions from the day.

"Do you not trust me?"

"I do." Tears roll down my knees seeping into the fresh cuts on my skin.

"I can't help you if I don't know."

The fear that has been gripping at my heart for the last few months becomes overwhelming as I let it all out. My sobs are uncontrollable, making it impossible to speak one word.

"C'mon, baby."

I float in the air, nestled in Tuck's arms. The living room is noisy and full of bodies when we enter. I keep my head tucked down and avoid all eye contact.

"I'm just going to take a bath," I say, as Tuck sets me

down on the bed. He kneels before me, forcing me to look up at him.

"Blue, what are you not telling me? Did more happen that night? Do you know this man?"

"I don't know. I really don't know." I drop my head again. "Can I just be alone tonight?"

"Blue."

"I need to be alone." My palm cups his face.

"I'll start you a bath."

He leaves without saying another word, and it hurts me even more when I thought I was at my lowest. I should go to Tuck and apologize, but I don't have the energy to do it. By the time I make it to the bathroom, he's gone, and I'm left with a hot tub of water. Sinking into it, I close my eyes and wish for everything and everyone to disappear, and I really do wonder if the inevitable blackness of death would even soothe this tortured soul of mine.

I let my body sink lower and lower under the water until I'm fully immersed.

Chapter 30

The morning sun is blinding as I roll over in the bed. It takes me a few moments to realize it's empty, and that's what wakes me up. I don't remember much from last night or even how I made it to bed. Everything is a haze and not making sense, but the most unsettling is that Tuck isn't by me.

Making my way down the hallway, I hear him and Noah out front talking, but have to stop at the bathroom first. Looks aren't even on the agenda this morning; it's the screaming bladder yelling at me. As soon as my knees bend, I feel the sting and crack of my fall in the parking lot yesterday. Two Band-Aids cover each of my kneecaps where the torn flesh lies. Resting my elbows on my thighs, I bury my face in my hands and cry for how I've fucked up this whole situation. I'm going to lose Tuck.

I pull up his boxers quickly, rolling over the top band so they stay in place, and rush down the hall.

Words fly out of my mouth before anything comes into view. "I'm sorry, Tuck, I'm so sorry."

I don't wait for his reaction before bounding smack dab in the middle of him on the couch.

"Please forgive me. I'm sorry."

"Shhhh, it's all right, baby."

He pulls me into a tight hug, and I find that place that feels like home against his chest. Soon his hands are running through my hair as he offers up a constant string of reassurance.

When I realize Noah is in the room, I finally lift my head and offer him a weak smile, and then focus back on Tuck's gorgeous face.

"Thank you for the Band-Aids, and I know it was an accident. You'd never hurt me, and I do trust you." I settle myself on the couch facing both men. "I know with my whole heart the guy who was arrested and charged with the rapes and murders wasn't my attacker. I'd recognize the eyes anywhere, and it's not him."

Noah stands and rubs his hands through his hair, with a pissed off look on his face. "And exactly when were you going to share this information with us?"

"Stop," Tuck roars, and I jump. He wraps me tight to his side. "We went through all this yesterday. The point is Blue tried to block it out and it didn't work. We think it was the asshole soccer player. He came to the gym yesterday."

"I'm not sure if it's him or not. I just don't know."

I keep the tears at bay. I refuse to break down at every fucking corner of this story.

"C'mon, I made breakfast. Let's eat and enjoy this day. I'll figure something out, Blue." Tuck pulls me from the couch and drags me into the kitchen. He sure wasn't lying about the spread on the table. It's covered with all sorts of breakfast foods, from pastries, to eggs, and all sorts of meat.

"I couldn't sleep."

"I can tell." I slide out the dining room chair and take a seat. "Tuck, I really am sorry. I just don't know how to act anymore."

"It's okay, Blue, we'll get through this." He ruffles the top of my hair, picks me up, and then sits with me in his lap. I pluck a strawberry from the table, making sure to lather it in the fruit dip he's prepared, and plop it in his mouth.

"Is that a promise, Tuck?"

"I don't do promises, I just do me."

"I know." This time I wipe some of the cream on the

tip of his nose and giggle at his reaction.

"You little shit."

I squeal as he rubs it into my chest, and then relax back into him.

"I just want to run away with you, Tuck, and start over."

"I know, Blue, I know."

***

A week passes with no more threats or sightings of any dangerous eyes. It's taken seven long days to finally not jump out of my skin at every corner. Tuck's tried his damnedest to stick right next to me, but with our hectic schedules, it's never easy. I finally gave in and talked to Trainer Jay and Steve about all my issues. To say Jay was pissed would be the understatement of the century, but thank goodness I have Steve, who has reassured me over and over. He checked the campus surveillance and found nothing. He's about the only peace of mind I have.

Tuck's been on a manhunt for the soccer player, but nothing has surfaced. He knows any mention of it puts me straight over the edge, so he keeps it all in hushed tones with Noah. And I can handle that.

"Blue, what are you wearing tonight?" My gaze goes from the cracked tile on the floor up to a damn near naked Sophie.

The football team is having a little get-together at Noah and Tuck's place. Actually, it will more than likely turn into a rager, but their parties always start out small. I overheard Tuck and Noah talking last night about needing a distraction.

"This." I gesture with my hands.

"Seriously, Blue."

"It's not like I'm trying to land a guy or anything."

"No, but you could at least dress up for Tuck once in

a while and get out of those damn gym clothes."

"He likes gym clothes."

"He'd probably like a little sexy dress too. Just saying."

"I'm not a whore like you."

Sophie cringes and sends me an offensive glare, but then softens.

"Point taken."

"Some things never change, Sophie. Let's get moving. Wear this." I toss a lacy dress her way, then make my way to the mirror to fix my hair up a bit and slap on some of Sophie's make-up since pretty much all my stuff is at Tuck's.

It was a damn battle letting me come here with Sophie. I'm pretty sure he stalked us all the way until we walked into the front doors. I thought it was quite odd when Steve waved to someone behind me, and then I only caught a glimpse of a black hoodie walking away.

"Okay, I'm ready."

I turn to look at Sophie with her amazing thighs showing, the crest of her ass peeking out of the bottom of her dress, and her tits on high alert.

"Yes, you are, slut biscuit."

Walking through the halls of the dorm sends chills through me. I know my attacker has been here lurking these halls, waiting for the perfect time to slip notes under my door. As I push the elevator button, I recoil before I touch it.

"Blue." Sophie stares down at me and I freeze. "What's going on?"

His finger has touched this very button. The finger attached to his hand that he beat me with before trying to rape me. My stomach lurches and I feel the bile begin to rise.

"Blue."

Sophie's voice is louder this time, and the elevator doors slowly glide open. Two men waltz by, and one of them brushes against my shoulder, snapping me back to reality. Mentally I scold myself for being so damn paranoid.

"I'm fine. Just thought I forgot something."

"Well, if I'm a slut biscuit, you, my friend, are sure as hell a shitty liar. Let's go."

My stomach drops once again as the elevator descends, whirling and spinning all my emotions together in one massive lump of confusion. I listen to Sophie ramble on the short walk over to Tuck's. I don't even try to add to her conversation and block most of it since the size and power of Lane's cock holds none of my interest.

Several vehicles already swarm Tuck's small house, but I don't see his truck, so I grab my phone.

Me: Where are you, lover?

Tuck: Running a few behind. Had to talk with coach.

Me: Everything okay?

Tuck: Couldn't be better.

Me: Okay, walking in.

The small gathering is more a frat party on steroids with bodies everywhere. Tuck is going to shit when he see all the people. I spot Noah standing in the kitchen with a herd of girls swarming him. He could have his pick out of the whole freaking university, but I've never seen him with anyone.

"I need a drink," I mouth to him over the heads of the girls.

He pushes up off the counter and stretches out his full glass to me. I take it and begin drinking it without a second thought. What I wouldn't give for just a quiet night at home with Tuck. Well, it wouldn't be quiet, but we'd be at home together, naked in bed, sweaty, and satisfied. That's it, I talked myself into it, and I'm jumping the man as soon as he walks in that front door.

I find a place on the edge of the couch near some of Tuck's teammates and sit watching the people moving about the house. Soon the living room is full, the front door is left open, and people start spilling outside. The fresh, cool breeze is welcoming, whirling around in the living room. Noah passed by once and handed me a new beverage. I'd expected Tuck way before this, and have checked my phone several times.

The crowd hasn't dwindled at all and has only become more rambunctious and out of control. My skin would be crawling by now if Noah hadn't been watching me like a hawk across the living room. His eyes haven't left me all night long.

Finally, Tuck's bulky frame fills the doorway and I practically leap from the arm of the couch into his arms. He's always good at catching me, and never even stumbles.

"About time." My lips brush his.

"Sorry, Blue."

I don't hesitate to attack his lips, planting a deep and sexy kiss. He walks backward until the backs of my legs meet the arm of the couch again. I growl at him as I break off the kiss, and he only chuckles at my clear disappointment.

"Here, this was in the mailbox for you."

He hands me a large manila envelope and turns to greet some friends, with his hand cupping my shoulder.

Rather odd to be getting mail at Tuck's, but maybe my mom realized I'd get it quicker here than the dorms. There's no return address, and I can only guess this is one of her surprises.

Peeking in the envelope, I see it's stuffed with papers. A hard shove knocks me from the back, and the contents spill from the envelope. It's us. Tuck and me, scattered all over the floor. Full color pictures of us on the beach that day, and one paper with bold letters: "How dare you fuck around on me?"

It's as if the papers on the floor are magnets for everyone's attention. My exposed body mingled with Tuck's lives for everyone's view. His burnt flesh, the billboard of the scene. I scramble from the arm of the couch to gather them and hear several hushed noises and gasps as everyone realizes who it is.

I look back at Tuck, who has gone white and devoid of any expression, and then scramble back to the papers on the floor.

"Get out," Tuck orders, but I don't quit picking up the papers and stuffing them back in the envelope.

This time his voice is louder, sending a vibrating echo through the living room. "I said get the fuck out, Blue."

My gaze rips back in his direction as I try to comprehend his words, and right when I do, he lurches for me, but Noah stops him and pins him to the wall.

"Get her out of my fucking house now."

I remain frozen on the floor, clutching the poisonous paper to my chest.

"You made me love you and promised not to hurt me." His voice is laced with more than anger. "Get out now."

The last three words have the power to shatter every single window in the house. But yet I don't understand one of them.

"Tuck." Tears run down my cheeks as I try to stand. "This isn't me. I didn't do this."

"You exposed me. Pushed me. Hope you're happy now."

Someone tugs on my arm.

"Tuck, no," is all I can get out before I'm dragged out of the living room by one of his linemen. Even the party outside has hushed from the scene that just played out inside. With one hard jerk, I break from the giant's grip.

A mixture of hatred and hurt rushes through me, transforming me into something unrecognizable, and before I even think about my next actions, I sprint back into the house screaming.

"Fuck you, Tuck Jones. Fuck you." I send the envelope of papers flying into the living room, and this time Noah comes for me. "I fucking love you and think you're beautiful. I'm not sorry for loving you. I didn't do this."

Tuck doesn't flinch from his stance and is now being held back by two of his teammates. Noah tugs on my arm, trying to pull me from the house, and with all my strength I pull from his hold.

"You were right about one thing, Tuck. You truly are a beast."

I don't give Noah the chance to so kindly escort me from the house. I turn and walk off on my own, and when my tears don't keep coming, but that odd mixture of hatred and hurt continues to course through my body, I know I'm in trouble.

Chapter 31

The dark dorm room envelops me. If there was a threat or letter slid under the door, I didn't notice as not one light was flipped on before I crawled into bed. It's been hours since the worst moment of my life played out before my very own eyes, and not one call or text from Tuck, Sophie, or any of my so-called friends.

My mind refuses to turn off as it churns the events over and over again and dissects Tuck's actions. It's enough to make me puke and crawl out of my skin. *Game over, assholes.* I tear away the blankets cocooning me and lace up my tennis shoes, not concerned with the rest of my attire. I don't flinch as I walk down the hallway and slam the elevator button.

"Blue."

I turn to see Steve standing behind his station. "Steve."

"Everything okay?"

"Perfect." The word is gritted out between clenched teeth.

"May I ask where you're going? I know it's none of my business." He rounds the corner of the counter and makes his way closer to me. "I mean, after all, I did promise your dad that I'd keep you safe and all."

"I'm going running."

I don't wait for his response before I exit the building and forgo stretching. My feet pound on the same exact route as the night I was attacked, and I wish for nothing more than a fucking neon sign glued to my forehead. I want the pain and second-guessing to stop. I crave nothing but that the attacker finish the fucking job he started.

I don't hold back on the pace or the length of my strides. I push hard to punish every single part of my body as I run along the darkest parts of the trail, letting the night air and sounds encompass me. Not music or Tuck's scent, just nature and the hopes of meeting my attacker. Sweat beads form and run down my back and arms. It only forces me to push harder and run faster. When the dorms comes back into view, I feel yet another stab to the heart. Life is nothing but a cruel fucking joke. When I'm forced to survive, I do, and when I'm begging to no longer survive, it's not granted.

Entering the dorms, I notice Steve is gone and his counterpart has replaced him. Fred, just as polite and inviting as Steve, but I feel no loyalty to him, so I just rush past him in my haste to get back to my prison. When my door shuts behind me, the silent confines beckon me and I go numb.

The sheets of my once soft and welcoming bed that smell of home are harsh on my skin. Every part of me cringes as I sink into them. Even though Tuck is dead to me, he's the only thing my body craves. My DNA needs him to function—no, yearns for him in order to survive.

My eyes drift shut, haunted by Tuck's face and his possessive anger tonight directed toward me, and only me. It's as if anyone else in the world saw him, and he instantly blamed me, but before I pass out completely I see the soccer player's face and develop a hunger to hunt him down and take care of him first.

***

Drowning, still drowning in my own guilt and others' stupidity. The world seems to keep spinning, but it doesn't matter to me at all. The sun beckons me to wake up, but again I don't care about attending class or even making it on time to practice. I've already lost the title of head cheerleader during basketball season, and it was actually a relief. It only took me showing up late to practice twice.

It's been five days since the worst day of my life spiraled out of control, but I've lost so much. Even in my depths of sorrow and self-loathing, my admirer hasn't given up. He's even gone to the extent of speckling blood drops on my kill notes. It's like I've made it near the top of his hate list, but have never secured the number one spot.

I've run every single night since, hoping and praying he revisits the same spot to finish the job. It seems easier than to explain to my parents the whole fucked up situation, and Tuck sure as hell hasn't tried to make amends in the slightest.

Walking into the gym, I get a glare from Sophie and the rest of the girls behind her. In their defense, it could be my unshowered and unkempt hair or her disgust of me. Either way, I don't fucking give a shit and hope more than anything…someone would slice my throat now and let me bleed out on the gym floor, since that's how all my invisible open wounds feel.

I fought to be here and now would die to leave.

Chapter 32

Tuck

"I didn't drive here to be turned away."

"Sir, again, do you have an appointment?"

I pound a fist into the weak countertop and raise my voice to a growl. "I need to see him…"

I'm cut off by someone mentioning my name, and when I look up it's as if I see her standing within her dad. Their eyes are identical, and even though Blue isn't here now, the resemblance is something I never noticed. It's not until this moment that I realize just how much they look alike. Her dad sees me, and I freeze. It's written all over his face that he's shocked to see me, but I keep on with my plan. I didn't come here to fucking dick around.

"Sir, Dr. Williams, please?"

His face doesn't hold anything back as he stares back at me. I knew it was going to be a gamble, but it's worth gambling for. It's been months without Blue in my life, and the last words she spoke to me ring in my ears every single morning. She's right, I'm a beast and don't deserve anything more. She's the only person on Earth who actually made me believe I was desirable. She was my one person, and I pushed her away like a piece of garbage.

"Sir, I'd like a consultation, please."

I know I've caught Dr. Williams by surprise, but just like his daughter, he welcomes me with open arms, and it's another dagger to my wounded soul.

"Follow me, son. I have about twenty minutes." He rounds the counter and opens the door. I follow him until he welcomes me into his office. It's nothing less than prestigious, with an over-sized dark desk placed in the center of the room. The walls are adorned with plaques and certificate after certificate, but my vision is magnetized to one picture. The picture of Blue leaning into her dad with the biggest smile plastered on her face.

She's a true beauty like I've never met before. It's not just her perfect skin, gorgeous eyes, and killer body; it's more than that. It's her desire to fight for what she believes in and her ability to love. I owe this to her.

I sit in the large leather chair across from him and try to form a thought.

"I need your help." I roll the sleeve of my shirt up to let him view my skin. "I need to be fixed, sir."

He leans forward, pitching his pen to the ground. "What did you do to my daughter?"

I lift my shirt the rest of the way, pulling it over my head and exposing everything to him.

"I let her love me and then broke her heart."

"Why are you here, Tuck?"

"I want these gone." I rub the thick scars over my abdomen. "I want Blue back."

He relaxes back in his chair and shakes his head. "I have no problem helping you out if this is what you want, but I know Blue better than anyone in the world. You broke her heart, she loved you more than cheer, so I do know that she'd never want you fixed."

He air quotes the word "fixed."

"I need to be fixed, to be whole again, because there is no way I can lay next to her with this skin."

"Why?" He leans forward, resting on his elbows. "Has she ever made you feel inferior or ugly?"

"Never," I whisper.

"So, you're telling me that you don't think you're worthy of Blue."

"Sir, she only ever made me feel loved and on top of the world, but when I look in the mirror I see the nasty truth."

He raises an eyebrow at me, pushing me to go on.

"I'm not good enough."

"It's going down like this, Tuck." Dr. Williams rises from his chair. "I'll move ahead with this if you're doing it for you, but if it stems from not feeling worthy of Blue or doing it for her, then you'll have to move on."

It's the end of the discussion as he walks over to the door. "Oh, and Tuck, I think you're a damn fool. You have so much in your life and overcame obstacles, but you are willing to let the scars ruin you. Wear them like a warrior."

Three Days Later

I made an appointment this time and am ready to share my final decision with Dr. Williams. After several sleepless nights in a run-down hotel and countless conversations with my sister, I know exactly what has to be done.

"Tuck Jones." A nurse in baby blue scrubs stands beaming before me.

"That's me."

She weighs me, takes my blood pressure, all the normal shit you go through at a doctor's office. It was my life for years, surgery after surgery, with almost daily appointments. The only difference is Joe's not by my side.

"All right, Tuck, to the room on the right. Doctor Williams will be with you soon."

I hear the nurse swing open the room indicator and then pull the door half shut. She's distracted by someone in the hall and is off before shutting it all the way. It doesn't bother me since I'm still fully clothed and my mind is still reeling from everything I've processed over the last few days. It's been numbing, then spirals into painful.

"Where is he?"

The voice coming from the hall now is very familiar.

"I don't care if he's busy or not. It's about our daughter."

The words slowly process in my foggy brain, and then I realize it's Blue's mom. I don't wait for her to speak another word before I jet into the hall and come face to face with her. Blue's dad joins us moments later.

"What is going on?" He grabs his wife by the elbow and begins hauling her to his office. I follow them, not caring if I'm invited or not.

"What is wrong?"

"It's Blue," she sobs before I can close the door behind us.

"What about her?"

"She made me promise not to tell you until she got home." Her mom wails again before collapsing into the chair. "She quit the squad two weeks ago and was supposed to fly in today. She never showed up and isn't answering her phone."

"She what?" I ask before anyone else has a chance to speak.

"She quit, Tuck." Her mom rises and comes for me. "You broke her heart, and she's done nothing but spiral out of control. I even went and spent a week with her trying to get her back on track."

"Stop." Her husband pulls her back and she instantly crumbles into him.

I'm left reeling from the thought of Blue quitting cheer with Nationals just a week away. There's nothing that would stop that girl from cheering and kicking ass at it. It was her heart, life, and passion. It was everything to her, until…I collapse onto the floor as the realization of my selfish actions seeps through.

I kicked her out of my life straight into her own personal hell without a second thought, and it all stemmed from my fucking insecurity. When thoughts of her lifeless body lying on the running trail flood back in, my mind goes into overdrive. I tear my phone from my pocket and dial Noah's number. When he doesn't answer, I try Lane, then Sophie, and then go back to blowing up Noah's phone. He finally answers after the tenth time.

"Dude, I'm in class, where your ass should be. What do you need?"

"Blue. Go find her now."

"She's not there," Blue's mom interrupts.

I turn my back to her and try to focus on Noah since he's probably closest in distance to Blue. "Go find her now. She's missing and quit cheer."

"Oh, fuck." His voice conveys his understanding. "Fill me in."

I hear some rustling in the background and then silence on the other end and know Noah just left class.

"I'm in Colorado. Had a doctor appointment with her dad."

"What the fuck are you thinking, Tuck?"

He's pushed me to go back after Blue, but I never have. He knows about everything and still claims I was a fucking fool.

"Just listen, Noah. She was supposed to fly in today, but didn't show. She quit cheer and won't answer her phone. Go to her dorm."

"On my way. I'll call you."

My first urge after he hangs up is to throw my phone across the room, but in this moment it's my only hope.

"What's going on, Tuck?"

I look up to her parents, and for the first time really feel the floor of my world fall out. The time away from

Blue was torture, but this has no meaning or explanation of my feelings.

"She was attacked this fall on a running trail." Tears stop me from going on. I keep them back and try to find my voice again. "That's the weekend you guys were gone for fall break. I made her go to the hospital, but she refused to report it."

I feel like the scum on the bottom of scum looking into her dad's eyes and revealing this information about his only daughter. A wave of anger passes over his expression, but doesn't last long before he goes into saving mode.

"Tuck, go find her. We'll call the cops and campus security. Everyone stay focused."

He bolts from the room before another word is spoken, and I'm left staring into the pained eyes of Blue's mom.

"She was beaten." Her words are barely a whisper.

The pain is too overwhelming, and I can't stop my next actions. I stand and wrap her up in a hug and hold her as she sobs, trying offer some sort of comfort.

"I tried and tried, but she refused to get help or talk to anyone. I'm so sorry."

"Was she…was she…" Her voice trails off into sobs. "Did he…"

"No." I make her look up at me. "She was not raped."

"So, you're the voice?"

"What?" I step back from her, confused.

"She had nightmares when I was there, and she would always say it was a voice that saved her and would wake her up from it. I knew the dark lines under her eyes and the way she trembled weren't Blue."

My phone startles both of us as it starts to ring.

"Noah."

"She's not here. I talked to the security guard, and he

claims he hasn't seen Blue for weeks."

"Ask for Steve. Blue always felt comfortable with him."

"I talked to Steve. She's gone, Tuck."

"Fuck, I'm flying back on the next flight." This time I do throw my phone as fucking hard as I can against a cabinet, sending glass in every direction.

"Tell me, Tuck, what did he say?"

"Nobody at the dorms has seen Blue for weeks."

"Impossible. She's been in school. She quit cheering, but told me she was still going to classes."

Chapter 33

Three Weeks Earlier

The letters don't even faze me anymore, and text messages are long gone since I've blocked number after number. The dead mice in shoeboxes have been quite the romantic touch.

I finally broke down and told the one person who's been by my side everything. Steve. He's checked in on me and made sure I had food or was leaving the dorm in time to get to class. He's walked me to and from class when he has the time. Having him is the only thing that helped me keep my shit together while my mom was here, and I was barely able to fool her.

Steve's uncle is a local detective, and he's taking me to talk to him. I'm still unsure about telling a stranger everything, but I'm at a point of no return.

"Are you sure your uncle is a good guy?" I nervously rub my hand over the metal handle of the door.

"Blue, I can't reassure you enough. I still can't believe the shit you've put up with. He'll help you." Steve drives his piece of shit Oldsmobile like it's a brand new Trans Am.

Steve's physique and looks are far from that of a college student. One night he told me he still lives with his mom and hopes to make it out on his own one day, and that he's currently working a side job to make extra cash. He may not be the knight in shining armor on a white horse to save the day, but he's fit the bill for me.

"Thanks again, Steve."

"I told you I'd always help you."

Steve pulls up in the front of a run-down house with missing shingles and a broken picket fence.

"Are we here?" I ask, peering at the shamble of a

house.

“Yeah, my uncle works a lot and doesn’t have time to keep up.”

Well, he could at least trim the grass, I think to myself, but when my gaze falls upon the broken windows, I begin to squirm in my seat.

“Steve.” I look back over to him sitting in the driver’s seat, and for the first time I see those eyes again. The dark ones that attacked me that night. He places his hand on my shoulder, and the whole violent attack plays out in slow motion in my mind. Several times I will myself to stop, knowing very well it’s just my mind playing yet another nasty trick on me.

The sound of a door shutting grabs my attention, and when I look forward, Stephie is standing in front of the car.

“Fuck.” Steve pounds the steering wheel. “She’s fucking early.”

The next thing I know, he’s out of the car and rounding the hood on her. Her belly is the only thing I notice, and it was a lie because she has no belly. It’s flat, and she’s in the best shape of her life. I try like hell to count back the months, but everything is a blur since Tuck turned his back on me. I can’t hear them, but one thing is glaringly obvious. They’re in a whisper-screaming match.

I focus in on Steve’s body movements, and it’s as if I’ve never seen him before. It’s clear that he’s my attacker. Vomit flows onto the floor all over my shoes, and then I begin to scramble for the door handle. My foot catches on the floorboard while the rest of my body tumbles out on the ground.

I begin to run, but a heavy hand lands on my shoulder and knocks me to the ground. It’s the moment I’ve prayed for the last few months. My attacker has finally made his reappearance in my world and come to finish the job. Now all I want is one final glimpse of Tuck's beautiful face and to take back my nasty last words to the only man I've ever loved.

Chapter 34

Tuck

"I'm not fucking crazy and I'll never stop the search, Noah."

"Tuck, it's been over two months since we've reported her missing."

"I don't fucking care." The coffee table in the living room flies up into the air as I stand and look out the window.

Noah, Lane, and Sophie all talk in hushed voices, but their words come through crystal clear.

"He's a mess and it's time Joe comes back and takes him home."

"He won't leave here until she's found."

"We've looked everywhere. It's only a matter of time before her remains turn up."

My fist flies through the window, not fazing my already raw, bloody knuckles. They've been raw since the day in Dr. Williams' office. Punching and hitting are my only outlet when everything decides to consume me at once.

Knowing my friends will stop me if I give them any warning, I head out the front door to my truck and zip off to the beach, to the place that was the best day of my life and ultimately ruined it. It wasn't the beach as much as my fucking shallow train of thought.

Looking back, I'm a fucking idiot for never allowing Blue the whole me. The day she told me she loved me, I should've ripped my shirt off in public for her. She saw it all and adored me like a god, and all I could do was push her away. At night, in the stillness of the dark, I can picture her loving eyes soaking up every single one of my burns, and in the sweetest and rarest of moments,

I feel her lips on me again. But it all vanishes as fast as it comes.

Settling onto the sandy beach, I take my shirt off and let the breeze hit my skin, not caring who sees me or might judge, and send prayer after prayer up to whomever might be listening to bring Blue home. Her dad calls me every day with updates from the private investigator they've hired and the dead ends they've hit.

I still don't understand why her father would ever even speak to me again after hearing my statement at the precinct, but he's never given up on me and reminds me of the fighter heart that Blue has. Instead of pushing him away or punishing myself over it, I've embraced him like my own father figure, and have even opened up to him. Her mom, on the other hand, is a mess and has been admitted to a hospital for help.

I spend my evenings like this on a regular basis, blowing up at my friends, retreating off to my haven at the beach, and then scouring the town. My truck has packed on the miles roaming up and down the streets and alleys. I've given up hope that she's in town anymore, but never that she's alive. I'll never give up that hope, or at least I try to convince myself of that fact.

As the sun begins to set, I send off one more silent prayer for Blue and decide to wander the streets tonight on foot. Most of the shops are occupied by exuberant college kids living like I should be with Blue on my arm. I quicken my pace through these blocks, knowing there's no way she'd be here or she'd be spotted by now. Her picture has been blasted all over town, and the nation for that matter. Every single time I see her face on the news and that bright smile shining back at me, it hurts.

When I drive, I lose track of time and just keep searching for her. I've made it through the college part of town, through the ritzy mansions, and now into the slums. I lift several lids of trashcans, knowing I'm a fool to even look, but I can't help it. Several of the homes are run-down with broken windows and shitty roofing. It doesn't stop me from scouring everywhere. I know this is a place I haven't ventured, so it intrigues me.

I come across a homeless shelter and feel a tug on my arm. When I look back, an elderly woman looks up into my eyes as if she knows me.

"Never give up hope. You are so close."

"Excuse me?" I ask her, bending down a bit.

"She's here."

"Who?"

"Your love."

"Eleanor, leave him alone."

A brunette pulls the woman away, but it doesn't stop her from talking.

"She's here. The one you want."

"I'm sorry, sir, she rambles all the time."

They disappear into the homeless shelter, sending goose bumps all over me. The woman's eyes were haunted, but it seems I read way too much into even the tiniest clues, and they all lead to nothing.

I pass the same desolate homes on the walk back, and even though it's darker as night settles in, you still can't miss the broken windows of the houses and the shitty environment. Then it's like I cross over an imaginary line where the homes become nicer and the college campus begins to permeate the air. All hopes of finding Blue tonight drift away as fast as they entered my mind.

My truck is the only one left in the parking lot, and barely lit by the streetlights. Starting my engine, I begin to lose my shit again. It seems to be a daily routine, and whatever is near gets the shit thoroughly beat out of it. My poor steering wheel can't take much more. My head slams back into the glass as I stare up into the dark night sky speckled with shining stars, and I wonder for the first time if Blue is one of them looking back down on me. I've refused to believe the worst, but at times like this, what other choice do I have?

Sleep will never come, so I drive and drive in the darkness, knowing even if Blue was near I'd miss her. I find myself in front of the homeless shelter and replay the lady's words in my mind. Something about her pulls me from my truck.

The shelter is not buzzing like before. It's clear supper has been served and everyone has moved on. When I enter the building, a strong stench hits me, nearly causing me to gag. It's a mixture of piss and filth. I try not to stare at random people loitering around or lying on the ground. I finally spot someone with a name badge and wave them over.

"Sorry, sir, we're full tonight. Try the shelter on the other side of the city."

"I'm actually looking for an older lady who I talked to earlier tonight."

The volunteer isn't impressed as she raises an eyebrow at me and cocks a hand on her hip.

"Yeah, I want a million dollars and to marry Santa Claus."

"Ma'am, I'm being very serious. I'm looking for a missing person, and an elderly woman said some pretty random stuff to me earlier. I'd like to talk to her."

"You need to vacate the premises or I'll call the cops. We don't have room tonight."

I try again to reason with the overworked volunteer, but she threatens me again with the authorities, leaving me no choice but to walk away.

"Wait, sir." When I turn around I see the volunteer who escorted the elderly lady off earlier. "Did you need something?"

"I know this sounds odd, but I'd really like to see the woman who was talking to me earlier."

"Oh, honey." She touches my forearm as an almost comical expression covers her face. "She's a drifter, and was only here for a few hours today and then wandered off again. Maybe stops in every couple of weeks. Who knows where she is now."

"She's not a regular?"

"No, not many are, and when they are, we try to set them up in a home or turn them in to the authorities."

"I was just looking…Never mind." I grab the back of my beanie in frustration. "Thanks for your time."

Stepping out of the shelter, I look for something to punch, and the two women's voices fill the quiet space as I walk.

"He's hot."

"Yeah, but seriously, focus. We need to call the cops on blondie. It's the same gal who was here a few weeks ago."

It doesn't even amuse me anymore when random chicks check me out or make comments. In fact, it makes me want to beat the fuck out of something even more. I quicken my pace to the truck to find something to punish. Too bad, tonight I pound my fist into the metal side of my truck. The sting feels amazing, and then the throb of everlasting pain shoots through my hand as I pound it again.

Then it's as if someone slaps me in the fucking face. I bolt back into the shelter and find the two volunteers still deep in conversation.

"Excuse me."

They both look up at me.

"Did I hear you say something about a blonde?"

"Listen, super jock," says the first volunteer, who

was less than welcoming. "Get the hell out of here and move on."

Something catches my attention, and when I turn, I see a mass of blonde hair. Walking closer to the corner, I can make out a frail body huddled in the corner with matted blonde hair draped over most of her legs. Stepping close to the person without invading their personal space, I feel something I haven't in months…hope.

My hearts stills in my chest when I see the scars on her knees, and then my breathing hitches when I spot the large freckle peeking through the dirty, messy blonde hair hanging over her forearm.

"Blue."

The figure doesn't move a bit.

"Blue, it's Tuck."

A deep, husky voice comes from the huddled mess. "Leave me alone."

"Sir, please don't talk to her. We need to call the cops. She's a mess."

I don't rise to my feet or quit staring. This is Blue, and it takes everything inside of me not to tug her face to look up at me.

"It's Tuck, Blue. Your boyfriend. I love you and have looked for you every day."

"My name isn't Blue."

I feel a light tapping on my shoulder and turn slightly to see the friendly volunteer.

"She doesn't know her name or who she is. We've kicked her out for soiling herself and not trying to better her situation. She's beyond malnourished, and needs help. We are turning her in tonight."

"Please." It comes out louder than I expect. "Call the cops now."

I turn back to the person huddled in front of me, and

this time I touch her. The moment my hands touch her skin, I know it's her. I feel that electric connection and the way she used to make me feel. Then I spot the Preston logo on her shorts and begin to panic, but try to keep my cool on the outside.

"Blue," I cry. "Look at me."

In slow motion she lifts her head, and I watch as each thick, matted dreadlock falls to the side of her face. Eyes I once knew stare back at me, but are so far away with nothing behind them. Her gaze darts away an instant later. Her fingers tremble upon her knees.

"Blue, look at me."

"I'm not Blue." Urine seeps out onto the ground as her body begins to shake violently. "Lea…lea…leave me alone."

I can't help but grab her hand and hold it in mine, trying to calm her poor body. I have no doubt this is my Blue, and I can't even begin to process what in the fuck got her in this condition. I place my other hand on her cheek and gently force her to look in my eyes.

"Look at me, Blue, I'm here for you."

She nestles her head into my touch, relaxing into my palm, and her hand stops shaking so rapidly. Tears form in her eyes and begin rolling down her cheeks.

Turning around, I see the two volunteers staring at us. "Call 911 right now, and the cops."

My voice comes out harsh, and I feel Blue tense in my hold once again, so I go right to calming her back down.

"Blue, do you remember me?"

She's frozen and slowly drifting back into a dark state.

"You're a cheerleader. I play football. You make me do your homework." I ramble on and on, trying to remember everything about us. "You loved me, Blue, and I love you. I was an asshole."

She eases back into my hand, resting her cheek in it, and closes her eyes. I take her trembling hand and bring it to my shirt. Lifting my shirt, I run her palm up and down the ripples of marred skin she used to worship on a nightly basis. Blue opens her eyes, lifting her head to look at me, and then her gaze goes straight to where her hand is placed.

"Tuck," she whispers.

"Yes, Tuck. Blue, I'm here for you."

Her body convulses again. I swoop her up into my arms and roll her into my lap. Blue buries her head in my chest, burrowing into a tiny ball. Her body doesn't still as she repeats my name over and over again. I sob into her filthy mess of hair as I feel her wet herself again. I keep talking to her while we wait for help.

"Your mom and dad are looking too, Blue. We never gave up. I love you. Fuck, I love you so much and was such an asshole. Fuck, I hope you can forgive me. I'm never leaving you again."

My last sentence strikes a nerve with her, breaking the trance she's trapped in. Her hair flies up, and then her hollow face is in mine. She's beyond unhealthy. The word fragile doesn't even begin to describe her.

"You put a curse on my heart, Tuck. I can only love you."

I watch in slow motion as her eyes roll back in her head and her entire body goes limp in my arms. Sirens and flashing lights fill the room in the next moment. Emergency workers swoop in and take her from my arms. Before standing, I grab my phone from my pocket.

"I found her. She's alive."

Blue's dad's response is a click of the phone, and I know he's on his way here. I fall back on the floor, staring up at the water-stained ceiling tiles, and squeeze my temples and finally feel for the first time in months. I found her. Blue is alive.

Epilogue

"Mommy, what does that say again?"

"The curse of my warrior."

"Tell me the story again."

I ruffle little Will's hair and scoop him up in my lap. There's plenty of time before the game starts, and we really don't have much to entertain ourselves in the bleachers, and I never miss a chance to stare in his beautiful and very curious eyes.

"Remember, silly boy." I poke the tip of his nose. "It's part of my vows from my wedding day. I got it tattooed on my arm to never forget."

"But who's your warrior?"

This little four year old's questions never get old, and it still amazes me how curious he is.

"Your daddy."

"But then who am I?"

"My hero." I ruffle his dark hair again and wait for him to swat my hand away.

"Grandma," Will yells with absolutely no control on the level of his voice. Tuck is constantly worried he'll grow up and want to be a cheerleader the way he can yell. It's our running inside joke.

Will bounds down the bleachers and flies into the arms of my mom. I'd like to think I was his favorite person on this Earth, but that would just be a lie. My mom and Will are inseparable. They are always a bittersweet picture of perfection, yet my heart cringes every single time I see them embrace.

My dad was diagnosed with a fast-acting cancer when I was three months pregnant and passed away three months after that. The man who raised me, loved me unconditionally, and forced me to get back to living after my attack simply wasted away before my eyes. Tuck stood by my side while I lay in bed with my dad day after day and watched him lose the fight.

Tuck and my dad became best friends after finding me, and were shits at times, but completely lovable shits who adored me. We spent three sweet years together with my dad and mom before he passed. It's those memories I cling on to. My father walking me down the aisle, handing me off to Tuck, then wrapping Tuck up in a hug before turning to sit with Mom. It's not tradition, but he gave away Tuck that day as if he were his father. It had nearly all of the attendees at our wedding in tears. I've seen Tuck Jones cry three times in my life. When he opened up to me about his past, the day my dad hugged him at our wedding, and when Will came into our lives.

Yet my selfless king stood by me the entire time, watching my father fade, and then held me through grieving, never being selfish even though he was hurting as badly as I was. When my little wild child miniature Tuck came shooting out in the world, there was only one name suited for our perfect prince, Will W. Jones. And since the universe never gets tired of playing jokes on me, he has my dad's sense of humor, intelligence, and Tuck's athletic abilities. The boy is constantly wandering the house with a pigskin tucked under his arm. My dad would've had the boy running plays already.

I never went back to Preston after my freshman year. I stayed at home with my parents and immersed myself in online classes and several sessions of counseling. The day it was released I was found, Steve turned himself in, and then shortly ratted out Stephie. Their mission…to force my hand and make me leave. They won, and that fact haunted me for months. She wanted head cheerleader and wouldn't stop at anything. But if it weren't for Tuck's endless love and continued support, I'd still believe they won.

My dad's words rang true. Once a snake, always a snake. Stephie and Steve simply fucked up because Dad was the ultimate snake killer, putting them both away for life. He hired the best lawyers and didn't relent. I've never fully remembered the elapsed time in my life. My last memory was being knocked out and then coming back to with my palm pressed against Tuck's skin. Doctor after doctor tried to get my memory back, but it never came. I know it's the best blessing of all.

But what actually happened is Stephie and Steve instilled a drive and passion in me that will never die or be extinguished by another threat. I found my niche in life, and that's in counseling and coaching. And ultimately they landed me right in the middle of Tuck Jones' hurricane life. Neither of us would've ever been brave enough to peel back all our protective layers until we saw the real person standing on the other side.

Tuck was never an option, rather a force I had to face, and against all odds we've made it. He finished his senior year, winning a national championship with me and my parents, and of course, his family by his side. I never missed a college game. The day he refused to enter the NFL draft was more heartbreaking for me than for him. He wanted nothing to do with it, even though he was expected to be drafted in the first round.

Tuck wanted to buy a home, open his accounting business, marry me, and knock me up. He made that statement every single time I brought up the conversation. He's still bullheaded as fuck and an asshole, but he's all mine.

I rise to my feet and hug my mom as she and Will

make it up to the top row of the bleachers.

"Hi, Mom."

"Hey, baby Blue, I love you."

"Look what grandma bought me." I feel a light tug on the end of my shirt. When I look down, I see Will smiling brightly back at me with a large bag of blue cotton candy.

"Of course she did." I roll my eyes in my mother's direction.

She shrugs. "I brought wet wipes."

The Friday night lights flip on, bringing the football field to life, and I see my very sexy husband lead his team out on the field. He's dressed in a short sleeve team t-shirt, with sexy gym pants, and a backward ball cap. He's followed by the star quarterback and his biggest fan, Ruger. We moved back to his hometown after my father passed and made our home. My mom is our next door neighbor, with Joe on the other side, so yes, I've become the pro at not screaming out in pleasure as Tuck works his magic on my lady bits.

I refuse to sit by Joe at games because of her hot head, screaming, and well, she's just downright embarrassing, and typically ends up pacing the sidelines. I know one day she and Tuck will break out into a wrestling match behind the bench.

Even through all of our trials and errors—or as my mother likes to refer to them, our growing pains—I'm still proudest in the moments when Tuck is Tuck. He rips his shirt off to wrestle Will and answers every question the little toddler asks him. Sometimes the scene is so heartbreaking for me that I leave the room, but Will will always know who his dad is. Then there are times I'll catch him coming from practice in a tank top or wearing a super tight tee like tonight. In moments likes these he's Tuck, exposed and completely whole.

"Daddy," Will begins squealing. "Daddy."

I know Tuck doesn't hear him, but always scans the crowd for his little man and waves up to him like an idiot. Ruger always follows suit, making Will feel like the hometown hero. I stand and wave back, rubbing my swollen belly and praying like hell for a little girl. I'd never be anything without Tuck and his endless love. He cursed me the day I saw him and never relented. He's my curse and my warrior…my happily ever after.

THE END

"Fairytales do exist if you're brave enough and have just the right dash of badass in you to chase them down and fight like a warrior to live them out."

-Blue

Acknowledgements:

Thank you to all the readers who support me on a daily basis. I love receiving your messages and support. But truly this book wouldn't have even been born or thought of without Lauren Perry. I literally saw this cover picture and instantly messaged her and BLUE was born. Lauren, you are a rock star and I love your guts.

Social Media Links
Website: www.hjbellus.com
Facebook:
https://www.facebook.com/AuthorHjBellus
Goodreads:
https://www.goodreads.com/author/show/7079478.H_J_Bellus
Twitter: https://twitter.com/HJBellus

Next Release From HJ Bellus
8 Second Decision
Add to your TBR list on GoodReads
http://bit.ly/1MpSR2k

Blue Playlist

Beverly Hills- Weezer
We Be Burning- Sean Paul
Roses- Outkast
Pop (Radio Version)- NSYNC
I'm Like a Bird- Nelly Furtado
One Thing- Finger Eleven
Don't Stop Believin'- Journey
Uma Thurman- Fall Out Boy
Don't- Ed Sheeran
American Bad Ass- Kid Rock
Let Her Go- Passenger
All These Things That I've Done- The Killers
Time of Our Lives- Pitbull, Mr. Vegas, & Lil Jon
Fireball- Pitbull, Mr. Vegas, & Lil Jon
Make Me Feel My Love- Adele
You Give Love a Bad Name- Bon Jovi
Hot in Herre- Nelly & Tim McGraw
Honey, I'm Good- Andy Grammar
Home- Dierks Bentley
Halo- Beyonce
Bills- LunchMoney Lewis
Funky Cold Medina- Tone-Loc
Without Me- Eminem
Lonely Eyes- Chris Young
Hey Mama- David Guetta & Sia
Outside- Calvin Harris
Everybody- Backstreet Boys
Budapest- George Ezra
Goodbye- Who Is Fancy
Little Red Wagon- Miranda Lambert
Counting Stars- OneRepublic
Cool Kids- Echosmith
Me and My Broken Heart- Rixton

Can't Blame a Girl for Trying- Sabrina Carpenter
Dumb Love- Sean Kingston
I Would- One Direction
Sugar- Maroon 5
Nothing Without Love- Nate Ruess
Cheerleader-Omi
Demons- Imagine Dragons
The a Team- Ed Sheeran
Radioactive- Imagine Dragons

Made in the USA
Lexington, KY
17 June 2015